Nantucket Five-spot

Books by Steven Axelrod

The Henry Kennis Mysteries
Nantucket Sawbuck
Nantucket Five-spot

Nantucket Five-spot

A Henry Kennis Mystery

Steven Axelrod

Poisoned Pen Press

Copyright © 2015 by Steven Axelrod

First Edition 2015

10 9 8 7 6 5 4 3 2 1

Library of Congress Catalog Card Number: 2014951259

ISBN: 9781464203428   Hardcover
      9781464203442   Trade Paperback

Poisoned Pen Press
6962 E. First Ave., Ste. 103
Scottsdale, AZ 85251
www.poisonedpenpress.com
info@poisonedpenpress.com

Printed in the United States of America

For my Mother, Gloria Goforth (1920–2012)
Who always knew this would happen.

Acknowledgments

Thanks to Nantucket Police Chief William Pittman for his continuing advice and support; to Rob Dunbar who gave me the first title; to Jim Berkley, Ginger Andrews, and Karen Palmer, whose shrewd early readings caught many embarrassing mistakes; to Annette Rogers whose editorial letters always make me cringe because she's always right; to Annie Breeding, who always had the right word through the hole in the ceiling; and finally to Domenic Stansberry and Diane Lefer, who helped shape this book when it was my MFA creative thesis at Vermont College of Fine Arts. I'll never forget Domenic reading those original first hundred pages and asking "Are you planning to start the story any time soon?" People ask what's the practical use of an MFA degree. As far as I'm concerned, you're holding the answer in your hands.

"Meekness: Uncommon patience in planning a
revenge that is worthwhile."
—Ambrose Bierce, *The Devil's Dictionary*

"An effective campaign must be sensible in its
planning and reckless in its execution."
—Brigadier General Prescott Trainor, USMC

"Rock blunts scissors, scissors cut paper,
paper covers rock."
—Rules to the Han Dynasty strategy game

Contents

Part One:
Rock Blunts Scissors

Chapter One

Arrivals

Finally, I was having dinner alone with Franny Tate. It was a mild summer night, we were dining at Cru, overlooking Nantucket harbor. I was leaning across the table to kiss her when the first bomb went off.

A hole punched into the air, a muffled thump that bypassed my ears and smacked straight into my stomach, like those ominous fireworks that flash once and leave no sparks. The blast wave hit a second later, shaking tables and knocking over glasses, rattling windows in their frames. Franny mouthed the word 'bomb,' her lips parting in silence and pressing together again, not wanting to say the word aloud, or thinking I couldn't hear her through the veil of trembling air.

I pushed my chair back, pointing toward the Steamboat Wharf.

We ran out into a night tattered by running feet and sirens. Our romantic evening lay across the stained tablecloth behind us, tipped over and shattered with the restaurant stemware.

Something bad had arrived on my little island, an evil alert, a violation and a threat like a dog with its throat cut dropped on a front parlor rug. It was up to me and my officers to answer that threat, to make sense of it and set things right.

I didn't explain this to Franny. I didn't need to.

She was running right beside me.

◇◇◇

At that point, I thought it all began with the first bomb threat, two weeks earlier, but I wasn't even close. It takes a long time to make a bomb from scratch. Lighting the fuse is the quick part.

I can tell you the exact moment when the match touched the cord, though.

It was a bright humid morning in June. An eleven-year-old girl named Deborah Garrison stepped off the boat from Hyannis and skipped ahead of her mother down into the crowded seaside streets. As it happened, I was at the Steamship Authority that morning, picking up my assistant chief, Haden Krakauer. We actually saw Debbie in her pony tails and Justin Bieber t-shirt. She didn't seem special, just another adorable little girl on a holiday island crowded with them.

And Debbie didn't actually do anything. Nothing that happened later was her fault. The simple, irreducible fact of her presence was enough. Even years later, the consequences and implications of Debbie's arrival seem bizarre and implausible, far too weighty to balance on those thin sunburned shoulders.

It was like setting off an avalanche with a sigh.

The next time I saw Debbie, it was a week later and she was holding hands with my friend Billy Delavane when he came to the station to report a stolen wallet. She'd been tagging along with him everywhere, since the day she came to Nantucket. They had met in the surf at Madaket when he pulled her out of the white water after a bad wipeout.

"She'd launch on anything, but she kept slipping," Billy told me later. "She couldn't figure it out. No one told her she had to wax the board."

She was happy to let Billy get everything organized and push her into some smaller waves and even happier to share a cup of hot chocolate with a few other kids at Billy's beach shack when hypothermia set in.

They'd been inseparable ever since.

Barnaby Toll took Billy's stolen property report and then buzzed my office. He knew I'd be pleased that Billy had shown up at "Valhalla" as he liked to call it. Billy had been one of the more vocal opponents of the new police station, dragging himself to several Town Meetings and fidgeting through all the boring warrant articles to take his stand against the giant new facility on Fairgrounds Road.

I understood his point. I had been against the construction myself, initially. But, like driving in a luxury car or eating at good restaurants, I adapted to the change shockingly fast. Now I couldn't imagine working in the cramped crumbling building on South Water Street.

I found the two downstairs in the administration conference room.

Billy tilted his head as I walked in. "Nice place. Lots of parking. In America, where nothing else matters."

I ignored him, looking down. "Who's this?"

Debbie spoke up without waiting for him. I liked that. "Debbie Garrison." She extended her hand and I tipped down a little to shake it.

"Police Chief Henry Kennis."

"Glad to meet you, Chief Kennis. Can I have a tour? I think this place is awesome."

"Absolutely. How old are you?"

"Eleven," Billy volunteered.

"I'll be twelve in September," Debbie corrected him.

"That's my son's age," I said. "You should meet him."

"Most eleven-year-old boys are extremely immature."

I let that one go and offered Debbie my arm. "Shall we?"

"Yay!" She grabbed my hand and led me into the corridor. "Can we see the jail cells?"

"Sure."

The place was buzzing on a June morning. We had Girl Scouts gathering in the selectman's meeting room and people milling in the front lobby, complaining about the neighbors' noise violations and picking up over-sand stickers. Last night's DUIs, the unlicensed, uninsured, or unregistered drivers (a couple of them always hit the trifecta).

On the way down to the booking room I asked Debbie what she thought so far.

"Well, the upstairs where we came in reminds me of a mall. That hole in the ceiling where you can see up to the second floor? I was like—is there a GAP store up there? This part is more like my school. But nicer."

"Well, it's new."

"New is good," she announced decisively and I thought, you've come to the right place.

"So are you spending a lot of time with Billy?" We pushed through into the booking room. It was crowded, phones were ringing. A bald geezer who looked like he was constructed out of sinew and tattoo ink was being hustled inside from the garage. Debbie stared at him. He was obviously sloshed out of his mind at ten in the morning.

I took her hand and led her around the big horseshoe-shaped desk toward the holding cells. "Debbie?"

"It—what?"

"Billy? You're spending a lot of time with him?"

"That guy is creepy."

"He's sad. His kid was killed in Afghanistan. He drinks a lot, that's all."

"Ugh. Those tattoos."

"They're bad." She'd probably have one herself by the time she was sixteen, but you can always hope.

She moved on. "Billy's great." Then, "What's behind that door?"

I followed her gaze to the corner. "That's our padded cell."

"For crazy people?"

"Well…for people who might try to hurt themselves."

"Cool! Can I see it?"

"Sure."

We went inside. "Padded" is a slight exaggeration—the beige walls and floor have the consistency of a pencil eraser. "Billy's not like I expected." She pushed the walls, bouncing tentatively on the balls of her feet. "I mean, he's not crazy or dangerous or anything."

"Who told you he was dangerous?"

"Oh, I don't know…just—people."

"They were probably talking about his brother, Ed, who actually is crazy. And dangerous. But he's going to be in jail for a long, long time. So I wouldn't worry about him."

"Billy is so the opposite of that. He wouldn't hurt anyone. I mean, he's sad about all the changes here, but he knows he can't stop them. He's not like some kind of terrorist or anything."

I put a hand on her shoulder to stop the bouncing. "Debbie." She looked up at me. "Someone's been calling Billy Delavane a terrorist?"

"I don't know. I guess so. It's just—people talk. People say stupid stuff all the time. Gossip and stuff."

"I guess. But you've only been here a week, and you're already hearing hardcore gossip about Billy Delavane? I don't see how that's possible. Are the kids talking about him?"

"The kids love him."

"Then who? Your mother? Your mother's friends?"

"Yeah, right."

The idea of her talking to her mother's friends was obviously so crazy only a clueless grown-up could entertain it.

We went to the jail cells next, three for the women and six for the men, simple rooms with built-in stainless steel sinks and toilets and a blue cement slab bed. The men's side was full, so I walked her into the women's block which was empty for the moment.

Debbie pointed at one of the slabs. "How can anyone sleep on that?"

"We have special bedding, but people don't usually stay here overnight."

"What's that for?" She was looking at the stainless steel rail than ran along the length of the slab, eight inches off the floor.

"That's called a Murphy bar—it's for handcuffing people."

"Oooo." She shuddered.

"We don't use them much."

"That's good. That would be scary, being handcuffed in there. Is that a phone? It looks like a phone."

It was—we have a metal plate set into the wall with touch tone buttons and a speaker, so prisoners can have their mandated phone call without any complications. It might seem like an unnecessary luxury, but it beats trying to wrestle a cell phone away from a two-hundred-fifty-pound PCP addict at four in the morning. Someone inevitably gets hurt and the town can only absorb so many seven figure lawsuits.

Debbie was fascinated with the phone. "That is so cool. It almost makes up for the handcuffs. Can you call long distance?"

"No. Local calls only."

"So you take people's cell phones away?"

"Oh yeah. We take their iPods, too. And their PlayStation portables."

"That's so mean."

"Actually most criminals don't have PlayStation portables."

"Billy hates cell phones. He refuses to text me. He was watching me yesterday and he said, everything is opposite now. In the old days being 'all thumbs' was a bad thing."

I smiled and she pounced. "See? He's really funny. I've never heard of a terrorist with a sense of humor, have you?"

"No, I guess not."

We walked to the last cell and turned around. "So—you have no idea who's saying this stuff about Billy?"

"No, but if I hear anything else, I can tell you. Plus I can snoop around. Like an informant."

I led her back out to the lobby where Billy was waiting. On the way I asked her what else she planned to do on the island this summer—she couldn't spy for the police full time.

She shrugged. "Nothing. I guess I'll go to that stupid whaling museum, or the oldest house or whatever, or just sit on the beach."

I had an idea. "You should tell your mom about Murray Camp. It's fun. My kids go."

"Really?" She sounded dubious.

"It's great. You meet all the island kids and there are kids from all over the world whose parents stay here for the summer. They have tennis and kayaking and windsurfing and biking and cook-outs, and…I don't know. You name it. They explore the island. You really learn about this place. My kids love it."

"Okay." I could see she wasn't convinced. I made a mental note to call her mother.

I said my good-byes and went back up to my office. Two big windows showed a view across the parking lot to Fairgrounds Road and beyond. It was a big improvement over the sub-street-level closet I'd worked out of for my first few years on the island.

I hooked my chair and sat down.

◇◇◇

The arrest reports on my desk were a standard summertime array. The fat Midwestern couples who insisted on riding mopeds down Wauwinet Road, taking blind turns side by side. The tradesmen who ran them into the bushes after too many beers for lunch at the Chicken Box. The girl caught stealing earrings from The Souk. The boy caught stealing a sweater from Murray's. I had no leads on the oxycodone suppliers plaguing the island, and nothing new on the underground prostitution ring I'd been hearing rumors about. For the moment all I had was the strong suspicion, developed through too many years of too many after-work drinks with the hardened cynics of Administrative Vice in L.A., that the two were connected somehow.

Then there were the angry yuppies to deal with. For instance, one Tyler Gibson, who bullied himself into my office a few minutes later, brandishing a handful of parking tickets like a magician starting a card trick.

"What am I supposed to do with these?"

I stood up. "Good morning. I'm Chief of Police Henry Kennis. I don't believe we've had the pleasure."

He was a slender man with lots of well-groomed blond hair framing his hawkish face, blue eyes set tight together, sharp nose, thin lips clenched around his indignation, sucking it like a sourball. He spoke with a slight southern accent. I stuck my hand out as I walked around my desk.

He shook it. "Tyler Gibson."

"Good to meet you, Mr. Gibson. Why don't you sit down and tell me the problem."

We settled ourselves and then he launched. "I'm not going to pay these tickets. It's outrageous."

"Well…all the streets are marked, Mr. Gibson. If you keep your car in a thirty minute spot for an hour, someone will probably ticket you."

He stared at me, features pinched in the effort to control his temper. "I am a resident of this island until Labor Day, Chief Kennis, and I am paying dearly for the privilege."

"I appreciate that, but—"

"So I demand to know why I wasn't given a resident parking sticker."

"Where are you living? What's the address?"

"On Deacon's Way. 10 Deacon's Way. Off Cliff Road."

I shrugged. "There you go. Those stickers are issued to homeowners within the core historic district. There's a big sign in the lobby explaining the rules. Take a look at it on your way out."

"This is absurd. You're telling me I have to pay these tickets?"

"I'm sure you can afford it."

He jumped to his feet and brandished the tickets at me. "I'll tell you what I'm going to do. I'm going to sue this town, and the Board of Selectmen, and you personally. You're going to lose and you're going be giving back all the money you've extorted from people like me for decades. It's going to be expensive and I'm going make a point of seeing that a good chunk of it comes out of your pay check. Maybe then you'll think twice about biting the hand that feeds you!"

I didn't offer any of the obvious responses to this petulant tirade. I was more or less under orders not to gratuitously alienate people who were paying in excess of two thousand dollars a week to rent a vacation home, and spending twice that on jewelry and restaurants. I never got a chance to answer him anyway, because that was the moment when Chief Selectman Dan Taylor showed up.

I heard him first. "I'm seeing Chief Kennis right now and you can't stop me!"

I had arrested Dan's younger son Bruce the night before, at a rowdy beach party in Madaket, but that was no excuse for this confrontation. I had also saved his older son Mason from killing himself, but that was more than six months ago, and Dan's memory was short. One thing for sure—I needed to tighten up the security downstairs. It was turning into Grand Central station around here.

"Dan, come on in. Mr. Gibson here was just leaving."

I brushed past Gibson, stepping out into the hall to greet the burly Selectman. Gibson lingered behind me. "You'll be hearing from my lawyer," he said.

"I need you to go."

I turned around. He was standing at my desk, looking for something actionable, no doubt—some memo about harassing summer visitors.

"Now," I said.

"Fine."

He strode past us. Dan hadn't even noticed him. He was glaring at me, a squat pugnacious troll, balding with a fringe of gray hair and a big square face designed for temper tantrums. He filled my office, incongruously sporty in Nantucket red shorts and a Lacoste t-shirt.

"What do you think you're doing, Kennis? What the hell kind of—"

"Sit down, Dan. Take a deep breath and—"

"I will not sit down! I have no intention of sitting down! How dare you patronize me! You threw an innocent boy in jail while real crimes were happening on this island—my lawyer will be checking the 911 logs! The only question is—who was paying you to do it?"

I spoke quietly, not so much to calm him as to underline the difference between my professional demeanor and his absurd hysterics. "Your son was caught performing a sexual act on a minor, Dan. There were roughly fifty witnesses. He had enough weed on him to get all of them high, and he took a swing at me when I pulled him off the girl. He's in serious trouble. You have to calm down and start dealing with the situation."

"The situation? You want me to deal with the situation? I'll tell you the situation, Kennis. This nonsense is going away like it never happened. I'm taking Bruce out of this station with me. Right now. You're signing the necessary papers and clearing all the bureaucratic bullshit and walking us to the door with a big grin on your face and waving bye-bye as we drive away. Or I will make your life a living hell here. I will ruin you. I will destroy you in this town!"

It was a flimsy blizzard of words thrown like confetti at a wedding, filling the air for a second but falling immediately, bluster as litter, scattered on the floor.

"How's Mason doing? I saw one of his poems in *Literati* a couple of months ago."

"I don't know what happened in that room, I don't know what you said to him, but—"

"He had a gun that should have been locked away in your gun safe, Dan. We could have prosecuted you for that. I wanted to, but you have important friends, and they went to bat for you. Nice lesson for your kids, by the way."

"That's the way the world works Chief. That's how you get ahead. Not by writing fag poems for some socialist school magazine."

"I don't know. He's dating the prettiest girl in school, and last I heard, he was planning to get an MBA. That doesn't sound like a socialist fag to me. Just the opposite. Not that I care either way. One of my best friends fits that definition. So do most of my favorite writers. I'm rereading Gore Vidal right now. Great stuff. You should check him out."

I sat down, settled my feet on my desk and leaned back into a bar of dusty summer sunlight. "Let's cut to the chase, Dan. The bail hearing is set for one o'clock. Bring a lawyer. And be on your best behavior. Or I will happily throw you in jail right next to your son."

Barnaby Toll stuck his head in the door, belatedly. He must have heard the shouting.

"Show Mr. Taylor to his car, Barnaby."

"Yes, sir."

In the quiet of my office after he led the fuming selectman away, I picked an envelope off the blotter and stared at my name scrawled across the front, under the unfamiliar riot of blue and green Irish stamps.

It was a letter from Fiona Donovan, a woman I'd fallen in love with and then arrested the winter before. The envelope bulged with photographs, and part of me wanted badly to see them. But I knew that was pointless. She had been extradited, she was never coming back to this country, and I was never going there to visit her. It was over. Nothing she had to say could matter to me anymore.

I threw the envelope into the trash. Then plucked it out again. I turned it over, weighed it on my palm, still uncertain. But the decision was taken out of my hands.

The first bomb threat came two minutes later.

Ezekiel Beaumont: Ten Years Ago

Zeke Beaumont knew they were coming for him. They had been stupid enough to threaten him first. The big one, Tony his name was, had approached him when they were walking the outdoor chain link corridor that afternoon. At first what Tony said was drowned out by a formation of low-flying F-18s.

"We're gonna fuck you up," Tony repeated, after the planes had vanished out over the Pacific. "You pushed Dooley."

So that was it. Beaumont shrugged. "He pushed me first."

"You don't fuck with Dooley, man."

Tony had walked away after that.

The midday sun was hot and the starched pressed uniform all the inmates had to wear was sweltering. Beaumont's arms and legs were prickling, chafing against the heavy material. He kept walking. He had to look calm, but he was furious at himself. He always did this. He had to make trouble.

He had left a cigarette butt near Dooley's free-weight set-up in the yard this morning. You weren't supposed to use Dooley's barbells, and you definitely weren't supposed to leave a mess behind. Dooley had walked up to him a few minutes later with the crumpled Marlboro pinched between two massive stubby fingers.

"What's this?" he asked.

Beaumont had responded without even thinking. "A moron with a cigarette."

Dooley had shoved him, and it had turned into a shoving match. Beaumont knew he should have apologized, but he couldn't.

He got to the end of the walkway and turned around. The F-18s were coming back. The thunder was growing in the air beyond the walls. No wonder the Iraqis hated the United States. Send those planes over a village a couple of times and you'd scare the crap out of them permanently.

Beaumont clapped his hands over his ears again, letting the roar of the big jets rumble through him like the IRT express subway through a local station. Finally, they were gone. He stuck his hands in his pockets and kept walking, easing around a group of tough Hispanics. They nodded to him without saying hello. He made a small salute in return. They hated Beaumont, but they had to put up with him. He used his job in the stockade commandant's office to get them cigarettes, Spanish language newspapers and occasionally more exotic items like pornographic playing cards, Caifanes and Maldita Vecindad tapes, or brass knuckles. They had no idea how he did it, so they regarded him as prison shaman. Beaumont was happy with that. Science always looked like magic to the barbarians.

He had gotten the office job in the first place because he had the highest tested IQ at Miramar. The Commandant's office gave him access to the facility's computer system, and he had been fucking with computer systems since he was in high school. It was easy to alter merchandise order manifests and stock supply lists. Covering his tracks was a little more difficult, but for the moment no one suspected anything and no one was looking.

His access to the brig computer system was his one advantage over Dooley's thugs. He certainly couldn't out-fight them. There was nothing on hand to blackmail them with. He had no particular standing in the stockade, no influence, no connections he could ask to intervene on his behalf. He had plenty of lackeys, though—helpless, lonely freaks who needed allies and craved the little treats Beaumont procured.

Enemies and lackeys, that summed things up. But he liked it that way. Friends were a liability. You trusted them and trust could be lethal. He had trusted his commanding officer in Kuwait. The CO had wanted to help and the deal he suggested seemed fair: if Beaumont turned in his supplier, he would walk away with a general discharge, no questions asked.

The trouble was, he didn't exactly know who the supplier was. They used no last names, no ranks, no serial numbers. It was always just Zeke and Eddie. They worked on a handshake and dealt in cash. But that wasn't a problem, the CO told him. All Beaumont had to do was let the MPs know when the next meeting was going down.

They had met in a dingy café off Fahd Al Salim Street and done all their subsequent business there over the joint's specialty Indian tea. It gave Beaumont heartburn and made him long for a shot of Johnny Walker. But there was strictly BYOB in Kuwait City, and you better not let them catch you. It was actually kind of funny—discussing hundreds of thousands of dollars in illegal drug sales in an upright Muslim restaurant where they'd call the cops on you for drinking a glass of wine. Beaumont gave the MPs the address, ditched the meeting, and waited.

A week after the bust he was still waiting for his papers to be processed when he picked up the new issue of *Stars and Stripes.* There was a front page profile of Major General Edward Claymore, 3rd Corps Support Command.

Eddie.

It made perfect sense. No one in that godforsaken desert was better setup to get his hands on any item he wanted, from fan belts to ceiling fans, emery boards to MREs. 3rd COSCOM supplied food, water, and clothing to more than a hundred thousand troops. It kept their vehicles rolling and their guns loaded. It brought everything an army could possibly need into the country and shipped it out in the trucks it serviced, over the thousands of miles of roads it maintained, all over the theatre from Mishref to Baghdad. COSCOM was the lifeline, the supply line.

And, it turned out, in the case of Eddie Claymore's illicit drug business, the pipeline.

Staff Sergeant Beaumont closed the paper with a sickly chill. Nothing was going to happen to Claymore. If Beaumont's CO went up against the command structure of COSCOM, they'd crush him. He wouldn't even try. No one ever really helped anyone else. People didn't risk anything for each other. They didn't even inconvenience themselves. They turned away. The CO was no different, for all his chummy talk.

Beaumont had seen the CO one more time outside his office and offered enough evidence to make an airtight case against the Major General, talking fast as they walked through the parking lot, flop sweat evaporating in the furnace heat. The CO wasn't listening. He wasn't interested. Beaumont could tell it was over. He considered running, but there was nowhere to go—just a thousand miles of desert, a ring of crumbling Arab towns where he'd stick out like a Ken doll in a dumpster. Fleeing was useless. He'd just get the crap kicked out of him and add a few years to his sentence.

In the end he went quietly. The CO never even showed up at the court-martial. Major General Edward Claymore was quoted in the newspaper when the verdict was announced, something about not letting "a few rotten apples spoil the barrel."

Sanctimonious prick.

He was still making a fortune out there, probably close to twenty thousand dollars a day after expenses, while Zeke Beaumont was doing hard time in Miramar. Well, no one said life was fair. Actually his Dad had told him something much more to the point—life was plenty fair, if you made it that way. "Don't let things happen to you," he said, "Make things happen to other people."

Good advice. Today he was going to make something happen to Dooley and his friends, something bad. They'd get caught kicking the shit out of another inmate, and that would mean an extended sentence and a transfer to Leavenworth, where they'd never be heard from again. It meant taking a beating, but hopefully not much of one. Timing was everything here. No margin for error. Once those boys started it wouldn't take them long to do permanent damage.

Zeke looked at his watch—a few minutes before noon. They'd be hustling him inside for lunch soon. You never had a moment to yourself at Miramar. Or at least, you weren't supposed to. Dooley and his pals shouldn't have been able to jump him, but they had obviously worked something out, which meant they had to have at least two or three guards on the payroll. The most likely prospect was Boatswain's Mate 2nd Class Brad Liddell, a thin balding kid from Jersey with acne scars and giant teeth. Rumor was the originals had been knocked out and the Navy had fitted him with dentures a size too big. Liddell walked Beaumont from the brig commander's office to his cell every night, after he was finished with the inventory spreadsheets on the computer, or the requisitions or the payroll…whatever busy work they had loaded him up with that day. Of course he did his own work, too.

He was on the List of Users—someone had changed it to Lusers in the old days. The old ITS system was a Smithsonian exhibit now, but the jargon remained. It suited him. He was a loser—and a cracker. That was the hacking term for crooks. Beaumont was born in South Carolina, but he had only been a real cracker, the kind people respected, since high school, when he'd used that crude system's buffer overflow to launch his first format string attack—one simple code injection and he was a straight A student.

The brig system incorporated a program that attempted to track private computer use, a Jedgar they called them at school, after the FBI director. But the Navy was using the same Unisys MCP he had played with in the old days. The tracking program was easy to dike, just two lines of code.

He changed the schedules and posted two additional guards in the last long stretch of corridor that led to his cell. He posted their duty call for 8:15, just as the attack should be starting.

He was setting up a print run for the immediate distribution protocol when Angela said, "What are you doing?"

He looked up. She was smiling.

"Just checking on the bed linen inventories."

"And I thought my job was boring."

Was she flirting with him? "I'm sure there are lots of things you're good at, Angela. I bet you have some hidden talents. And quite a few that are…right there in plain sight."

She actually blushed. "Zeke!"

"For instance—I bet you knitted that sweater yourself."

"How did you know that?"

"Well, you don't see that kind of workmanship in store-bought clothes. And my sisters knit—I know a homemade grafting stitch when I see one."

She pushed her hair back from her forehead, stood up a little straighter. "My, my. You are full of surprises."

She had no idea how accurate that comment was. Startling people into a vulnerable moment of contact, an intimacy he could exploit—that was Zeke's real talent, his most valuable one, and it didn't show up on the IQ tests. He absorbed facts and details and archived them and used them for leverage. He had overheard two women talking about knitting on a cross-country bus. Ten years later he could convince a prison secretary of a whole fictional family full of handcraft minded siblings with one telling detail.

He could teach a class in the technique if he wanted to give away his trade secrets. He even had a name for it—the tip of the iceberg theory. If you could construct a plausible jagged three-foot chunk of ice and float it in the right spot, people would naturally assume there was a whole iceberg underneath. You couldn't sink a ship with your little decoy, but you could get it to change course, and that was all Zeke ever wanted. That was the real fun. But dangerous—you could easily wind up in a military brig scamming for your life. Even now, even here with imminent danger pressing like a hand at his throat, it still gave him a rush.

It wasn't that much different with computers, except that machines were much easier to fool than people. You just had to know the language and he knew them all, including C++, the core language of the Unix machine he was manipulating right now.

He finished up and Angela ambled back to her desk. Nice girl. She might come in handy some day.

◇◇◇

The corridor was empty. Liddell slammed the big door behind them. It had all seemed so easy in the office, sitting at the terminal. But so much could have gone wrong. The orders might not have been delivered. His tampering might have been discovered.

Zeke took a deep breath as Liddell griped on about missing his Toronto Blue Jays. He had season tickets, but they did him no good stuck in the smog on the other side of the country. He was sure the Jays were going to win the World Series this year. Zeke agreed. He could feel the blood pounding behind his eyes. The far door opened. Dooley and Tony and two others started rolling toward Zeke and Liddell like a phalanx of Bradleys. They filled the whole corridor. Zeke tilted his wrist so he could see his watch. The digital read out said 8:13. He had two minutes.

If the orders had gone through.

If his tricks were undetected.

He let his breath out through his teeth in a low hiss. His body was already flinching, trying to draw into itself. This was going to hurt, which was part of the plan.

The group stopped. Liddell faded back.

"Hey, Beaumont." Dooley grinned.

"I suppose it's too late for an apology."

Dooley snickered. "Oh no. You're gonna say you're sorry, Beaumont. But you're gonna do it with a shattered knee, and a collapsed lung and a ruptured kidney. And that's for starters. Every time you try to piss or walk upstairs for the rest of your life you're gonna say you're sorry. We're gonna break you so you can't be fixed."

Zeke risked another glance at his watch, 8:15 exactly.

"Expecting somebody?" Dooley asked.

"The cavalry."

"Right. The cavalry. Like in those old movies. But in real life there ain't no cavalry. The Indians just massacre everybody. Nobody shows up to help. Nobody gives a shit."

"You may have a point there, Dooley." Zeke admitted. "You're not as stupid as you look. On the other hand—how could you be?"

Dooley's face hardened. "Grab him."

Tony took one arm and an even bigger guy grabbed the other. Dooley took a step forward and the first punch hit Zeke's stomach like a police battering ram blasting through a cheesy motel-room door. He was wide open and Dooley charged in, knocking Zeke's head left and right with two roundhouse punches. Agony exploded behind his eyes, he could feel his sinuses rupture and his jaw break. He sagged forward and Dooley grabbed a handful of his hair, yanking him up face to face.

"How stupid do I look now, fuck face?"

Zeke could barely open his mouth to talk. "About the same," he managed to say. "But there's three of you."

Dooley grunted and drove his knee up into Zeke's groin. The flat glassy wave of pain raced through him like voltage.

The next punch ended it.

Zeke woke up in the brig emergency ward, his nose bandaged, his ribs taped, and his jaw wired shut. It was day time, that was all he could tell. They had him on some powerful painkiller, probably oxycodone. He had no idea if it was a day or a week after the attack and he didn't care. He was high as a kite, being fed through a tube and drained through a catheter. It was the perfect life style for a lazy shit.

He faded again and when he came to, Boatswain's Mate 2nd Class Brad Liddell was staring down at him.

"Good news, Beaumont," he smiled, showing his oversized teeth. "Dooley and his pals shipped to Leavenworth yesterday. They were caught in the act, committing felony assault on a fellow prisoner. Open and shut. It added five years to their sentences and that's an automatic transfer. So you're OK. You pulled it off. Good for you. Funny thing is, no one could quite figure out how the guards who broke things up happened to be in D block at that time of night. They were normally assigned to the northeast perimeter detail at that hour. But they got new orders that very afternoon! What a coincidence. Some people think there's a glitch in the computer. I know it's true. I even have proof. It's you, Beaumont. Am I getting through there? You're the glitch in the computer. I'm no alpha geek, but I was good enough to hang a bag on the side of that little worm you wrote. I was stuck for a while. I had to reboot twice. But I nailed it finally."

The terminology penetrated the drug haze. There was another hacker at Miramar. Suddenly, he felt sea-sick, as if the bed was floating in deep water, rocked by groundswells, about to tip over. He closed his eyes but that made it worse. He opened them again. The kid was grinning down at him.

This was bad. If Liddell turned him in, they'd transfer him to Leavenworth, too, and Dooley would be waiting. Actually, that would be the good part—a familiar face. He knew he couldn't survive there.

He tried to talk—was he going to beg or bargain? It didn't matter; nothing came out.

Liddell held up a hand.

"Don't bother, Beaumont. I'll do the talking. And I'll make it short since I'm not even supposed to be in here. How about this? You're mine now. Whatever I want you to do, you do it. Whatever I need, you get it. Sometimes I just need to hit someone. Sometimes I need other things. I may keep you to myself and I may rent you out. All you have to do is keep me happy. Me and my friends. Think about that while your jaw heals. Look for me when you get out of here. Because I'll find you if you don't."

He squeezed the oxygen tube until Zeke's eyes bulged. Then he was gone. Zeke started to fade again after that, but his last thoughts were of Kuwait and his commanding officer, his great friend with the sure-fire deal to keep Zeke out of prison. His true comrade who never even showed up at the court-martial.

There was going to be a day of reckoning for that Judas. It would be intricate and cruel and Zeke knew exactly how to do it. The fool talked too much when he was drunk. Planning it would be logistically complex, but so what. It would take time, but that was okay. Zeke had all the time in the world.

When he finally fell asleep, he was smiling.

Chapter Two
A Person of Interest

I hit the rewind button, held it down for a few seconds and then released it, exactly at the start of the message. The voice resonated through a distortion box, an electronic baritone. "I'm going to bomb the Pops concert. I'm taking out the ruling class of America and there's no way you can stop me. Sell your little houses soon, because this island is finished. I'm going to turn it into a ghost town. Think about that future. I'm going to start it with a bang."

I pushed the off-switch. Haden Krakauer stared at me. "Do we have to hear it again?" I could smell the familiar tang of HALLS menthol cough drops on his breath, and under it the faint hint of vodka. Haden, Haden, I thought. Get it together. He had been doing so well.

"Not right now," I said. "Tell me what you think. Some kind of prank?"

"Maybe. I hope so. But I doubt it. "

A small group of cops had gathered around the big table in the upstairs conference room. Detectives Kyle Donnelly and Charlie Boyce hovered at my shoulders, crowded by some uniforms and even a couple of summer specials. Randy Ray stood in the back with Barnaby Toll, who was supposed to be on dispatch.

News traveled fast at the Nantucket Police Station. Sometimes the place seemed like a bad Disney movie from the fifties, with me starring as the harried single dad trying to manage a house full of orphans. What hijinks would these adorable scamps get up to next? I had a pretty good idea, in this case. I could feel them reaching for their cell phones.

I faced the group. "The information on the tape stays in this room. Tell no one. If the news gets out, I'll know one of you was responsible. Are you listening to me, Barnaby?"

Toll looked up nervously. "What? What did I do?"

"You left your post to see what all the excitement was about. Go back. And don't talk about this to anyone. Including your girlfriend."

Barnaby left and the group dispersed. Randy Ray stopped on his way out. "They're gonna send some heavy hitters in here on this one, boss," he said. "FBI, NSA, DHS—don't let 'em push you around. My dad always told me, there ain't nothing nobody can do to you, if you don't let them push you around."

Haden grunted. He had a language snob's distaste for double negatives. Or was this a quadruple? I didn't feel like untangling it. "I think we'll manage somehow," I told Randy.

When I was alone with Haden and the detectives, I looked around the big handsome room with its flat screen TVs, banks of laptop computers, and sun-filled windows. I felt like a bachelor who had impulsively cleaned his house before a surprise visit from his girlfriend. I wouldn't have wanted the FBI and the Department of Homeland Security poking around the old police station. It had been cramped and shabby, smelling vaguely of rotting wood, burned coffee and mildew. The new building was substantial, professional. Still, I felt a flicker of dread. Randy was right—we were going to be overrun, and I was about to set the whole process in motion. I had no choice.

I turned to Haden. "Get Lonnie Fraker on the phone."

"Wait a second, Chief. Why do the State Police—"

"They have to be notified. So does the FBI. And Homeland Security. This recording has to be viewed as a terrorist threat. There was a detailed memo on this from the DHS in my files when I first got here. Did anyone ever read it?"

Kyle and Charlie studied their shoes.

Haden said, "I did. It was fifteen pages of in-the-event-of-an emergency-shut-up-and-cooperate-with-the-JTTF. That's the Joint Terrorism Task Force—Homeland, the FBI, the Coast Guard, the CIA, the National Guard, FEMA…basically everybody but us. I got together with Chief Bradley and we told everyone the gist of it. It was all bureaucratic jargon and frankly it didn't seem relevant. What do we have here? A whaling museum? We're not exactly a prime target."

I nodded. "That's true, ten months a year. But we're talking about July and August. For those eight weeks this island turns into a Core Priority Terrorist Activity Location, according to the Homeland Security memo. It makes sense. The stock market crashes when the Fed hints that the recovery might take a few more years. What do you think it will do when fifty CEOs are killed in one night? Not to mention John and Theresa Kerry, Colin Powell, Joe Biden, Governor Patrick, and God knows who else?"

"So what do we do?" asked Donnelly. "Cancel the concert?"

I stared him down. "No, Kyle, we do not cancel the concert. We do our jobs. We catch this guy. And we do it before half of the Federal Government stomps in here and takes this department away from us."

"Do you think it's really a terrorist, Chief?" asked Charlie Boyce.

"No, I think it's some kids playing a stupid prank, just like last time. Let's check it out, Charlie. Talk to the guidance counselor at the school. If you know any of the kids, talk to them. The rest of you, ask around. Haden, check the websites that sell these voice distortion machines. And find out who manufactures them. I'm going to get a court order from Judge Perlman. I want to know who bought one of these toys recently. If it's someone on-island we'll know when we get the credit card information."

"Anything else, Chief?"

Kyle Donnelly's open attentive face irritated me. I felt like saying "You tell me." But I controlled myself. "See if you can get a trace on the original phone call." Donnelly took a pad out, and he started scribbling. "Also—someone should get over to Valero's and find out if there've been any unusual fertilizer purchases in the last few weeks. And check the gas stations for big diesel buys. Find out if there's any manure missing at Bartlett's." The detectives looked blank. "Tell them why, Sergeant."

"Homemade explosives," Haden said. "ANFO—Ammonium nitrate/fuel oil. It's what Timothy McVeigh used in the Oklahoma bombing. And while you're at it, check out Marine and Stop&Shop, too. Ask about bulk orders of paint thinner and toilet bowl cleaner. You mix them up with any antiseptic first aid solution and you get the shoe bomber explosive TATP—very unstable, very tough to make. You definitely want to brush up on the science before you fool around with that shit. Also, has anyone bought or borrowed any chemistry textbooks recently? That might be a lead."

"You need a hell of a lot of it for a decent sized bomb," I added. "We should check bulk deliveries from off island, too."

"And military explosives." Haden said. "C-4 and thermite. Semtex, too."

"Check your sources, see if anything's been moving."

"My sources are pretty old and I owe most of them favors already. But okay."

"One more thing," I turned to the others. "Be alert. Put on your regular clothes, go out to dinner and Little League games and dart tournaments—and listen. There's a lot of gossip and innuendo out there. People love to talk. Pay attention. And if you hear anything, report it to me directly. All right?"

They nodded.

"Good then. You have enough to keep you busy for a few days. Let's get to work."

I gestured for Haden to stay behind but immediately regretted it. He didn't need to know what I was really worried about. He had enough on his plate. I studied him for a few seconds. He was just over five foot seven, his body thick with the kind of hard fat that comes from years of weight lifting, years in the past, thinning brown hair and not one of them out of place, scalpel-sharp creases in his spotless uniform. He seemed much too solid to be falling apart.

He was staring at me expectantly. I needed to ask him something, so I chose his favorite subject. "How's your year list coming?"

"Chief?"

"Did you break a hundred yet?"

"Yeah, but—I mean…what do my bird sightings have to do with anything? We have a serious situation on our hands here, and—"

"Maybe we do. Maybe we don't. Meanwhile I have an officer on the force who pays a lot more attention to the world around him than anyone else I know. If you notice some shore bird migrating back from the Arctic early—what was that bird you saw last week?"

"A Whimbrel."

"Right. You notice the Whimbrel, you also notice the shell casing or the heel print in the mud, or the window where someone put up new curtains—or whatever. Those boys out there see nothing."

He ducked his head. "Thanks, Chief. Most people don't get that."

"So? Did you see anything interesting lately?"

He smiled. "There was a Blacknecked Stilt out at Hummock Pond yesterday. That guy should be in Florida right now. Check it out if you're driving by—bright pink legs, white front, black back. Gorgeous bird."

"Okay, Haden. Let's keep an eye out for that other bird—the red breasted Nantucket bomber. That would be a great addition to our year list of criminal species."

"Yes sir."

I stayed in the conference room after he left. The subject of bombs and terrorists had come up with Debbie Garrison just the day before, and the bomber in question was Billy Delavane. If our investigation collapsed among the usual unproductive clues and bogus confessions, Debbie's innuendoes would be my only lead.

I got State Police Captain Lonnie Fraker on the phone. We had sniffed suspiciously around each other for my first few years on the island. There was a natural antipathy between the State Police and the locals. But a big murder case the previous winter had changed things between us. We weren't friends and we never would be, but grudging respect and reluctant affection had begun to poke through the institutional rivalry, like weeds through cracked asphalt.

"I've dealt with these Homeland Security people before," Fraker was saying. "I had to liaise with one of these JTTF outfits when I was working out of Springfield two years ago. And let me tell you, Chief, Joint Terrorism Task Force crews are a fucking misery. I mean, how many assholes can you stuff into one room without everybody killing each other? You got DHS, the goddamn FBI, firemen, National Guard GI Joes. We even had some spook from the NSA fucking things up. I took orders and let them fight it out, you know? I can handle these guys. I speak their language. I'll make some calls, set everything up."

Donnelly stuck his head into the office.

"We traced the call, Chief," he said. "The phone company gave us an override on the number block. It came from Billy Delavane's house."

"I have to go, Lonnie," I said. "Thanks for the help. Keep me posted."

I hung up, rolled my chair back, and stood. "I'll deal with this myself. Assistant Chief Krakauer is in charge until I get back. Refer everything to him."

Haden stuck his head in the door.

"Hey Kyle," he said. "Before you do any more paperwork— try to figure out the difference between 'which' and 'that.' You're a high school graduate."

"Sorry. I will."

I shrugged in mock despair, but Haden wasn't done yet. "You're no better, Chief. And you're supposed to be a writer." I gave him the occasional poem to proofread and he always found something to correct. "The kid has to work on 'which'

and 'that'—you have to brush up 'less' and 'fewer.' 'Fewer' is
for specific things you can count. Like weeks—'fewer than three
weeks.' You wrote 'less than three weeks.'"
  "It sounds better."
  "It's wrong."
  "It's idiomatic. Anyway, what about poetic license?"
  He shook his head. "You barely have a learner's permit, Chief.
Don't push it."

◇◇◇

Driving around the new rotary on the way to Billy Delavane's
Madaket jobsite, I could feel the toxic changes in the island. I'd
been living on Nantucket less than four years, but even in that
short period of time it seemed like the population had doubled.
There was real crime now—ordinary squalid city crime, mug-
gings and road rage and rape.

I had put out a press release at the beginning of the summer
urging women not to walk alone at night. Every time I walked
into the Stop&Shop, the courtesy desk was swarming with immigrants cashing pay checks or using the Western Union service
to send money home to Brazil or Ecuador, Belarus or Bulgaria.
Nantucket had been a white-bread, upper-class enclave. Now it
was turning into a beehive, with workers from all over the world
feasting on the building boom. That boom was sputtering to a
halt. Would all those workers stick around? What would that
do to the crime rate? I was going to have to keep pushing for
more officers, and not just summer specials.

On the long drive down Madaket Road I hit the flashers
for a second to slow down a Hummer. The big car pulled over
but I just drove by. There were twenty or thirty Hummers on
the island in the summer. I would have banned them if I wrote
the laws. They weren't just cars, they were another piece of class
war iconography, a constant reminder of the divisions that were
spoiling Nantucket. The middle class was being pushed out from
above and below, selling property if they had it, or quietly going
bankrupt if they didn't. Town meeting had voted me a pay raise

last year. Good thing—without it I would have had to leave the island myself.

The last real bulwarks against change were people like Billy Delavane, cranky islanders who held onto their properties, loving them because they were old, leaving the horse-hair plaster and clay mortar chimneys intact.

It occurred to me as I neared the western end of the island that things had come full circle. In the whaling days, Nantucket had teemed with sailors from all over the world, looking for the 'greasy luck' of a successful voyage. Wild men of every race and color jostled each other in the crowded streets. The opportunities were different now, but the sense of buccaneering adventure and jackpot optimism remained.

That Brazilian working three jobs was buying real estate in Sao Paolo. That Jamaican riding the bike he found at the dump had scrounged the money for a down payment and was moving his family into a little condo near the airport. That Rumanian tailor had set up shop in a mail-order military tent and was now re-upholstering couches for the Cliff Road set. Sure it was crowded and messy, but that's what was the American Dream looked like when it was coming true. The only people left out were the actual Americans. But maybe it had always been that way. You got lazy and then you got displaced. People loved the idea of competition until they were forced to compete. It was a ruthless process, maybe it was the real social Darwinism, but it kept the country alive.

Nantucket certainly was lively these days.

I found Billy Delavane's jobsite, a sprawling mansion at the far end of Warren's Landing Road, perched on a bluff above Nantucket Sound, surrounded by churned mud and work vehicles. Stone cutters sorted rocks, piecing together the elaborate wall that snaked around the house. A web of scaffolding surrounded the giant chimney under construction thirty feet overhead. Shinglers moved across the roof, crab-like on staging planks. Someone had set up a table saw outside. Painters stood priming trim boards across a pair of work benches. Cedar dust

scented the air and music from at least two different stations
blared from the house, along with the whine of planers, the
bang of hammers, and a Jamaican electrician who kept yelling,
"We're on a ROLL!"

Billy Delavane was in the two-story living room, facing down
a gray cement fireplace.

"Hey Chief," he called out.

A compressor clicked on at that moment and its pneumatic
roar rendered inaudible anything I might say. I lifted a hand in
greeting. When the air pressure had built up again and the big
machine cycled off, I said, "Busy around here."

"Check this out. The fireplace was supposed to be plaster.
Now the people decide they want painted brick. But the bricks
would extend it out another two inches and we'd have to buy
another hearth piece. That's about a thousand bucks worth
of polished granite right there, and these zillionaires are 'on a
budget.' So what do we do?"

"Explain the problem?"

Billy laughed. "That'd work. No, Chief, what you do is find
someone who spent his summers in high school working for
a crazy old Irish mason and tell him to fix it. That'd be me. I
troweled on this cement ten minutes ago. It's about ready, so
stand back and prepare to be amazed."

I retreated a step as Billy started pushing straight lines across
the cement with his thumb, using a wet rag to clean the sludge
off his finger between strokes. When he finished he took a breath
and started making the vertical gouges. By the end it looked
exactly like a wall of gray brick.

I stared. "How the hell did you do that?"

Billy wiped his thumb one more time and threw the rag into
a trash bin. "Talent and practice, Chief. Just like police work.
Or poetry. I used twenty bucks worth of Portland cement and
saved Pat Folger a grand. You'd think he'd give me a bonus. But
all I get is a free lunch."

He glanced over my shoulder. Billy's girlfriend, Abby Folger,
was walking toward us, carrying a brown paper bag and skirting

the step ladders, coils of copper wire, tangled power cords, miter saws, and boom boxes. The cut-off shorts and work boots showed off her legs.

The Jamaican stapled a wire to a stud and shouted, "We're on a ROLL!"

Abby tossed her head toward the electrician. "He's happy."

"We're all happy now," Billy said.

"Except the chief. I have the feeling he'd prefer me to wear baggy pants. But I like the air on my legs."

"You like the eyes on your legs," Billy said.

She smiled. "That, too."

The compressor kicked on again.

"Let's get out of here," Billy shouted.

We followed him to sit out on the deck, our backs against the new shingles, watching sailboats track across the Sound. A ferry headed for the mainland, plowing steadily into the azure distance. Hyannis smudged the horizon. The immense cloudless blue sky arched above us. A gentle breeze shifted and cooled the sunlight. The air brushed our faces like silk.

Billy waved an arm expansively at the view. "This is what people pay a million dollars for. And we get it for free."

I nodded, then shut my eyes and tilted my head back and let the heat press against my eyelids. It felt good. I was tired. I didn't want to have this conversation. I should have sent Haden Krakauer, but I had never learned how to delegate.

"So what's up, Chief?"

"It's police business." My eyes were still shut. "It's private. You probably don't want to have—"

"It's fine. Abby won't even be listening."

I opened my eyes, squinting against the bleached glare of noon. Abby was putting on a pair of earphone buds.

"I have the new Modest Mouse on my iPod," she said.

I sat up straight, turned a little to face Billy. "We got a bomb threat phone call today. It came from your house."

"So I'm a suspect?"

"Not to me. Not yet. You're a 'person of interest' to the investigation."

"In other words—almost a suspect."

"Look, I think some kid made that call. There were a lot of them at your house last night. They trust you. Did any of them say anything odd?"

Billy laughed quietly—a humorless little cough. "One reason they trust me is they know I won't rat them out to the cops."

"I understand. But there's more at stake here than some underage drinking. We had to alert Homeland Security and the FBI. This is serious."

"Okay, okay. But I didn't hear anything."

"Listen, Billy…do you have any idea who might be talking to Debbie Garrison about you?"

"Saying what?"

"That you're capable of setting off bombs. That you're a potential terrorist."

"What the hell? Me? Are they nuts? That's crazy. Who'd say something like that?"

"I don't know. But I'd sure like to find out."

"Me, too, but I mean—"

My cell rang, with the first concussive piano notes from Jackson Browne's "Fountain of Sorrow."

I cut Billy off with a raised hand as I wrestled the phone out of my pocket.

"I just got off the phone with DHS," Lonnie Fraker said into my ear. "They're sending a couple of guys over. No big deal, it's just, you know—SOP. They have to snoop around a little and we have to let them."

"Thanks, Lonnie."

I slipped my iPhone back into my pocket—a hand-me-down from my ex-wife, who always had to have the newest version.

"Anything?" Billy asked.

People always want to know police business. "Nothing." I stood up. "But I have to get moving. I'd tell you not to leave the island, but I know you won't. And talk to Debbie. Someone is spreading some bad rumors about you. Do us all a favor and find out who."

Billy gave me a little salute. I stepped around Abby. Inside the house things were still going well. "We're on a ROLL," crowed the Jamaican.

Back at the station, Haden Krakauer was sitting in my office. He handed me a fax as I walked around the desk. "Is this who I think it is?"

The note was printed on Department of Homeland Security letterhead: protocols and instructions. The gist was that DHS would require the full cooperation of the Nantucket Police Department. In the event of an ongoing investigation we were "tasked" with support services and expediting Federal initiatives.

Donkey work, in other words, if it ever came to that.

Two agents temporarily attached to the Boston office were flying over for a preliminary on-site evaluation—John Tornovitch and Frances Tate. I put the paper on my desk. Haden lifted his hands, palm up.

"What?"

"Come on. Is that Tornovitch from L.A.?"

"Unless there's another one. I heard he got promoted."

"The prick who made your life miserable for six months?"

"People change."

Krakauer laughed. "No they don't. He gave the staties that recording of Diana Lomax talking to her boyfriend, remember? And it wasn't because he wanted to help close our case. He just wanted to make you look bad. Lonnie said so, himself." Haden was right. I remembered thinking I'd never get away from Jack Tornovitch.

Good instinct.

The muted rush of the air-conditioning filled our silence. Haden was waiting. I let him. "Well?" he said finally.

"Well what?"

"Jesus you are a pain in the ass sometimes! *Well*, is this the Frances Tate you've been telling me about since you got off the boat four years ago?"

"They worked together. And Tornovitch always managed to take the credit. So, yeah, probably."

Krakauer was squinting at me. "You're OK with that?"

"I'm delighted."

"Yeah, that's what worries me. They're on the two o'clock flight from Boston. That's forty five minutes, Chief. So get yourself together." He rolled his eyes. "And if you're thinking of writing any poems on NPD time, make sure you let me proof them before you give them to her."

He left and I picked up the fax again.

Franny Tate, after all these years.

Of all the police stations on all the islands in all the world, she walks into mine. I grabbed the brush out of my bottom drawer and slipped out of my office to the bathroom.

I actually needed a haircut, but I didn't have time.

Chapter Three

Reunions

Driving out to the airport, Lonnie started to brief me about the Homeland Security agents. I let him talk for a while.

"I guess what goes around comes around, right Chief? You messed with this guy in L.A., he messed with you on the Lomax case and now, boom, he's right here, out of the blue, taking over this one. Karma's a bitch, am I right?"

I looked out the window "We'll see."

"I don't know this Tate guy, but if he works for Tornovitch, he's gotta be a hard-ass. Check this out. When Tornovitch was with the California Highway Patrol, he used to pull people over for driving exactly the speed limit, that's the kind of dick this guy is."

I nodded. I'd heard all these stories before. "The most annoying part is, the system worked. Every time he pulled over a careful one, he found something. Guns in the trunk. Coke in the glove box. No registration. All of them driving double nickels and signaling for every lane change."

Lonnie grinned. "So how bad did you fuck up in L.A.? I never got the full story on that one."

I shrugged. "Everybody fucked up. Except Franny. I used the case in a novel I was writing. It didn't make the LAPD look good. The brass got wind of it. I had to let them read it. They confiscated the manuscript. It violated the non-disclosure form I had to sign when I was promoted to Robbery-Homicide. But a section of it was already running in *L.A. Weekly.* So I started job hunting."

"Frances Tate. Franny—I get it. So you worked with her, too."

"Tornovitch likes her. She gives him the credit when she figures things out."

"You write about that?"

I nodded.

"No wonder the guy hates you."

"The truth hurts."

Lonnie snorted out a laugh. "This is gonna be fun."

We pulled into the airport parking lot. The flight from Boston was fifteen minutes late. I left Lonnie talking to an agent behind the Nantucket Airlines counter and walked out to the chain link courtyard to wait for the plane, thinking about Franny Tate. It had been a long time, but it didn't seem that way this morning. Maybe she had gotten fat, maybe she had forgotten about me. Two unlikely prospects—Franny was a raw nerve of energy, constantly in motion, living on coffee and bagged salad greens.

And she never forgot anything.

Behind me, a man struggled with the *Boston Globe* in the gusty south-west wind. The plane taxied toward the terminal.

I had been married the last time. Maybe Franny was married now. But probably she wasn't. Franny didn't stand still long enough for that. If she were single, there'd be nothing stopping us, no reason to hold back, apart from work and the watchful eye of Jack Tornovitch. Chaperone was one of the few jobs he was qualified for.

When I turned back to the chain link fence the plane was coming to a stop in front of the terminal, a kid with a reflecting vest and two batons guiding the pilot. I watched Franny walk across the tarmac—the same half run. She always looked like she was about to break into a sprint. She was a little thinner than I remembered and her hair was longer, a great brown mane, scattered by the wind. She wore khaki shorts and a white t-shirt, flip flop sandals. She looked like a tourist. She caught my eye and waved. I waved back. Tornovitch trundled along behind her, squinting in the sunlight, wearing the same wrinkled gray suit and polyester shirt I remembered from L.A. He must have a closet full of them.

Lonnie Fraker stood behind me. "Frances Tate," he said admiringly. "Things are looking up."

"Down boy. She's out of your league."

Franny pushed through the gate and gave me a hug. "Hey, Hank. How are you?"

"Good, Franny. Much better all of a sudden."

"Always the right words."

She disentangled herself and turned to Lonnie with her arm out. "Frances Tate."

"Lonnie Fraker." He shook her hand.

Tornovitch brushed past them.

"Can it," he said. "We have work to do. Write any good books lately, Kennis?"

He was striding into the terminal before I could answer. Franny followed him.

Lonnie turned to me. "Hank?"

I raised my hands in surrender.

We walked out of the terminal, trotting to catch up with the Feds. As we passed the little Homeland Security shed by the taxi stand, Andy Cochran stepped out and raised an arm in greeting.

"Andy."

"Hey Chief. Orange alert today."

"Thanks. We're on it."

We caught up to Franny and Tornovitch on the access road into the parking lot. "I like the look of that kid," Tornovitch said. "I like his attitude."

"Really, Jack? I wish I could feel that way. But half the summer specials I didn't rehire are working for the TSA now. Like this Andy Cochran kid."

"He was probably just overeager, Kennis. The boy looks like a go-getter. No harm in that."

"He was a go-getter all right. He was tearing up girls' parking tickets in exchange for their phone numbers. If terrorists actually show up here, for Andy's sake I hope they're ugly old guys. If they're cute girls, he could wind up joining al Qaida. Which might actually be the most effective way he could help Homeland Security."

Franny gave me a little shove. "That's harsh."

"Yeah? Well, most people who want to be cops should be disqualified automatically. Lord Acton got it right. Power corrupts—even the power to write parking tickets."

Franny narrowed her eyes, her head tilted slightly with alert curiosity. It was an almost canine gesture. She was like a Pointer who had just heard a duck crash into the underbrush. But there was a very human challenge there. I remembered that expression. I used to get it a lot. "Who was Lord Acton, anyway?" she said. "All anyone knows about him is he said that one thing."

"I know a little more."

"Of course you do," Tornovitch snorted.

We had reached the car. Lonnie hit the remote entry, the Explorer honked twice and Tornovitch took shotgun. Lonnie got into the driver's side, and I was alone with Franny for a few seconds in the bright sunlight. A private jet was taking off. We watched it climb.

"So come on, who was this Lord Acton guy, anyway?" Franny asked.

Our first moment alone in half a decade was vanishing fast, and she had derailed it in typical fashion. But she had always enjoyed rummaging around in my steamer trunks of irrelevant information. She was smiling at me now across the SUV's hood.

I took a breath. "Okay. Sir John Emerich Edward Dalberg-Acton. He was a nineteenth-century English historian. When he said that, he was talking about the pope. There's more to the quote, something like—'Great men are bad men.'"

Franny smiled. "Amen to that."

Her parents were both Catholic, I remembered. "Good Catholics," she had said once, with a tired sarcasm that discouraged further questions.

Lonnie honked the horn, at Tornovitch's insistence, no doubt. We got in and Tornovitch was talking before the car doors closed.

◇◇◇

"Okay, let's set some ground rules," he said. "First of all, we are treating this telephone call as a serious infraction. Agency directives specify prioritizing any incident that occurs in a primary threat location, a category which happens to include Nantucket, among areas as diverse as the twenty square miles radius around Camp David in Pennsylvania, parts of lower Manhattan and all of Aspen Colorado. But even without reference to DHS policy, I have to tell you, I would pursue this matter, Kennis. I have a gut feeling about it." He waved a dismissive hand at the passing landscape. "This place is a catastrophe waiting to happen. Or it was. The wait may just be over."

"Jack, I think you're overreacting a little. We don't even know—"

"We know a great deal. I have been fully briefed by the State Police. Captain Fraker was quite informative—a model of inter-service cooperation. You could learn a lot from him." I could see Lonnie's self-satisfied little smile in the rear-view mirror. He lifted his head an inch, chin up, preening like an Afghan hound. I half expected Jack to scratch him behind his ears.

"I'll keep it in mind, "I said.

"Good. Now, here's what you can do for me, Kennis. We have a National Security Letter for The Souk clothing store at 32 Broad Street. I want to turn that business inside out—in town and also the warehouse on Teasdale Circle. I want phone logs, e-mails, billing and accounts receivable, customer lists, credit card records as well as complete personal breakdowns on both Rashid and Patel Lashari."

"The Lasharis are law-abiding citizens, Jack," I said. "What are you going to do—throw them in jail for being Muslim?"

"Maybe I will, Kennis. If that's what it takes. And maybe I'll send them to Guantanamo Bay and if I do, they'll never be heard from again, whether they did anything wrong or not. So back off."

"They're not the main focus of the investigation," Franny said.

"No. Obviously. The main focus right now is on this William Delavane. His credit card was used to purchase a voice changing machine on June 3rd of this year. The numbers are a lock. And that includes the three digit identification code."

"We've been trying to get that information," I said.

"Well, you never will. It's classified now and you need a higher clearance than 'local cop' to access it."

It was all flooding back to me. You couldn't work with Tornovitch for more than twenty minutes without feeling the urge to hit him with something wet and messy.

"I don't believe it," I said. "I have a crime report on file, Jack. Billy's wallet and credit cards were stolen last week."

"How convenient. But we'll be searching his house, Kennis— from the insulation in his attic to the subfloor in his basement."

I shrugged. "Good luck with that."

"Luck has nothing do with it, Kennis. You're about to learn that. We're going to be taking over the emergency response suite at your shiny new police station. On the second floor. I have the specs, Kennis. I do my homework. As you might remember."

"What I remember is that you have an office full of drones to do your homework for you. They work all night and you get a sheet of paper to read on the plane coming over."

"And what do you have? Thirty half-trained summer specials, ten keystone cops in uniform, a couple of detectives who've worked one major case in the last decade, with a twenty million dollar playhouse for them to trash. And, oh yeah, I almost forgot—an alcoholic second-in-command who could fall off the wagon tomorrow. That's nothing to boast about, Chief."

"Gee," I said, "I thought the organization was called 'Alcoholics *Anonymous*.'"

The laser intensified. "Nothing is anonymous. This is the twenty-first century. We're fighting the war on terror and our biggest weapon is information. We can't afford secrets anymore."

"And here we are," Lonnie broke in, cruising past the berm of plantings (like a bad haircut, they were finally starting to grow in and look natural) and into the wide parking lot that faced the handsome brick façade of the new station. The flags on our high poles snapped in the wind. Tornovitch climbed out first. Haden Krakauer was striding toward the car, over the big compass etched into granite by the front doors. He was walking in a straight line. I was pretty sure he could also stand on one foot and touch his fingers to his nose.

I got out and performed the introductions.

Tornovitch was examining the building. "Very nice. But all the new construction in the world can't replace real police work. That's what controls criminal activity—old fashioned leg work. Knocking on doors."

As if he had ever done any of that.

"We have the criminal activity pretty well under control—sir," Haden answered. The gap before the 'sir' drew Tornovitch's attention. He had a heightened sensitivity to insubordination, the faint crackle of disrespect, like Billy Delavane's pug bounding into the kitchen when I peeled the plastic wrapping off the cheddar cheese.

"Except for the bomber." He turned to Haden. "This is a little more serious than your usual island drug busts and two-bit DUIs."

"Let's not get ahead of ourselves," I said." We don't have a bomber. We have a crank call."

"Really? You also have the biggest drunk driving problem in New England. And remember—you're all suspect. One of the 9/11 hijackers was wearing a Nantucket t-shirt. All right? Someone sold it to him. Or maybe it was a gift. We're still investigating that. There's no statute of limitations on treason, Kennis. Now let's get inside, get oriented, and get busy. The clock is ticking, people."

Tornovitch strode into the station. Lonnie Fraker hurried after him. Haden shook his head. "Clock? What clock? There's a clock? Is it going to be ticking until the Pops concert? Because that could really get annoying."

"Get in there," I said. "Play nice."

I hung back with Franny. "Has he gotten worse or is it just my imagination?"

She pushed a hand through her hair. "The worse he gets, the faster they promote him. Maybe he knows something we don't."

"He knows you. That's all he needs."

I first met Franny on a case in Los Angeles. A twenty-five hundred-dollar-a-night hooker had been killed. The crime scene looked like a robbery. But the girl had been involved with some prominent drug dealers, and the FBI wound up big-footing the investigation. Franny and Jack Tornovitch were new partners then, long before their transfer to DHS. This was one of their first assignments. Franny was clearly the junior member of the team. He used to send her out for coffee. But she broke the case. She never bought the robbery angle and started poking around into the alibis.

Detective Sergeant Roy Elkins was lead investigator on the case, out of the Robbery-Homicide Division. He had been my mentor in the LAPD. He knew the girl. He had used her as a drug informant from time to time. Franny had a bad feeling about Roy from the start, but he had a solid alibi for the murder. He had been in line at the Silver Lake post office that Friday, express-mailing a package to his mother for Mother's Day. Friday was always the worst day for that PO, because all the Mexicans showed up to send home their week's wages. Long lines, no air-conditioning. A postal clerk verified Elkins' story. An ambitious, high-ranking officer with no motivation for the killing, the LAPD barely looked at him.

Canvassing the girl's neighborhood, several people told Franny that they could place the time of death exactly because of the daytime television shows they were watching when they heard the gunshots. It seemed an ostentatious way to murder someone in broad daylight, but it set the time of the murder with unique precision. Franny tracked the killer's escape route down through the brush below the house to the next street on the hill. One of the residents there mentioned seeing an unfamiliar Toyota pickup truck parked on the street that day. She thought it might be a workman's truck, but it was gone after she came back from some errands in the early afternoon.

Franny ran everyone involved with the case for their car registrations and got a hit with Roy Elkins. So she went to the actual post office the next Friday, poking around on her own time. When she saw that they opened up a courtesy window for express mail, she asked—did they only do it when the place got jammed up and they had the extra staff? How about the date in question? They looked it up: yes. Then she checked out the clerk on duty that day. And guess what? He had recently bought a flat screen TV with cash. He'd been eating at nice restaurants, shopping at Nordstrom's. There was a post office record of the express mail package. But that slip could have been filled out any time. It was obvious then. Elkins paid the clerk to mail it, using his home label, on the day of the murder, so he could plausibly paint himself as crushed on line behind fifty Mexicans when the crime was going down. All he needed was an official time-stamp for his whereabouts.

Elkins had been working in law enforcement for almost twenty years, so he knew how to manufacture an alibi. But he got careless. He missed one detail. He didn't know about the express window. The clerk didn't care. He took his money and did what he was told. The easiest five grand ever.

The only problem was Special Agent Frances Tate, who had to see everything for herself and never quit until all her questions were answered.

The FBI confiscated Elkins' computer and Franny retrieved his deleted e-mails. He was in love with the woman. He wanted to marry her. She was selling him drugs and he was using heavily. When she dumped him he lost it. An ordinary crime of passion, but Elkins was meticulous in its execution. All that care and planning paid off. The FBI had no hard evidence—no prints, no DNA, no eye-witnesses. Franny's evidence was circumstantial, and without a confession the DA warned that they could easily go to court and lose. They brought Elkins in on the drug charges, Tornovitch sweated him for seventeen hours in the interrogation room, but he stuck to his story. Even after two nights without sleep he knew it was good enough to save him from the lethal injection needle.

So they compromised. Elkins walked on the murder, which was never officially solved. They convicted him on the drug charges, and he got ten years in jail. With some counts suspended for cooperation with the ongoing investigation and time off for good behavior, he was due to be out of jail in less than six months. He might go back to cocaine and he might even commit murder again, but we had the cold comfort of knowing he wouldn't be financing his habits with a police pension or hiding behind a badge.

As Jack liked to point out, it was still a significant case, a major scandal rehabilitated by the vision of a new LAPD, stringent in its standards and willing to work with the FBI to police itself. Despite his failed interrogation, Jack was remembered as the man who broke up an important police drug ring. Franny was furious and heartbroken.

Jack told me, "Write it off as a victory and walk away." That was what he did. He got promoted and went back to Washington. Franny let it go and followed him.

I used the case in my "true crime" book. I told the truth about Elkins. He threatened to sue me and the city. He was still in jail, but he managed to hire one of the toughest litigators in L.A.

I withdrew the book, but I got fired anyway.

And that was it. Six months later, I was living on Nantucket.

Franny and I committed no crimes of passion in those days, though we both wanted to. When I kissed her cheek at LAX I suspected I'd never see her again.

But here she was.

"I want to look at Delavane's e-mails," she said to me now. We were standing by the car again, stealing another moment before we had to go inside. It wasn't the moment I would have liked.

"You're going to need more than the fact that someone bought a voice machine with his stolen credit card."

She pulled her fingers through her hair again. The sun beat down on us. She blew out a breath.

"I almost wish you were right about that."

"I am right about it! Being a random burglary victim doesn't constitute probable cause in a felony investigation. Not in America."

She winced, pulling all those pretty features together. Another familiar look. I was demanding too much. "Talk to Jack about it. I just do the tech work."

"Right. I remember that."

A gentle breeze stirred the damp air, ruffling the flags, setting their chains clanging.

"Well, this is romantic," she said finally.

"Yeah. You and me and Jack, like the old days. I can't help thinking the guy is an arrogant dick who has no idea what's really going on, and I know he feels the same way about me—and what really worries me is, this time we may both be right."

She took my arm. "All you can do is your job, Chief Kennis. Protect and serve."

"Yeah."

"And take me to dinner tonight."

I put my arm around her shoulder. "Eight o'clock?"

"We're staying at the Harbor House. I'll be waiting in the lobby."

She released one arm and pirouetted out from under the other. She trotted for the station and I hurried to follow her.

Chapter Four
Mountains and Molehills

Tornovitch took over Haden's office, which surprised me. I expected him to take mine. But Haden's was on the second floor adjacent to the Emergency Response conference room Jack would be using as a command center.

"Besides," he said to me, "This is still your bailiwick, Kennis. I respect that. I don't walk into a man's house and throw him out on the street. We're going to be working together. I want you on my side. And I want you at your best. Sticking you in a cubicle somewhere doesn't do that for me." He extended his hand and I shook it, startled by this new level of pragmatic civility. We'd see how long it lasted.

Walking out of the office, he noticed my police band scanner. "Keeping track of everybody, Kennis?"

"I find it soothing."

"Admit it, you're a control freak, just like me."

I paused in the doorway, blocking him. "A real control freak wouldn't own up and give you the satisfaction, Jack. So if I disagree I'm admitting you're right."

He showed me a mouth full of sharp white teeth, compressed cheeks narrowing his eyes in a predator's warning. Any resemblance to a smile was a trick of evolution, a Darwinian caprice designed to lull the unwary. "That's why I handle the interrogations, Kennis."

"I remember a seventeen hour one, Jack. How did that work out for you?"

"Take a look. It should be obvious."

I called a meeting half an hour later and he gave us our marching orders. Everyone settled in the Emergency Response room. Boyce, Donnelly, Krakauer, all the ranking uniforms. Jack stood at one end with Franny by his side. She stood quietly, hands clasped in front of her, letting him do the talking.

"All right, people. News travels fast so you know who we are. I'll learn your names as it becomes necessary. I'm aware of the fact that some of you don't take this threat, or our visit, seriously. But at Homeland Security we have to take every threat seriously. This isn't a game—we can't afford to lose a point. We have to win every time. If we lose, people die. I am tasked with preventing that and you are tasked with helping me in every way you can, including obeying orders that you don't agree with or even understand. I welcome your questions—after the fact. Obey orders and discuss them later. I know I have the Chief's backing on this."

Everyone looked at me. I nodded.

"We are currently looking at three suspects. Ricky Wynand, who called in a false bomb threat to the Steamship Authority two years ago. He is currently employed at On-island Gas on Sparks Avenue. I want him in custody this afternoon. The same goes for William Delavane, and for Rashid and Patel Lashari, proprietors of The Souk clothing store on Broad Street. I have National Security Letters granting me access to all business records of that store, as well as the gas station and Folger Construction, Delavane's employer."

"Pat Folger ain't gonna like that," Charlie Boyce said. A knowing chuckle rose up and subsided, extinguished by Tornovitch's glare, which descended like one of those dunce-cap candle-snuffers. There was nothing he could do about the curl of amused provincial smoke that rose off the chastened group, though. They all knew Pat, some of them had been on the sharp end of his temper, and they'd back him against most terrorists and any DHS agent, especially this one.

"Stick around," Tornovitch said. "I'll have your individual assignments in a few minutes."

People shuffled out. I could see Franny pulling him down a little so they could have a whispered conference. He nodded and started to answer, but she interrupted him and he went back to nodding. A change of plans was obviously in the works. I wondered if he'd acknowledge Franny when he made the announcement. Not likely. The room cleared out. Haden and I lingered at the door until Jack called us over.

"It occurs to me that bringing in this Delavane character might be a mistake," he said. Haden had noticed the brief conference with Franny. He shot me a look. Jack saw it, of course. "You have something to say, Krakauer?"

"No, sir."

"Good. Now let me lay this out for you. If Delavane isn't the one we're looking for, we'll have needlessly antagonized an ordinary citizen. More importantly, if he is the one, then we'll have alerted him, which will make it much tougher to monitor his activities and gather any substantial evidence. He might go underground completely until we're gone. Much better to put him under surveillance, at least for now. Franny can check out the gas station, talk to the owner. Wynand doesn't need to know anything. Kennis—you and I are going to pay a call on our Muslim friends. We'll have the element of surprise in our favor."

"I bet they've been expecting us for the last decade or so."

"Then we're long overdue. Get your people out on the street, pick someone to tail Delavane, and let's get moving. It stinks up here. Someone's been smoking. You'd better deal with that. I don't like cops breaking the law. I fired an agent for littering once. Franny can tell you. She was there."

I glanced at her. She nodded. Her eyebrows lifted a little in mockery and fatigue.

"He was a highly qualified agent," she said. "An encryption specialist. And he spoke fluent Arabic."

"That had nothing to do with it," Tornovitch snapped.

Franny looked down. "Of course not."

"Though you have to wonder—why study the language of Islamofascism if you're not interested, know what I mean? Most people study French. Or Spanish. This kid chose Arabic. I guess he wanted to read the Koran in the original."

Downstairs, I found Randy Ray by the coffee machine in the break room, dumping cream and sugar into a mug of Starbucks Morning Blend.

He still had his football physique and his fast metabolism, but his body had some unwelcome surprises in store for him. He was the perfect candidate for a middle-aged beer gut.

"How would you like to do the surveillance on Billy Delavane?" I said.

"Me? Really?"

"You're a local, you know Madaket. You blend in."

He set the mug down on the chipped Formica counter. "Listen, Chief, I was thinking about this. Some friends of mine are working on a crew, painting one of those houses on Maine Avenue. I think it's like two doors down from Billy's place. It's the perfect observation post. You're outdoors all day, you can see everything and the best part is, you're actually supposed to be there. No one looks twice at you."

I nodded. "Sounds good. You can have the day shift. Drive your own car down there and park it out of sight. Keep track of the mileage and gas."

"Thanks, Chief. I'm on it."

Tornovitch was waiting for me outside. I drove him into town and we found a spot in front of the old police station on Chestnut Street. It was clouding over and the wind had shifted around to the northeast. The streets were crowded. Summer specials were chalking tires and writing tickets. Most of the tourists looked miserable, gritting their teeth through another family nightmare, despite the ice-cream cones and smoothies and cell phones everyone was clutching. I was the only one on the street with my hands free. I reached down to catch a pair of five-year-olds as they careened into my legs. They twirled away from me and kept going. We turned the corner and their mom brushed past us, yelling and apologizing in the same breath. "I'm so sorry—Billy! Tommy! You come back here!"

Tornovitch blew out a disgusted breath. "No discipline. Those kids are running wild."

"At least they're safe here. In the city she'd be right to panic."

He laughed at that—the usual dismissive grunt.

"It's true."

"I have a term for people like you, Kennis. Truth procrastinators. You don't deny it. You put it off as long as possible. Like this bomb threat thing. You think I'm making mountains out of molehills. Maybe I am. But this place feels like Mount St. Helens to me. And you're the kind of guy who buys real estate on the side of a volcano because you don't believe nice places blow up. Well, they do. I've seen it happen. I know the signs."

Maybe, but he didn't find any at The Souk, or at their out of town storage space, except dull financial records and boxes full of clothes and trinkets. But Jack scared the crap out of the Lasharis. That seemed to mollify him a little.

And there was news waiting for us back at the station.

Charlie Boyce and Kyle Donelly shuffled and shifted outside my office. Charlie was ten years older than Kyle and his hair was starting to thin, but they looked like brothers—two big men who had held down the Nantucket High School Whalers' defensive line in different eras. Kyle had never gotten farther away from Nantucket than Christmas shopping at Marshall's in Hyannis. Charlie had been to John Jay College in New York City and worked for the Boston Police Department. He wasn't suited for big city life, though. Maybe none of us were.

He took my arm and pulled me a few steps away from Jack.

"What?" I shrugged free.

"It's about the drug thing, Chief. Pat Folger's still following the guys who got his kid hooked on oxy. They caught him taking pictures of people going in and out of the house. There was a scuffle. Pat punched one of the guys."

"Did we get a call?"

"No—that's the whole point. Why wouldn't they call the cops? Anybody normal would call the cops, right? But these guys are illegal immigrants and drug dealers so that's the last thing they want."

"How do we even know it happened?"

"Tim Lepore called from the hospital. Apparently Pat broke a knuckle on this guy's jaw. So Pat got on the line and starting yelling at me to go in there and bust these guys. With no warrant and no evidence—nothing but some crazy contractor's random snap shots. Guy needs to be sedated."

"I don't know. He's making more progress than we are."

"That doesn't surprise me." Tornovitch strode up to us. "But as it happens, we have a real case to work. And I need to see some results."

Charlie started to speak, then deferred to Kyle. "Tell him."

"Well, we brought in the Wynand kid? He was scared witless but he didn't do anything. He hangs out with Billy Delavane though. He gave us some names. Kid's in the group, one of Billy's favorites."

"So?" Jack was still gruff but I could tell he was interested.

"We went to the houses."

"How did you get a warrant so fast?"

Charlie shrugged. "We didn't need anything like that, sir. We know these people. They were happy to help out. Kyle played football with Corey Herrick's big brother. I bought my used bug from his dad, and his mom always helps out with the firehouse Halloween party."

Jack shook his head. "You drive a Volkswagen beetle? How do you fit into it?"

"He looks like a turkey in a microwave," Kyle said.

"I bet he does. Not the recommended way to cook a turkey by the way. So let me guess the rest, Boyce. You found the voice changing machine in one of these houses."

Charlie ducked his head. He could feel his moment being cut short. "Yes, sir."

"Of course the kid and his parents knew nothing about it."

"Uh—that's right."

"But you confiscated the machine and checked the serial number against the credit card sale, so you know it's the same machine."

"Yes we did."

"So put it together for me."

"Excuse me, sir?"

"Do the rest of your job, Boyce. The important part. Put it together for me."

"Well… Billy is the Herrick's caretaker. He makes sure the pipes don't freeze when they're away in the winter, stuff like that. So he has a key. He could have hidden the machine there. Assistant Chief Krakauer called Barnstable prison. Apparently Billy's been visiting his brother a lot lately. Ed was in the Army in Kuwait. He has military connections. If Billy wanted military grade explosives, Ed would be the guy to ask. Just saying."

"There's another way to look at this," I put in. "Corey stole Billy's credit card and bought the voice changing machine with it. He's friends with the Wynand kid, so he decided to do him one better—adolescent copy-cat behavior. He made the call from Billy's because he was there all the time and he wasn't dumb enough to call from his own house."

"Did you find the stolen credit card?" Jack asked.

"No."

"Did you look for it?" I said.

"No, it didn't—I didn't think of that, sir."

I turned to Jack. "I'm not sure the caretaker angle means much. Most people leave their houses unlocked around here."

"That's not the point. These people know him. If they caught him inside their house he could make up a dozen reasons for being there. Are you defending this Delavane character, Kennis? If you have some connection to this individual that affects your judgment or your ability to act decisively, you are obliged to disclose that information."

"Forget it. I'm happy to arrest Billy Delavane or anyone else. If I have any reason to believe they're guilty."

"Well, congratulations, Chief. You have fulfilled the minimum basic requirement for any police officer in any jurisdiction. Even this one. I'm glad to see you set your standards so high."

I almost said, "And I'm glad to see that you're capable of sarcasm. You're inching your way toward an actual sense of humor," but I thought better of it. Like most people, Jack could laugh at something he knew in advance was a joke. He could laugh at other people's embarrassments—but never at himself. And nothing else counts, unfortunately.

"All right," he said. "With the Lasharis looking clean and the Wynand boy informing on his friends, Delavane is the best lead we've got. I want someone senior watching the house for the next few nights. Donnelly—rendezvous with officer Ray at five, debrief him and set up your position."

Donnelly squeezed his throat with his thumb and forefinger, pulling at the loose skin below his Adam's apple. It looked like he was trying to massage the words out of his throat.

"I, uh—I have a date tonight, sir."

Tornovitch clapped him on the shoulder. "Not anymore."

Donnelly gave me a pleading look, but I was in no position to help. I was sure his surveillance would come to nothing. Tornovitch reminded me of those UFO freaks, stalking the perimeter of Area 51 in Nevada, hoping for a close encounter. But all the Air Force has squirreled away in Area 51 are unmanned stealth aircraft and cruise missiles. And all we had were bored teenagers with free phone service and time on their hands.

Or so I thought.

Ezekiel Beaumont: Ten Months Ago

Zeke Beaumont watched the panda. All he could think was, you're still in jail, my friend. You're a lifer. A swarm of kids tumbled past his legs, shouting and laughing. The panda glanced up, chewing meditatively on his bamboo. He didn't care.

Zeke had been inside for ten years but he had spent every waking minute of that time thinking about freedom, making plans, and organizing the future.

The brig shrink had always advised him to 'forgive and forget.' Zeke had nodded, but he was laughing inside. That was for saints and Alzheimer's victims. Zeke was proud of his memory. He collected grievances and this one was special. This was the biggest one of all, and ten years didn't mean anything next to that. Neither did thirty years, or forty. It was never too late to set things right.

He strolled back to the hotel on the wide, sun-hammered streets, the tall palm trees lined up like an honor guard against the cloudless blue sky. Zeke was wearing shorts and sandals, a light cotton t-shirt. He could feel the warm air on his arms and legs. That was freedom, wearing shorts on a hot day.

Later he sat in the air-conditioning watching the TV with the sound off, nursing a room-service Tom Collins, assessing his progress. Things went so much faster in the outside world. Scooter had been depositing his money in the downtown Bank of America branch, just as he promised. Well, Scooter had good reason to keep his word. Scooter had his own grievances.

Zeke had checked into the hotel, bought himself a laptop, wiped the operating system and installed Linux so he could work comfortably.

He needed to find someone rich, someone casual about the purchases he made online, someone with a job that kept him moving around the country, someone single, someone with no immediate family, someone who wouldn't be missed.

Because the only foolproof way to steal someone's identity, the only way to really make sure it stayed stolen, was to kill them—unfortunate but true. One slip and the ATM machine would eat the card. Two minutes later the police would have you flat on the sidewalk with your hands cuffed.

Zeke narrowed the candidates to ten, but after studying their employment histories, as well as all the public information on real-estate transfers, driving records, insurance claims, school transcripts, marriages and divorces, income tax returns, travel itineraries, phone logs and e-mails, most of them had some disqualifying detail—a steady girlfriend, a nosy boss, a pimped-out car, some odd habit. One of them always played squash with the same partner. Another one owned a falcon. Any pet was a disqualifier—a dog was bad enough. But a falcon? Well, it took all kinds. This guy's bird had just saved his life, though he would never know it.

Zeke crossed another name off the list.

Fourteen hours later, when the work was done, Zeke Beaumont was officially someone else, someone much more prosperous and sophisticated, someone who had only two things in common with the ex-con from Miramar he used to be: a face, and a mission.

The next step was contacting Scooter. Zeke had maintained an e-mail correspondence with him from a secure address in the Brig office. He had followed Scooter's career as closely as he had monitored those monthly deposits to the war-chest bank account. It was typical of Scooter that he had gotten personally burned in the big bust just as badly as Zeke, but nothing showed. He buried it inside, out of sight. It didn't affect his Army career or his discharge. Scooter's genius for the quick escape, his ice cold ability to just turn and walk away had made everything possible—for both of them.

They both would have loved to nail Eddie, but the General was on the Joint Chiefs of Staff now, all the evidence long buried. Back then, Zeke's CO could have taken Eddie down. The CO could have made a difference, but he didn't. The CO chickened out and walked away. The CO made promises he couldn't keep, and Zeke had paid the price. Nothing else changed. The drug trade was up and running again by Christmas. A few little people got trashed, so what? A few bodies by the side of the road, who cares?

That was the CO's attitude.

But that attitude was going to change. Because the CO was going to find out some old school home truths now—actions have consequences and betrayers pay for their crimes. That was why Zeke had kept quiet for once. He had been offered a sweet deal—he could have ratted Scooter out. They both knew it. But he didn't, and now he was reaping the benefits. It wasn't only the bank account. It was the unity of purpose that mattered now. Scooter owed him and Scooter was still angry and Scooter was still hurting and Scooter was committed to seeing this thing through to the end.

That was worth more than money.

The waiting was over now. For both of them.

Zeke touched the screen of his new iPhone and listened to the ring on the other end. When Scooter picked up, Zeke said "I'm ready."

In the pause that followed he could hear Scooter's breathing. Zeke understood it. He knew that hesitation. He had felt it himself. It was one thing to know you were going to do something important and dangerous, at some point in the future. It was something else when the future ran out and there was nothing but the present, and you had to commit.

"I'm there," said Scooter.

Then he hung up. As always, Scooter knew exactly what to say—just two words, but they told Zeke everything he needed to know. Now he had a plan and he had a partner. He had a trap and the means to set it.

All he needed was the bait.

The girl was innocent, but so what? She wouldn't get hurt. She was just the primary ignition, something both trivial and cataclysmic—the discarded cigarette in the late August hay barn. The fire was what counted.

And the fire itself, a bizarre scheme, a preposterous conspiracy of bombs and planted evidence? That had nothing to do with Zeke Beaumont. He hadn't thought that one up. No way—that was the CO's idea, coming out of his fucked-up head and his drunken mouth, night after night in the officers club bar at Camp Doha. It was all about him. He figured it out and brooded and added all the neat little extra touches—always adding little curlicues to his perfect revenge fantasy. And that was the point, right there. For the CO, that's all it was—a fantasy, a game he played with himself to stay sane in the desert.

Zeke's inspiration was to take that drunken desert mirage, and make it real—to steal the CO's daydream and turn it against him.

Zeke stood up and stretched. He walked to the big picture window with its view of the cluttered roofs and the smog. It would be time to order dinner soon.

He walked back to the computer and opened the file he had created for relevant data, scrolling again through his pictures of the girl lifted from the hard drive of her mother's computer. He had hacked into it from the girl's Facebook page that afternoon. The mother's e-mails told him everything he needed to know. She was going back home for the first time since the kid was born. The grandmother had died, there was a lot of property, and the will was complicated. The idea was a last family summer on the island, but the girl didn't want to come. There was nothing to do on Nantucket, she didn't know anyone and she didn't want to leave her friends. She couldn't imagine any possible reason for spending a month "during the most important summer of my whole life" getting sunburned on some beach and traipsing through a stupid museum full of harpoons and whale bones whenever it rained. Which was most of the time, supposedly.

She couldn't imagine a reason? That was all right—she didn't need to.

Zeke had a reason for her—the best reason in the world.

It was time for Mommy to learn that no one can keep a secret forever.

He had already composed the posting to the girl's Facebook page. The fuse was lit. Now he had to get to Nantucket. He wanted at least two months lead time. There was a lot to do and he wanted to make sure everything was ready when the girl arrived. He closed the computer and sat back with a contented sigh, whispering to himself, rolling the words on his tongue like ripe fruit.

"It's on, it's happening. I'm making it happen."

At last.

Chapter Five

Dinner at Cru

Eighty minutes before the first bomb went off, smashing our cozy resort-island summer into a season of rage and blood and terror, I was having a swell old time on my first evening out with an old flame.

I got to the Harbor House early and Franny was waiting for me. She emerged from behind a potted ficus tree while I was checking out the lobby. She was wearing a pale green silk dress that brought out the color of her eyes. The dress left her shoulders bare and fell to just above the knee. Her hair was down and the sight of her caught my breath in my throat for a second. The phrase 'dressed to kill' flitted through my mind.

"Are you all right?" she said.

I swallowed some air. "That dress should come with a warning label. You need to learn the Heimlich maneuver before you wear it."

She stepped forward and pressed herself to me. I held her, buried my face in her hair. She smelled the same, the citrus shampoo mingling with some sharp musk of her own. It was overpowering. I eased away from her. People were staring at us. The police chief was making a spectacle of himself with some off-island woman.

She took my arm as we walked outside, along the bottom of the town on South Beach Street toward the strip. The streets were crowded. The rain had finally cleared off to the south. Kids on bikes and bicycle cops whipped past going both directions. Couples of all ages strolled by. You could also see the requisite "Mr. Man" types, captains of industry, talking into their iPhones. A pack of high school girls swarmed past us. They'd spend the rest of the evening hanging out in front of the fast food restaurants on the Broad Street strip. I generally posted a couple of summer specials there. Tonight it was two kids named Jimmy who'd been loitering on the fringes of the in-crowd themselves a few years ago. I nodded to them as we walked past. They straightened up and tried to look—not busy, since there was really nothing for them to do—alert, anyway.

"So," Franny said. "Did you ever finish that book?"

"It was bad."

"Not to mention libelous."

"I could have gotten around the libel part if it was any good." I pointed ahead of us with a slight chin lift. "I hate these crowds."

"I'm with you." We walked along, forced apart frequently as we bucked the heavy pedestrian traffic. "So what else do you hate?"

I thought for a second. "Fat people. Successful writers. Tourists. People who yell at their kids in public."

I cocked my head to the left, and Franny looked across the street, where a frazzled looking woman was leaning down over her six-year-old, wagging a finger in his face.

"I told you to go to the bathroom before we left the hotel! Now you're just going to have to wait!"

"Well, that's child abuse," Franny said.

"And the worst part is, she'll never admit she was wrong and she'll never say she's sorry. At least if she's anything like the women in my life. They just can't do it. I don't know why."

She took my hand. "I was wrong. I'm sorry."

"Thanks. That was nice to hear. But it doesn't count unless there's something at stake."

"You just wait. Apologies are my specialty."

A Cadillac Escalade roared by us, twenty miles over the speed limit. Two kids had to leap back onto the sidewalk to avoid getting hit. The momentary urge to sprint after the big SUV was overwhelming. I must have actually started because I felt Franny tug me back.

"Down, boy."

"That's something I hate. People who drive like that. Sometimes I want to arrest everyone—throw them all in jail, impound their cars and their cell phones and their computers and their TVs, and give their stupid McMansions which they use two weeks a year to the homeless people who need a roof over their heads."

"Do the selectmen know you're a communist?"

"I'm not a communist. It's summer on Nantucket, that's all. And I hate the selectmen, too. They're useless. All they do is put up unnecessary stop signs at random intersections so we can write more traffic tickets. Parking tickets and traffic tickets! This town lives on that money. I have forty people working for me and ninety percent of what they do is write tickets."

We turned the corner onto Easy Street. We passed a few ramshackle galleries and then the harbor opened out to us, amber in the evening light, dense with boats, a whole separate city of pleasure craft, every mooring taken at this time of year. The North Wharf houses marched out into the incoming tide.

Franny stopped to look, caught by the scooped coves of Coatue looping away beyond the boats, merging with the shadow line of Great Point at the head of the harbor. The serene vista opened her face, relaxed it. She looked young and vulnerable.

I remembered the last time I saw that expression. I had taken her high up on the backbone trail above Will Rogers State Park in the Santa Monica Mountains. It had finally stopped raining after a four day monsoon and the air was as clear as stream water. She had paused, out of breath from the steep grade, in the middle of a wood plank bridge that spanned a deep ravine. The dry air was scented with manzanita and eucalyptus. The city spread out below us, vast and intricate all the way to the ocean where Catalina dozed on the Marine layer like a porpoise on a rock. No sound from that glittering mosaic of buildings and traffic reached us—just the respiration of the wind. She took it in, wide-eyed, and I grabbed her and kissed her. It had been a mistake, submitting to that impulse. It might be an even worse mistake now. I let the pulse of desire move through me and disperse out into the harbor, following her gaze.

"It's beautiful," she said. "You get to see beautiful stuff every day."

"Washington is beautiful. All those white buildings and monuments."

"Spoken like a true tourist. There are maybe twelve pretty buildings, and they're surrounded by some of the worst neighborhoods in the Western Hemisphere. I'll give you a tour of south DC sometime. Anacostia is especially nice. If you're wearing body armor."

I slipped my arm around her shoulder. "So you're an old crank, too."

"I guess."

"Well come on, let's hear it. What do you hate?"

Her nose bunched up a little, as if sniffing the air for an idea. "People who don't clean up after their dogs," she said, sidestepping a little Tootsie Roll turd and lightly kicking it into the gutter with the side of her foot, soccer-style.

"That was brave, for a woman in sandals," I said.

"Ugh. You're right." She paused and cocked a knee to check out her foot. "All clear."

We started off again. "So, go on."

"Okay…I hate—sports on TV? The old bread and circus."

"You have to do better than that."

"How about shoes? I hate the shoes women are supposed to wear. It's like a hundred years ago in China. Binding women's feet."

"And? Come on—gimme."

"How about the glass ceiling at Homeland Security? We both know I should be Jack's boss."

"How about Jack?"

She tossed her hair out of her eyes with a flick of her head. The wind coming off the harbor scattered it again. She held it down with one hand. We were walking beside the Stop&Shop parking lot now, past the cheap tourist stores.

"Jack's all right," she said. "He's not worth hating."

"So that's it?"

"What?"

"Tight shoes, football and bureaucrats?"

"Don't forget dog shit."

"Yeah, that's controversial."

We passed Harbor Square, the plaza at the base of Straight Wharf. The cupola at the center was jammed with people and every outdoor table at the Tavern was taken. People jostled past us. Franny took a breath, started to speak, then released it as a sigh.

"That was something," I said.

"Not really."

"Come on."

"Okay." She pulled in another breath. "I was pretty pissed off at you for a while there."

"What did I do?"

"It's what you didn't do." We headed up Straight Wharf toward Cru. She veered off to look at the harbor. A pair of sea gulls were fighting over some discarded junk. A white paper bag floated on the dark water. "I kept track of you after I left L.A." she said. "I used the computer."

"You were a Google-stalker?"

"No. That's for amateurs. There's a program at DHS called CARGO—Coordinated All-Region Government Oversight. It can track anyone's personal data. Not just meta-data, like the NSA. We monitor phone calls, web searches, and e-mail. Combined with the new facial recognition algorithms and license plate identification and the real-time information from your smart phone, we can figure pretty much everything you do, everyone you know and everywhere you go."

"Well, Snowden blew the lid off all that," I said.

She shrugged. "Not really. Everyone knew it was happening and nobody really cares. Kids don't even want privacy any more. They want to post their drunk party pictures on Facebook. They get pissed off when no one reads their blogs. Nothing is real if you don't tweet it."

"And that's all fine until the government decides you're a problem. So everyone stays in line. Fit in, don't draw attention to yourself."

She smiled. "Sounds like small town life."

"Ain't it the truth?"

"Anyway…I worked on the CARGO software and I had access. I didn't initiate any surveillance protocols—I didn't snoop on you. But I knew you got divorced. So I got your number and I called you."

"Yeah. And I called you back. Three times. It was a work number. I tried using my own contacts to figure out your home number, but I got nowhere. Finally I called the D.C. police and tried to con them into letting me have it. No dice."

She was staring at me through the gloom "You called me back?"

"Three times, over two weeks."

"Shit. Goddamn it."

"What?"

"People suck. And just when you think you've figured all the ways they suck and how much they suck, they find a new way to suck and they suck worse."

I had to laugh. "Okay, but I don't see what—"

"It's Jack. All my calls went through his office. They screened every in-coming message."

More seagulls had joined the fun. They got the bag open and were feasting on water-logged potato chips and crusts of bread, cawing at each other to protect their share of the booty.

"Why would Jack—?"

She shrugged. "A couple of reasons. I'm sure he'd say that the Department of Homeland Security had mandated a moratorium on personal calls during high alert episodes. Which is about ninety percent of the time."

"What if I had called on a low-risk day?"

Franny took my hand and we started back up toward the restaurant.

"He suspected we'd been…intimate." I started to protest. "Well, you did kiss me that day." I subsided, pleased that she was willing to acknowledge the kiss after all this time. "You had made some negative comments about religious profiling…kind of like what you said today. That made you a security risk. Our connection rendered me unreliable. It was his responsibility as the special agent in charge to eliminate any possibility of a breach."

"And he was jealous."

She nodded "Mostly he was jealous."

"What a turd."

"Come on. He had a crush on me. I think that's sweet. It shows his human side."

Cru was perched at the end of the pier, with big open windows looking out on the water. A girl at the podium in front checked our reservation and then turned us over to an eager young Brazilian guy who showed off his English as he led us to our table in the front room, recommending special entrees and encouraging us to take a walk along the longer spit of dock beyond the restaurant, if we "chose to partake of some postprandial exercise."

Franny saw the look on my face and bit down on a laugh as we seated ourselves.

"No postprandial exercise for you, buddy," she said. "You're lucky you're getting dinner."

"That is so unfair. My motives are pure."

"That's what I'm afraid of." I must have made some little grunt of amusement as we passed the bar, because Franny said "What?"

"See that guy, the tall thin blond one—blue blazer, khakis, top-siders?" I realized I could have been describing half the men in the restaurant, but Franny followed my glance and nodded.

"Check out the girl next to him," Franny said. "She's drinking her Scotch with a straw. That's bizarre."

"At least it's not a flavor straw."

"They still have those?"

"My kids love them. The last hold-outs against healthy products and natural flavors."

The girl laughed at something the man said. The smile lit up her austere Slavic features. She laid a hand on his knee. I was impressed. "Anyway, this guy—Tyler Gibson—."

"You remember his name?"

"I remember all their names. It's a curse. So, anyway—Gibson storms into my office a few weeks ago. He wanted a resident parking sticker because he was renting a house. He'd have been in the office all day if some other angry jerk hadn't shown up. I remember thinking, what a useless bullying punk this guy is. No style, no charm, no social graces—just money and a mouth. But somehow or another he's about to score with that incredible girl over there."

Franny shrugged. "Money helps. So does a mouth, some-times." Franny stole another look as we sat down at our table. "She looks Eastern European."

"I'm sure she is. Every attractive woman from Krakow to Vladivostok seems to wind up here eventually."

The waiter came to the table and I ordered a Mojito. Franny chose white wine. She looked around the bright, high-ceilinged room. The last light was just touching the yachts moored nearby.

"Look at those boats," she said.

"Some of them are so big they can't even get in to the harbor. It's a whole little subculture. I eavesdrop on them at fund raisers. All they talk about is their stuff. 'My yacht has a bigger sky bar than yours' 'But mine carries two helicopters.' They can't under-stand why the old money Nantucketers won't talk to them. One of them actually said to me after some old Yacht Club Yankee walked off in the middle of a sentence, 'Why did he do that?' I answered, 'because you're greedy and boring.'"

"What did he say?"

"'Don't expect any donations to the Police Benevolent Asso-ciation this year.' As he stamped off I said, 'Petty and vindictive, too.' I actually got yelled at by one of our selectmen for that one."

"You always had a knack for public relations."

"So did anything ever happen between you and Jack?"

She sipped her wine. "He did ask me out finally. In violation of all his own policies about co-workers seeing each other socially. I took the occasion to tell him I was getting married."

I set my drink down and double-checked her left hand. "You're not married now."

"It was a mistake."

"Let me guess. He wanted you to quit and be a stay-at-home mom."

"Something like that. I was supposed to dust the town house and change diapers while he went off to teach."

"A teacher with a town house. He must have had family money. I'm sure they thought you were a gold digger."

"Ugh. I'd rather be broke. Which I was anyway. I had to sign a seventeen page pre-nup. When we got divorced I even had to give back the presents he bought me. Including the BWM 330ci coupe I got for my thirty-second birthday."

"Sorry about that."

"Don't be. It was an automatic."

"Yeah—who wants a sports coupe without a stick shift?"

"He didn't know much about cars."

"He didn't know much about you. That's my reading."

She drained her wine. "Let's order."

I had swordfish. Franny chose lobster. She worked the meat out of the claws expertly, bit down and sucked it out of the legs while I told her about my own divorce, which had been unusually temperate. Miranda got custody of the kids and the house had been in her family since the 1940s. I liked my little apartment, I loved my time with the kids, but I relished my time alone.

"You walk into the empty house, and the TV is off and no music is playing and there's no mess and the place is—I don't know…it's like—resonant with silence. Like the walls have finally stopped vibrating. You ease yourself into it like a hot bath. And by the end of the night you miss them again."

She put her fork down, wiped her mouth with a napkin. "But doesn't it bother you that the State of Massachusetts automatically gives custody to the mother?"

"It did at first. Then Haden Krakauer set me straight. He said, 'Don't kid yourself, Chief. When was the last time you made a Halloween costume?' No, really—he's right. Sometimes I'm picking up a pizza on a night when I barely got home in time to feed them, and I think 'At least they'll get a decent meal from Miranda tomorrow. There'll be a vegetable.' It's a huge relief."

Franny took a sip of wine and set the glass aside. "You're a good dad," she said. "I must be getting older, because I find that incredibly attractive."

"Good," I said. I stood up, with the backs of my knees pressed against my chair and leaned across the table to kiss her.

And at that moment, the bomb went off.

Chapter Six

Circumstantial Evidence

Haden Krakauer was standing at the edge of wharf, looking into the black water when we sprinted up to him. Barnaby Toll lingered a few feet away. Two uniforms, Bruce Hussey and Dave Praeger, were stringing crime scene tape and three cruisers were pulled up to the terminal building, red and blue lights flashing. A crowd had started to gather. We pushed through them and ducked under the yellow tape.

"Are you all right?" I asked.

"Still half deaf," Haden shouted. "But otherwise okay, I guess. Jesus, Chief. Look at this place." The corner section of the pier tilted down toward the water and a raw crack cut through the asphalt toward us. One of the big bulkhead dolphin-shaped supports canted to the left.

"I picked up an officer-down call from Barney and on the way over dispatch caught another one from the Steamship Authority office."

Barnaby was edging toward us. I gestured him over with tipped head and a hand curl. "What happened?"

"It—I was…someone jumped me, sir. I was on patrol. It was quiet—between boats. I had gone down to Jim's to get a cup of coffee. I was only gone for five minutes. Everything seemed okay when I got back. Next thing I know, someone's got me in a

headlock, the coffee spills all over me. I let him take me down—
playing possum in case I could do something later, get the drop
on the guy. He went around the corner of the building—that
was when I called it in. Then, I don't know—someone inside
must have heard something, because this guy from the office
came running out. He didn't stand a chance though. I called an
ambulance. Then Lieutenant Krakauer showed up."

The ambulance was approaching through the Steamship
parking lot. I glanced at Haden and he walked off to meet it.

"So you didn't actually see anything," Franny said.

"No."

"Or do anything? You never got up?"

"No."

"Did you hear anything?"

"A scuffle. But then it was over and I didn't want to, you
know…complicate things. I thought it was better to just stay put."

"Smart move."

"Nothing like that ever happened to me before," Barnaby said.

She stroked his arm, calming him down as she might gentle
a horse.

"It's okay, Barney. Is that what everyone calls you? Barney?"
He nodded. "Just think, now. Did you notice anything? Was he
wearing cologne? Did he have bad breath? Like—garlic? Or…
he had you in a headlock. You must have seen his arms. Were
they hairy? Any scars? Any tattoos?"

Krakauer was back. I took a few steps with him.

"Find out where the Steamship guy fell. Get some pictures. I
have a camera in the car. I want to take a good look at this later.
So will Tornovitch."

"Okay."

Haden trotted off for the camera. One of the EMTs approached
me, a tall kid with thinning hair and big hands. "Anything we
need to know before we load the guy up, Chief?"

I walked him around the corner of the building to where
Dave Macy knelt, taking care of the Steamship clerk. His name
was Howie Patterson. He looked small and crumpled on the

curb. Macy had tucked his uniform jacket under Patterson's head. He was just waking up. He tried to sit and then lowered himself back to the pavement with a groan. The EMT kneeled beside him. "Mr. Patterson?"

"Hey, John Macy. How are you? How's your mom?"

"She's doing much better, Mr. Patterson. But let's take a look at you. Any nausea? Dizziness?"

"Oh yeah."

"Headache?"

Patterson laughed. It turned into a groan. "Good guess."

The other EMT pulled a gurney out of the ambulance. Over his protests, they got Patterson on, slid him inside, and closed the doors. We followed them around the building. Haden took some more shots.

"Meet you at the hospital," I said to the EMT.

Macy nodded and they took off. The boxy red truck rolled away silently, red and blue flashers blinking. The lights were ostentatious but secretive, like a whispered conversation in a crowded room.

We walked back to where Barnaby was standing with Franny. "What was it, Barney? What did you see?"

"I told the lady—agent Tate." She nodded, encouraging him to continue. "He was wearing a watch. The guy who grabbed me. I mean—a fancy watch. It was silver or platinum, it looked heavy. Roman numerals on the dial and some other fancy stuff."

"Did you notice the brand?"

"Sorry. It wasn't no Timex, though. I can tell you that much."

I patted his shoulder. "That's great, Barney. That could be a big help. Go on home and get some sleep. I'll see you in the morning."

"Thanks, Chief."

We watched the boy walk away. The slouch was gone. A little encouragement worked wonders.

Franny and I drove over to the hospital with Haden, along the edge of the dark harbor. There were lights from some of the boats, and across the inlet, the length of the White Elephant hotel was lit up, reflecting in the black water. It looked like a giant cruise ship, garish and out of scale. Haden was sucking on another HALLS cough drop.

"Tell me about the bomb," I said.

"Military grade C-4, Chief. Tucked away by the north side of the building, right against the foundation. They didn't even bother to hide it. Thing would have taken out the office and the furnace. I saw the red light blinking. That's an embedded timer. There was no way to reach it and it could have gone off at any time. Like holding a live grenade with the pin pulled."

"You couldn't cut the wires?"

Haden smiled. "Like in the movies? No, Chief. Sorry about that. No wires. I had to get rid of it somehow, so I threw it into the water."

I glanced at Franny. She nodded. "Quick thinking."

We turned away from the harbor, up Washington Street and onto Union. We hooked a right on York Street and passed my house, heading for the hospital.

"I guess it's time to arrest Billy Delavane, Chief," Haden said finally.

I glanced across at him. "Why now?"

He stared out the window. He exhaled a long stream of breath into the cool night air and sagged against the seat back.

"Haden?"

"Fuck."

"Tell me."

The five corners intersection was deserted. We cruised up toward the windmill and turned left, down the hill to the hospital parking lot entrance. The ambulance was parked by the emergency room doors. I pulled up next to it and turned off the engine. The night dispatcher was talking about a loud beach party in Dionis, near 40th Pole. I killed the radio.

Franny leaned forward from the back seat, her chin on the seatback between us.

Haden took a breath, let it out as a sigh. "That's a Patek Philippe watch Barnaby was talking about back there. I have one just like it. Somebody stole it from my apartment two weeks ago. I filed a report. They took my DVD player and a brand new Lexmark printer, some other stuff. The watch was the bad part. It was the most valuable thing I owned. Including my car, which I finally paid off last Christmas."

"Seriously?"

"It was worth almost twenty grand."

"Was it insured?"

"That's not the point."

"You're losing me. Are you saying the burglar planted the bomb? Because that makes no sense. He would have fenced it the next day, and besides, the profile—"

"That's not what I'm saying, Chief. That watch was a gift. From a woman. A long time ago."

"You never told me about this."

"Damn right I didn't. I wouldn't be telling you now, but—"

"But what?"

I twisted around in the seat. The steering wheel pushed against my ribs. Haden was still looking out the widow. Franny gave me a warning look—let him talk. I swallowed my next question. We sat in silence. A car drove by leaving a pulsing wake of rock baselines. Two nurses came off duty and started around the building to the dormitory.

"She gave one just like it to someone else," Haden said, then. "This other guy, he wears his. All the time. Surfing, ripping cedar trim, even in bed. Some girl told me that, never mind who. Point is, I don't think he's taken the thing off once since the first George Bush was president."

I sucked in a tight little breath. I remembered the nervous carpenter, obsessively checking his watch, the glint of sun on platinum.

"He was wearing it today," I said. "I went by the jobsite at lunch."

"That's what I'm saying. Jesus. Of all the goddamn people."

I shook my head. "I don't buy it. Billy couldn't be that careless."

"You prefer the mad bomber-burglar-dude theory?"

"I don't know. I just—"

"We're all creatures of habit, Hank," Franny put in. "And what difference would it make—if the bomb was going to take them all out anyway?"

"That's cold."

"It runs in the family," Haden said to her. "Billy's brother, Ed? He's a stone psycho. Drug dealer, murderer. He killed someone out here last winter. Maybe you read about it. When they find a rich guy stabbed to death with a fistful of hundred dollar bills shoved down his throat, it usually makes the news."

Franny nodded. "I heard."

"Well, he almost killed the Chief, too. During the arrest. Funny thing is, the parents were good people. They were around when mine weren't, you know? I probably ate them out of house and home in those days. Anyway, I drove Ed home when he was drunk, talked him down from some fights, tried to get him into some rehab programs. We were in the service together. I helped get him transferred to my battalion, called in a few favors, got him a job doing vehicle repair—welding armor onto Bradleys, that kind of stuff. But he still fucked it up. Clocked an officer in the officers club where he wasn't supposed to be in the first place. Wound up in the stockade. Court-martial, dishonorable discharge, the works. That's when I gave up on the guy."

"But Billy—"

"He was pretty wild himself, back in the day. Believe me. That guy could go off big time."

We sat and let the history settle between us.

"Who was the woman?" Franny asked finally. "The one who gave you the watch."

"Does it make any difference?"

"I don't know. It might. Come on. It has to be ancient history by now."

"That's what I thought." He turned to me. "You want to go inside, Chief?"

"Not until you tell us."

"Jesus."

Another ambulance pulled up to the big glass doors of the ER. Another accident, drunk drivers probably; maybe a Chicken Box brawl. Gurneys rattled and squeaked. They rolled inside and it was quiet again—just the faint sound of a jet, heading out over the Atlantic, bound for London or Paris. Haden was watching that pale line of exhaust, sharp against the stars in the moonlight.

"Every time I saw one of those contrails, my whole childhood, I wanted to be on the plane, getting out of here."

"How about now?"

"I got out, Chief. And all I could think about all day every day was getting my sorry ass back here."

The silence closed around us again. I felt like a cigarette, but I almost always felt like a cigarette and I hadn't smoked one in five years.

"So who was she?" Franny asked again.

Haden gave up—people usually did under the gentle relentless pressure of Franny's questioning.

"Joyce Garrison. Her name was Thayer then."

I straightened up. "Debbie's mother?"

"That's the one."

"They're back."

Krakauer let out a long breath. "Yes they are. Can we go inside now?"

"You didn't say anything."

"I never would have, either, Chief. I don't go for talk therapy."

I knew we'd taken this as far as we could, at least for now. I thought back. The first time I saw him popping the cough drops to hide the whiff of vodka on his breath was a little less than a month ago. That would dovetail perfectly with Joyce Garrison's arrival. These thoughts flickered through my mind in the space of a second or two, then vanished, like rabbits darting into the rosa rugosa.

Haden opened the car door. "I'll check out the patient," he said. "Be right back."

I started to follow him, but Franny gestured me to stay put. "You know what we have to do. What you have to do."

"Franny—"

"If you don't arrest Billy Delavane, Jack will. Only he'll do it with SWAT teams and helicopters, and a planeload of State Police and somebody will get careless or trigger happy and Billy could get killed trying to escape because he didn't hold his hands high enough or he tripped on the porch stairs."

"I don't know."

"Yes you do, Hank. He's a solid suspect. We have the voice changing machine, found in a house where he had access, the proof that he bought it, the original phone call traced to his house. And now the watch."

"But that's what I mean. It's like I was saying—why would he be wearing his watch at that moment?"

"Why would Son of Sam let himself get a parking ticket in front of the house where he killed someone?"

Her phone rang. It actually rang, like an old fashioned land-line. I wondered where she downloaded that one.

"Tate," she said. "Yes. They—it was taken care of at the scene. All right. What time? I'll be there. No—the local police are going to handle it. I know. Yes, but—Jack, this is better. He'll come quietly and we can do it under the radar. Absolutely. Of course I do. Yes. Not yet but—all right. I'll handle it. Yeah. You have a good night too."

She closed the phone.

"Let me guess," I said. "Tornovitch."

"The whole JTTF is flying in tomorrow. He wants Lonnie Fraker to do liaison work with the FBI and the Secret Service. Your primary job is going to be smoothing things over with the town, keeping everyone calm. And any errands that Jack needs taken care of."

"So I'm picking up his dry-cleaning?"

"You know Jack. That's just talk. There'll be a lot for you to do. There already is. He wants a suspect in custody when he talks to the press tomorrow, with the watch and the voice machine in an evidence locker."

Haden came back to the car, and folded himself in beside me.

"What's happening?"

"How's Patterson?"

Haden shrugged. "He'll live. So?"

I keyed the car and backed out of the space. "The Joint Terrorism Task Force arrives tomorrow," I said. "Tornovitch wants Billy in jail tonight."

"He wants to set the bail at half a million dollars," Franny added.

Haden laughed. "That should work."

"Why wouldn't it?"

"Billy looks like a beach bum. That's the old money look around here. Drive a beater and let your house fall apart around you. Get your clothes at the take or leave it pile. They don't show off. The new rich people pretend you're rich, too—'Come to Gstaad with us for the weekend.' As if you could. The old money act poor. That's the difference."

Franny gave him a slow, assessing nod. "You've made quite a study of it, Lieutenant Krakauer."

"Well, this is the place to do it, Agent Tate."

I blew out a breath. "The bail seems high, anyway. Given the evidence."

We were rolling down Pleasant Street, heading back to the Harbor House. Franny started to say something, stopped, started again. "There's more."

"What?"

"I searched Delavane's e-mail records."

"Since when? You told me you were just thinking about it."

"Jack put me on it as soon as we could boot up a computer. I spent most of the afternoon working it. I wasn't supposed to tell you—Jack wasn't planning to use the information unless enough other evidence developed and we could show just cause."

I stopped at the corner of Pleasant Street and Upper Main— one intersection where we actually needed a stop sign. A couple of pickup trucks rattled by on the cobblestones, heading for the center of town.

"It usually works the opposite way," I said.

We all sat in silence for a few seconds. Franny didn't make the rules, but she had always been expert at breaking them. I turned the car, and we jostled over the cobbles toward Gardner Street. I knew what Haden wasn't saying. I'd be hearing it all in full detail, later, anyway. He tended to be fairly old school about the Bill of Rights.

"The e-mails are bad, Hank," Franny said. "He's constantly talking about the island being ruined and getting rid of the rich people, 'burning off the leeches before they suck the island dry.' And using bombs to 'scare off the parasites' and wreck the property values here. That's what I found in his sent messages file."

I pulled over. A line of Escalades and Navigators swerved around us. At the back of the line was a battered Chevy Metro, a lone hold-out from the pre SUV era. Finally the street behind us was empty.

"Billy talks about bombs?" I said.

"He's obsessed with them, Hank. Read the e-mails yourself. I have the printouts at the station."

I pulled back out into the street. I drove a couple of blocks before I said the obvious thing. "So Tornovitch was right."

"It happens." After a little silence, she added, "He thinks like a terrorist."

"Tell me about it."

We dropped Haden off at the station and I drove Franny back to the hotel. We got out and she hugged me.

"Thanks for a lovely evening," I said into her hair.

She disengaged an inch. "You still owe me dessert."

"And I had such a good one in mind. We could have had it in your room."

"Not tonight."

She pulled me toward her and kissed my cheek. I kissed her neck. We couldn't seem to align our faces properly. Franny was good at that.

She reared her head back and our eyes met. She looked away first. "Go do your job. I'm going to watch C-Span for a few hours and write my report."

"Party girl."

"You have no idea, buddy. I may iron my work clothes, too. And floss. It's gonna be wild."

"Good night, Franny."

I grabbed her one more time.

Then I drove to Madaket and arrested Billy Delavane.

Ezekiel Beaumont: Ten Weeks Ago

Zeke Beaumont stood at the rail of the Eagle and watched Nantucket slide toward him across the harbor. It was Daffodil Day, a chilly April 28th and the local holiday had packed the boat with tourists. Zeke counted half a dozen antique cars on the vehicle deck, polished and preening, draped with baskets of yellow flowers, tucked between the Stop&Shop trucks and the eighteen-wheel lumber trailers.

The little town was crowded when he ambled off the boat, the cool wind touching his face. The Chamber of Commerce had dressed up the wide, cobblestoned Main Street today as an antique car showroom. Each Buick Roadmaster and Willys Jeep and Winton Flyer, each VW camper and wood-sided station wagon festooned with yellow ribbons and daffodils. The street swarmed with people, grandmothers in straw hats, Dads carrying their kids on their shoulders, gangs of boys circling packs of girls, people greeting their friends from the beds of World War II vintage pickup trucks, a thousand cell phones, texting and tweeting, or taking pictures.

Zeke walked awhile, away from the center of town, trying to get a feel for the place, past meticulously restored grand old houses standing side by side with teetering derelict piles that looked like the mansions in a gothic horror story. Other homes perched on temporary wooden footings, windows impaled by rusting steel I-beams, their foundations excavated for new basements. It reminded him of Charleston, where he'd grown up, all that encapsulated money, newly released, the kids high-fiving each other at grandma's funeral, waiting out the probate court, taking Granny's haunted relic and converting it to cash.

Zeke felt a quick twinge of Scooter's loathing for them all, the spoiled and the spurious, the happy ones, the lucky ones. Zeke smiled to himself.

Be patient, Scooter.

Happiness is fleeting and luck can change.

Zeke rented himself a car and took a quick tour. The grotesque, oversized police station on Fairgrounds Road. Security would be state of the art, so he'd need a clever little con to get into that fortress. The Garrison house off Polpis Road, not nearly as secure as their bigger place in Newton. Not that the fancy Walnut Street palazzo had given him much trouble. The Garrisons turned their high-end alarm system off when they came home, so all Zeke had to do was wait until three in the morning, people are most deeply asleep at that hour, pick a few locks, tiptoe into Debbie's room, and spend five minutes with her iPhone.

That was it.

Then he was gone, slipping out the way he'd come in, nothing disturbed and nobody the wiser. It was all so easy, that was the part that shocked him. He had almost burst out laughing in little Debbie's bedroom.

The next house on his Nantucket itinerary turned out to be even less of a challenge. The neighbors had already gathered on the green lawns at either side of Milestone Road, where it swelled into a broad, tree-shaded Main Street on its final run into the little town of Siasconset, organizing tables and blankets and lawn chairs, baskets of food, coolers of wine and beer.

The police had already set up barricades closing the avenue to normal traffic, but Zeke told the uniformed kid on duty that he was renting a home on Morey Lane. Zeke calibrated his tone to a perfect pitch of potential threat. For the wealthy, anger was a weapon you brandished but rarely used. The kid didn't want any trouble. He backed down, moved the barrier to let Zeke through.

Zeke nodded, and a few seconds later he turned down Morey Lane, looking for the address. He found it, parked fifty feet farther on, and walked back. He glanced around—the street was deserted for the moment. He slipped through the untrimmed hedge under the peeling arbor, and stood facing the old gray-shingled house with its tilting shutters, its twin dormers like a pair of startled eyes. Even the man's house looked drunk.

Zeke found the key in the shower and let himself in, exhaling a short laugh. You had to love small-town life.

He found what he was looking for in the first five minutes. The rest was just set dressing.

Driving to the third house, at the west end of the island, a sense of correctness settled on him. This place deserved what it was going to get, over and above Zeke's personal vendetta. All these weathered houses, plain and unadorned with their gray shingles and simple white trim, there was something so goddamned smug about the fake austerity of them, and the entitled careless pharaohs in faded denim who sipped their drinks on the porch. Scooter was right about that.

From what Zeke had read, he expected the third house to be full of kids, but they surfed around here, and he could hear the waves booming across the dunes. Between that and the Daffodil Day pig-out he had the whole neighborhood to himself. The house was unlocked. Of course it was.

Zeke found the wallet in the front pocket of a pair of blue jeans on the bedroom floor. The temptation to steal it tickled him for a second, but timing was everything. All he needed now was the credit card number and the security code off the back.

When he saw the computer, he gagged. Who the hell were these people? Where did they think they were living? Mayberry RFD?

This idiot had all his passwords written on Post-it notes stuck to the side of the screen, complicated ones with lots of numbers and punctuation marks. He scribbled the passwords and left.

He drove too fast on the way back to Madaket Road, and banged the undercarriage on a couple of deep craters in the dirt track, but he didn't care. He was flying. Everything was going perfectly. He was charmed this morning. He could do no wrong. Maybe that was why he wound up shooting his mouth off again, talking too much, getting himself in trouble. He just couldn't resist.

He made his mistake with a real estate lady, Elaine Bailey her name was. She was showing him the house on Deacon's Way and made some comment about the area between the Washing Pond stand-pipe and the microwave tower on Eel Point Road. "Very exclusive," she said. "Very desirable. But in my mother's day no one substantial would even consider living out here. My grandmother called it 'utility acres.' That's how things change."

"Now it would be a perfect spot for Occupy Nantucket," Zeke had blurted. "I guess no one ever thought of occupying Nantucket, though."

"I don't think that movement could ever take hold out here." She drilled him with a long, assessing look. She was smart and tough, good-looking for her age but hard-edged, packed, constructed.

"It's quiet." He tried to shift the conversation to neutral topics. Occupy Nantucket? What the fuck was wrong with him? But he had wanted to needle her, to shake her up a little, crack that porcelain composure.

"You can't buy that for any amount of money," she said.

"I know, believe me. Where I live, in Westwood, in Los Angeles…I'm half a mile from Supplevita Avenue and you can't open the windows on the west side of the apartment without hearing the San Diego Freeway."

She laughed. "Supple Vita? What a city! Even your street names sound like health drinks."

He sensed that he'd fucked up at that moment. Later on, in his room at the Jared Coffin House, he went on line and confirmed it. He'd take the next flight off the island, before he could make any more mistakes. He was okay so far—the blunder didn't seem to have registered. Elaine Bailey might not even remember what he said. She was much more interested in the rental agreement than any of the small talk that preceded it. She was happy. She was starting her rental season 'with a bang.' Zeke had to smile.

He couldn't have put it better himself.

Part Two:
Scissors Cut Paper

Chapter Seven

Tourist Season

The rest of Tornovitch's DHS team arrived the next morning, along with a pair of special agents from the FBI, a contingent of State Police, three bomb techs, a group of surveyors from the Army Corps of Engineers, a quiet man named Gould from the Secret Service, a fleet of local press trucks, reporters from every national newspaper—and my ex-wife.

She had my kids with her, that was the bright spot. They had been visiting her parents in Los Angeles for a few weeks, as they did every summer. I met them at the airport. The NTSA had tripled the security and there were National Guard soldiers, armed and in full uniform, patrolling the terminal.

"Well, this is going to wreck the rental season." Miranda gave me a brief hug as we waited for the luggage. The kids grabbed my legs.

No matter what subject Miranda was talking about, she wound up talking about real estate. I could laugh about it now. Someone was dying of cancer? Were they selling the house? 9/11? Oh, it was devastating for the real estate market. Chernobyl? You can pick up a nice three bedroom ranch style next to the reactor for a song these days.

Miranda was in her element on Nantucket. She was fascinated with the wealthy people she worked for. She told me one day after a parent teacher conference, that the man to whom she'd just sold a house made—she had actually figured it out with a calculator—he made my yearly salary every three and a half hours. Of course that was before my cost-of-living raise.

I looked down at the kids, Tim in shorts and a t-shirt, Caroline in a summer shift that Miranda must have paid a small fortune for. I couldn't begrudge her the expense, though I knew Caroline would grow out of the dress in a month or two. Buying kid's clothes was one of life's great pleasures, fleeting as a four-star restaurant dinner, doomed as a sandcastle. Tim's brown hair was wind scattered, Caroline's red hair was tied into a pair of perfect braids. But they were a matched set of smiling round faces. You could almost forget they were at war with each other.

"Did you get us something?" Tim asked.

"Hey—you went off-island. You're supposed to bring me something."

That gave him pause. "How about a hug?"

"Sounds good." I lifted him up, thinking, whoa, he's getting big. He was a sturdy little eleven-year-old, but he'd been a baby last week. Time was going by so fast it felt like a wind blowing hard out of the north, pulling the air out of your chest.

"I got you something," Caroline said. Tim writhed in my arms to stare at her, outraged at this bit of sibling one-upmanship. "When we were at Trader Joe's." She wrestled her back pack off and rummaged inside. After a few seconds she pulled out a bag of unsulfured dried apricots.

"Your favorite!" she crowed. It was true. She'd been studying my vices.

"I saw the new Ian McEwan novel at Barnes & Noble," Tim said. ""I wanted to buy it for you. But I didn't have any money."

"You spent your allowance," Miranda pointed out.

"I saved mine," Caroline said smugly.

Tim thrashed for a second, trying to get loose. I knew he wanted to pounce.

"I didn't even know there was a new Ian McEwan novel," I lied. "So that's a great present. We'll go to Mitchell's tomorrow and pick it up. Maybe we can find you a book, too."

"What about me?" Caroline demanded.

"Both of you. We'll have our own private book fair."

"You spoil them." Miranda grabbed the first of the suitcases.

"Oh yeah. Books. The scourge of today's youth."

I grabbed the other suitcases and we started out through the terminal toward the parking lot, the kids dancing in front of us, the squabble forgotten. They stopped to pet a pair of Bernese mountain dogs. We paused and watched them charming the harried woman holding the leashes. Tim said something and she laughed, while the dogs licked both sides of Caroline's face.

Standing there, it occurred to me that having children made regret impossible—at least for all the time up until the exact moment of their conception. If you had done anything different, or even done the same things in different order, your children might not exist. Certainly, given the way you rolled the genetic dice every time sperm met egg, they wouldn't be the same people. Looked at that way, not even a disastrous marriage could be considered a waste. I glanced over at Miranda, seething with impatience, worried about dog germs, distrusting strangers, eager to get back to the office and check the new listings. Across the floor, Caroline was teaching the dogs to give their paws, shaking them solemnly as if the dogs were graduating from high school and she was handing out diplomas.

I slung a duffel bag over my shoulder, took Miranda's arm and guided her toward the kids, thinking—an ordeal and a tragedy—but not a waste.

I drove them back to Miranda's house on Rugged Road, and promised again to look for a new apartment. Mine only had two bedrooms, and technically the kids were roommates when they stayed with me. They were getting a little old for that, and in practice I often wound up yielding my room to one of them and sleeping on the couch. It wasn't a particularly comfortable couch.

I got the luggage inside and hugged the kids while Miranda checked her messages. I hurried out and no one tried to stop me. They'd all seen the newspapers and the ubiquitous TVs in the airports. Nantucket was the lead story this morning.

"Are there really terrorists on Nantucket, Daddy?" Tim had asked me in the drive home.

"I don't know. I don't think so. There's at least one crazy person."

Caroline closed the subject. "Daddy will catch them, whoever they are."

Miranda gave me a quick skeptical look but said nothing. I could have told her we already had a suspect in custody, but I had a feeling it would come back to haunt me. Despite the mounting evidence, I still didn't buy Billy Delavane as the mad bomber, though I hadn't read his e-mails yet and I wouldn't get a chance to this morning. I had to check in with the Army Corps of Engineers at the Steamship Wharf, and get back to the station. Billy was sitting in one of the holding cells there, waiting for his first interrogation. He had waived his right to have a lawyer present. His point was logical but naïve—there was no way he could incriminate himself, since he was innocent, and he wanted his family lawyer more productively occupied, getting ready for the bail hearing that afternoon.

I was going to be present at the questioning, but they hadn't let me see Billy since I'd brought him in the night before. Too bad. I would have told him that being innocent wasn't necessarily going to help him with Jack Tornovitch.

My first stop was the Steamship Wharf. Floyd Pollack, the chief engineer, gave me the bad news. Two of the cement support dolphins were going to have to be replaced, forcing the Authority to run the big car ferries and the fast boat out of the same slip for at least a month. The timing couldn't be worse.

But maybe that was the point.

When I got to the station, a State Police car was blocking the entrance to the parking lot. Two of Lonnie Fraker's boys, in full leather and crew cuts, dangling guns and handcuffs, sauntered up to my cruiser. They looked like twins, though one of them must have been from off-island, since I didn't recognize him. Joey Thurston, the local boy, approached the driver's side of my car. I rolled down the window and let in a dense wedge of warm air.

"I gotta see some ID, Chief."

"Move the car Joey. I'm late."

He just stood there. "Sorry. Chief. It's the new rules. Everybody has to show ID."

"So you don't let in any impostors?"

He shuffled his feet, glancing back at his new partner. "So I don't get in trouble."

I flashed my ID. The other kid took it out of my hands and examined it. You couldn't be too careful where National Security was at stake. Finally they moved their car and I drove through. There was another security check point at the side door. No one had looked at my badge with such interest since my kids on the first day I got it.

Inside, Haden Krakauer wasn't any happier than I was. Strangers were giving him orders, he hated his new cubicle, missed his Mr. Coffee, and pined for his FAX machine. There wasn't much I could do for him. I was outranked, too.

The JTTF had Billy in the main conference room on the first floor. Franny and Tornovitch were inside with Lonnie Fraker, the Secret Service guy and a couple of FBI agents. The two FBI guys, Daly and Knightley, stood with their arms crossed against the far wall. All the stupid jokes had already been made about that unfortunate piece of nomenclature—Lonnie referred to them as '24/7.' Daly was white, Knightley was black. They looked like the strong side of the Clemson offensive line. By contrast, Gould, the Secret Service agent, resembled nothing so much as my son's new math teacher—small but lumpy, with horn-rim glasses and a comb-over. Still, he seemed much more dangerous than the FBI goons. And he was smoking with impunity. I knew that had to be driving Lonnie crazy. He was allergic to cigarette smoke.

A big man with a reedy nasal voice, Lonnie was a startling mass of frailties—allergies to everything, weak wrists, fallen arches, asthma. He was always at the chiropractor or the acupuncturist, always coming down with some new ailment, from shingles to swine flu. He coughed deliberately, as everyone turned their attention to me and Gould exhaled another cloud. It made me want a cigarette myself, but then again, what didn't?

Jack and Franny had placed themselves seated across the desk from Billy. Jack sported his usual suit. Franny wore what must have been DHS dress code: khaki pants, a button-down shirt and a mannish brown jacket suitable for hiding a shoulder holster. Billy's jeans and a vintage Killen Construction "Death and Resurrection" t-shirt broadcast his contempt for the proceedings. If the JTTF meant to intimidate him, they were failing.

Billy was only forty but already graying at the temples, a twisted cord of sunburned muscle, his dark blue eyes clear and steady. He had surfed all over the world—the North Shore of Hawaii, Indonesia, Peru; big waves on remote coral atolls, cold winter heavies among the rocks and sharks at Mavericks. After the ten-wave hold downs in forty degree water, this motley law-enforcement clusterfuck must have seemed like a bad joke. But he was in trouble, and I hoped he knew it.

I eased myself inside and took up a position against the wall next to Lonnie.

I was late. The show had already begun.

Chapter Eight
The Interrogation

The room was air conditioned, presumably for the convenience of the inquisitors. A tape recorder was running.

"So, as I was saying," Tornovitch said. "Your father was a member in good standing in the Monkey Wrench Society. Yes or no?""

"The what?"

"The Monkey Wrench Society, Mr. Delavane. "

"Do you mean *The Monkey Wrench Gang*? It's a novel by Edward Abbey."

"I've read it. The book concerns a group of what you might call guerilla conservationists. The kind of people who spike redwood trees to kill loggers."

"What's the point? That my dad read it? He read a lot of books."

Tornovitch leaned across the table. "I'm saying your father was part of a real organization on this island, dedicated to Edward Abbey's ideals. I'm saying your father consistently attempted to sabotage the renovation and restoration of this island by Walter Beinecke—"

Billy snorted. "Green stamps."

"Excuse me?"

"My grandmother despised Beinecke. She used to mutter 'green stamps' under her breath every time she passed him on the street. Remember green stamps? Collect them and paste them into books, turn them in for overpriced junk? That was where Beinecke's money came from."

"And this little feud explains why your father disabled Mr. Beinecke's construction vehicles, picked fights with his construction foremen, filed lawsuits—"

"He short-sheeted Beinecke's bed, too. And tied his shoelaces together."

"Then there were the fires."

Billy straightened in his chair. Tornovitch had touched a nerve. "My father was no arsonist, buddy."

"But his friends were—his chums at the Wharf Rats Club. The fires did very little damage and the story was hushed up. But a felony is a felony, however incompetently executed. Your father turned his friends in for immunity from prosecution. I have the court documents, if you want to look them over."

"Those records were sealed."

"We unsealed them. We keep the secrets now, Mr. Delavane. We don't share that privilege."

Billy pushed the heel of his hand across his forehead. This was what I had tried to warn him about. "So you've been rooting through my dad's court case, digging up all the dirt, smearing him with this bullshit—"

"It's not bullshit, Mr. Delavane, as you well know. It was a cowardly betrayal of his values and his friends that ruined his life and led directly to his worsening alcoholism and—five years later—his suicide. He left no note. But I think these depositions say it all."

"Fuck you."

Billy lunged across the table and I saw why Daly and Knightley were in the room. They were primed to attack and when the moment came they moved fast, Daly slamming Billy back into his chair, Knightley immobilizing him with a headlock. Still, both Tornovitch and Franny flinched backward.

"We're not here to talk about your father," Franny said. She looked at Knightley. "Let him go. Joseph—let him go now."

Knightley released Billy's neck and he gasped for breath, clutching at his throat.

"Try that sometime without all your friends around, asshole," Billy said.

"Anytime, dirtbag."

Tornovitch held out an admonishing hand, like a traffic cop.

"Back off, Knightley. Mr. Delavane hasn't been convicted of any crime…though he just came perilously close to assault on a police officer." He smiled and a low wattage chuckle moved through the room, Maybe it was just people releasing the breath they'd been holding. "In any case, Mr. Delavane, Agent Tate is quite correct. We're here to talk about you, not your father. More precisely, we'd like to explore the ways in which you have chosen to perpetuate this feud. Beinecke sold a major portion of his holdings to First Winthrop Corporation in 1987 for fifty million dollars. Two years ago Winthrop sold many of its holdings to Stephen Karp. Would you care to tell us what you think of the island's newest majority shareholder?"

Billy smiled. "Sure. He's an uneducated, New Jersey thug. He has no taste and no class. He makes Walter Beinecke look like John Muir. When he's done, this island will be nothing but bad art galleries, overpriced restaurants, and rich people sniffing each others' money. Then he'll move on to the next target. Wherever it is, I hope your family has a house there."

After a brief pause, Tornovitch leaned forward and folded his hands on the table.

"On the contrary," he said. "Mr. Karp is a respectable businessman, a pillar of the community and a dedicated humanitarian who has only the best interests and continued prosperity of this island at heart. Based on your comments, I think he would be entirely justified in suing you for slander. He might even win some of those crumbling properties of yours in the lawsuit. That would an entirely fitting outcome."

Franny cleared her throat. Everyone turned to her. It felt rehearsed.

"You have something, Agent Tate?"

"Just…these comments correspond very closely to the confiscated e-mails."

That got Billy's attention. "Confiscated e-mails? You confiscated my e-mails? Based on what?"

Tornovitch stared him down. "Based on our suspicions, the circumstantial evidence against you, and the powers mandated to the Department of Homeland Security by the Patriot Act, H.R. 3162, signed into law October 24, 2001."

"This one, for instance," Franny said. She pulled a loose-leaf notebook out of the briefcase beside her chair. She opened it and flipped through a few pages. "The trick is to make this place undesirable. People scatter boric acid in the crevices of their homes to keep out the cockroaches. But how do you keep out these bugs? It doesn't take much. Just find something they're afraid of. And everyone's afraid of a bomb.'"

Billy lurched forward and the two FBI agents slammed him back.

"I didn't write that last part!"

"How about this one," Franny said, turning a page. "'Edna was right, refusing to subdivide her property. She said to me once that's how the new people are taking over, subdivide and conquer. She knew it was a war. But she could never admit we needed real weapons to fight it.'"

"It's the same thing! It's been changed. Somebody got in there and—"

"But you were friendly with Edna Thayer," Tornovitch said.

"What? What are you talking about? You're trying to drag Edna into this? How did you find out about her? How do you even know her name?"

"Just answer the question, please."

"Yes. We were friends. All right? Very good friends. I met her years ago, through—she was the mother of a girlfriend of mine, back in the day. But what does that have to do with anything? She's dead. Leave her out of this."

Tornovitch chose to ignore the outburst. "Agent Tate?"

"There's one more post I wanted on the record."

"Fine."

She looked around the room apologetically. "This one is short. It says—"'People are herd animals. They follow each other, do what the others do. That's why one frightened cow can scatter a herd. Paint a target on one of these people, the others will flee like mewling cattle.'"

Billy hit the table with the flat of his hand. Everyone jumped a little, except Daly and Knightley. They knew there was no real threat this time. "Come on!" Billy said. "This is bullshit. I never wrote that. Mewling? I've never used that word in my life."

"Not in casual conversation," Torrnovitch said. "Of course not. But this is your manifesto. The Unabomber never struck anyone as unusually articulate. Until they read his letter to the *New York Times*."

"So I'm the Unabomber now?"

"Of course not," Franny said. "But these e-mails present you as an angry man with a radical agenda. We have to address that."

Billy blew out an exasperated breath. "Who was I supposed to have sent these e-mails to?"

"Cute," said Tornovitch. "You now don't know where you sent your own e-mails?"

"I didn't even write them, so no, I really have no idea—"

"But you did write parts of them, the less incriminating parts."

"I—"

"You'd be better off denying everything, Mr. Delavane."

"The e-mails were sent to a Matthew Barton. The address is waveslider@aol.com."

"There you go, Matt uses Gmail."

"And hotmail, and an old one from his days in San Francisco—pacbell.net. Mr. Barton initially denied receiving the mail, but we showed him the AOL inbox on his own computer and they were all there. All of them had been opened. He had no explanation for that, but he had to acknowledge that the sentiments sounded familiar."

"Your friend isn't in trouble yet," Tornovitch said. "He demonstrated a touching but misplaced loyalty which the department understands, but cannot condone. When he realizes the gravity of the matter he may find that his memory improves. That often happens. If it's any comfort, I assure you he won't be penalized for those initial conversations…so long as he comes clean when it matters, under oath."

Billy straightened his arms behind him and stretched. "So, my dad was a troublemaker and you say I wrote some nasty e-mails. If that's all you've got, we're wasting our time. I have a staircase to build."

Tornovitch cleared his throat, set his elbows on the table, steepled his fingers, and let his chin rest lightly on them. He looked like a bird eyeing a worm. "You're right," he said. "This is dragging on. Let me summarize. On June twelfth of this year you purchased a voice changing telephone module online from a company called Viper Tech. We have the receipt and the card number. This is the machine that was used in the initial bomb threat phone call. It was found in the residence of one Corey Herrick…one of your known associates. Additionally, you do caretaking work for the Herrick family and had unlimited access to the house. You also have access to military explosives through your brother's Army connections. Despite apparent years of alienated affection, you have visited your brother four times in the last six months."

"Okay," Billy said. "I'm patching things up with my brother. That's not a crime. As for the rest of it…my wallet was stolen a couple of weeks ago. Obviously Corey Herrick took it and used one of my credit cards to buy this machine you're talking about. Then you find it at his house—and you blame me? Actually, it makes sense. You guys have a good track record for going after the wrong people."

Franny put away her notebook and settled herself back in her chair. "Would you mind telling us where you were last night around ten o'clock?"

"I was home, asleep. Like most nights. I work for a living."

Franny nodded, letting the wave of hostility surge past her. "Is there anyone who could verify your whereabouts at that time? Your girlfriend—Abigail Folger? Would she be willing to testify that—"

"Abby was off-island last night. As you know."

"Our surveillance team saw you leaving the house at 9:25," Tornovitch broke in. "You climbed into your truck and drove away."

"No I didn't."

"Then how do you explain this surveillance report?"

"That's supposed to be your job, pal. I was asleep."

"So…some unknown malefactor…presumably the same diabolical computer genius who has been doctoring your e-mails… this person slipped into your house, found you sleeping and then left conspicuously, driving away in your truck to be sure that you took the blame for his misdeeds."

Billy shrugged. "It's not great, but it covers the facts."

"It's ludicrous! How did they get into your house? How did they start your car?"

"My house is never locked. I don't even have a key for it anymore. And I leave the truck keys in the ignition."

"You expect us to believe that?"

"It's true. It's how people live here. Ask anyone. Ask the Chief." They swiveled around toward me. I nodded. It was true.

"Are we done here?" asked Gould.

"Not quite," said Tornovitch. He stood up and walked around the table, looming over Billy. "Tell us about your watch," he said.

"My watch?"

"It's a nice one. Where did you get it?"

Billy looked past Franny, to me. "Who is this guy, Chief? What the hell is he talking about? What does my watch have to do with—"

"Just answer the question," Tornovitch said.

"It was a gift."

"May I ask from whom?"

"An old girlfriend. It was years ago, What difference does it make?"

"Tell us her name, Mr. Delavane."

"Joanna Thayer."

"Edna Thayer's daughter."

"For what it's worth."

"It's worth something, Edna seems to have tutored you in civil disobedience. And her daughter must have left a profound impression. You wear the watch constantly. So I'm told."

"Yeah, I like knowing what time it is."

Tornovitch smiled. "And what time was it, exactly, when you were subduing Officer Barnaby Toll with a headlock last night?"

"You're telling me he identified my watch?"

"No. *You* just told *me*."

"Come on. This makes no sense. There's no way I could have—"

He stopped talking, the way you stop walking when you come to a cliff edge. The room was silent: six pairs of eyes, watching him. Someone in the next room was listening to a Red Sox game on the radio. You could hear the rising murmur, the excited announcer, the faint roar of the crowd, as someone hit a home run.

"Damn," Billy said.

"What?" said Franny "What are you thinking?"

Billy took a long breath and let it out in a hiss. Then he took another one.

"I just figured it out," he said.

"Tell us."

For that moment there were just the two of them in the room. Franny had conjured some evanescent cocoon of intimacy. Tornovitch stepped slowly back. He had seen her work before, and he knew better than to break the spell.

"Okay," Billy said. "I knew one thing as soon as the Chief grabbed me last night—Someone was framing me."

"And how could you possibly know that?" Tornovitch couldn't help himself.

"Because I'm innocent, asshole."

"Go on," Franny said. She reached across the table and touched Billy's wrist.

"I'm not the only one who got one of those watches. She gave one to Haden Krakauer."

"His was stolen," I blurted out. Everyone stared at me.

"So he says. It's a smart thing to say, under the circumstances."

"He filed a theft report."

Billy shook his head, amazed at my stupidity. "Well, it must be true then."

Franny squeezed his wrist. "I want to understand what you're telling us," she said. "I don't want any confusion here. You're saying that Assistant Chief Haden Krakauer is framing you for this bombing? Why would he do such a thing?"

Billy laughed a short bitter laugh. "Oh, he has his reasons."

"He wants to hurt you?"

"Let's just say—he knows how to hold a grudge."

"What did you do to him?"

"I fucked the love of his life. And even after I dumped her, she wouldn't go back to him."

"No. She married one Theodore Garrison instead," Tornovitch put in. Once again, he had almost derailed Franny's line of questions. Billy was talking to Tornovitch now.

"If you know everything already, why ask me?"

"Well, for one thing, to see if you're lying."

"So—she married Garrison?" Franny asked.

"It was his lucky day. He'd been chasing her for years. They went to the Justice of the Peace and they were gone a week later."

"And she never came back?"

"She's back right now. Her mother died and they're dealing with the estate."

"So you think Haden, seeing his old flame after all this time…"

"I don't know. But he took it hard. I don't think he's had another relationship since."

Tornovitch again: "And when did this little scandal happen, exactly?"

Franny gave up and sat back in her chair.

"2003."

"I see. Any idea why he didn't just beat you up at the time?"

"Try beating me up. You'll find out."

"So he was afraid of you?"

"Ask him. He was afraid of something, that's for sure. Because he ran away so fast it was like a fucking cartoon. I expected to see a puff of smoke and a Haden sized hole in the wall. He enlisted in the Army and we didn't see him back here for five years."

"So...any theories as to why he waited a decade to take his... revenge?"

"I don't know. Something must have set him off. Maybe seeing Joanna again, like you said. But he's never made any secret out of his feelings. I lost count of how many times he's pulled me over for expired inspection stickers and over-sand permits. I get into a hassle at the dump, trying to take some shutters out of the woodpile. Who shows up but Haden Krakauer. I spent the night in jail over that one. Plus all the noise violations. He even got Dave Fronzuto to bust me for taking more than my limit a couple of times last season." He registered the blank looks. "Scallops," he explained. "Dave is the harbormaster. But that's not all. If I drive at night you can bet Krakauer will pull me over for a breathalyzer. Which is hilarious, because he's the drunk. He had the drug sniffing dogs in my car last time. We were blocking Union Street for half an hour."

"And they found nothing?"

"Of course they found nothing! That's why he's doing this, now. He's your guy. Think about it. He dealt with explosives in the Army. You say bomb, I see a bowling ball with a fuse sticking out of it. He knows how I feel about the island. And he could screw with my e-mail. He knows computers. I can't even set the margins on Microsoft Word."

Silence dropped like a curtain. No one was quite sure where to go from here, how to proceed. Franny sat forward, rubbing her face, as if she was trying to massage the fatigue from below her eyes with her finger tips.

"All right, Mr. Delavane," she said. "Let's start from the beginning."

"Not right now," Tornovitch said. "We all need a break. I still have an ongoing interagency investigation to coordinate, and I think Mr. Delavane needs to think about what he's told us this morning, and reflect on the consequences of any further prevarication. We'll reconvene tomorrow morning. Nine o'clock." He glanced at me. "Sharp." He made a roundhouse gesture with his arm that included Billy and the two FBI agents. "Take him back to the holding cell. Don't feed him. We'll keep the lights on tonight. And play him some of that German techno music."

"No waterboarding?" Billy asked.

"You're a surfer, Mr. Delavane. I'm afraid you'd find the experience recreational."

Outside a state trooper trundled up to Tornovitch.

"There's someone at the driveway checkpoint to see Delavane, sir."

"Get rid of them."

"It's a girl. Her name's Debbie Garrison? Apparently she knows Delavane. She's making quite a scene. She won't leave the driveway."

"It's one girl. Do we need to call in the National Guard here, son? Or can you handle it?"

"Let me," Franny said. "I want to talk to her anyway."

"For what possible reason?" But before Franny could answer, his cell phone went off again. "Tornovitch," He waved her away. Franny hurried off. I started to follow, but Tornovitch gave me the traffic-cop raised palm. I stopped and he lifted one finger— cell phone sign language for 'I'll just be a second.' I waited.

'Well let me know when they arrive," he said. "I want a full report." He closed the phone, grabbed my arm, and pulled me closer. "Not a word of this to Krakauer,"

I was shocked. "You didn't actually believe any of that shit, did you?"

Tornovitch shook his head sadly, as if I was a promising student who just flunked a midterm. "This job has nothing to do with belief, or faith or trust, Kennis. I don't believe anything. I have no faith and I trust no one. I follow the evidence. I investigate. Delavane offered some interesting alternative paths for that investigation. Was he lying or telling the truth? We can determine that. I never argue about facts. And I will not ignore any new evidence, any new lead, any fresh thought—however dubious or unlikely, however unexpected the source. Preconceptions destroy cases, Kennis. Keep your mind open."

"Fine, I understand that, but I happen to know Haden Krakauer and there's no way—"

He barked a laugh. "The 'happen to'; construction! 'This-may-seem-like-a-coincidence-to-you, but-it's-much-more-significant-than-that!' The favored rhetorical flourish of the desperate and the defensive. And why should you be feeling desperate and defensive, Kennis? Perhaps because every step in this investigation brings it closer to you and your circle of friends. Perhaps when we get to the center of the labyrinth we'll find you waiting: the minotaur in cop's clothing!"

"You're losing it, Jack."

"Maybe. But no one is above suspicion here, Kennis. Not even you."

"Or you?"

"I welcome suspicion! I thrive on it. I have nothing to hide, Kennis. Can you say the same thing?" Before I could answer, he waved me away. "Let's get busy. We have a lot of work to do before tomorrow morning."

As he stalked off, his cell phone rang again. "Tornovitch."

Then he was gone, heading upstairs to Haden's office. I knew he was right, there was a lot to do, but at that moment, I couldn't think of a thing. The morning's events had immobilized me.

Franny appeared beside me. She was breathing hard, as if she'd been running. She took my arm and walked me toward the empty interrogation room.

"Come with me," she said. "We need to talk."

Ezekiel Beaumont: Ten Days Ago

Zeke Beaumont was feeling under-appreciated. Scooter was treating him like some witless grunt who couldn't do anything but follow orders. Here's your twenty pounds of C-4, here's your blasting caps, here's your throw-away cell phone to detonate them with.

Zeke had felt like saying—I don't need your government issue crap, I can make this stuff myself. All you needed was some RDX, some plastic binder material and a little motor oil. And my stuff is better, it's more pure because I leave out the DMDNB that the government puts in as a security marker. As if Scooter would have even known what Zeke was talking about! He was acting like it was nitro-glycerin from some old movie—shake it up and ka-boom. In fact the stuff was so stable you could use it for a cook fire if you ran out of Sterno. They'd done it plenty of times in Iraq.

There was no point in correcting Scooter, though. Better to nod, tip the forelock and go about your business. But it was tough sometimes. Scooter wouldn't even let Zeke remove the motor attached to the asymmetrical wheel and wire the circuit to the blasting cap. As if Zeke didn't know how a cell phone's vibrator function worked! It was infuriating. When he had tried to explain about the illegal batteries they were going to need, the ones without the self-shorting safeguards, Zeke knew where to buy them on the black market—Scooter had brushed him aside, like Zeke was a child, showing off at tying his own shoelaces.

"It's all handled," Scooter had said. "Bury the device out at the golf club, by the clubhouse, next to a load-bearing wall. And make sure you hide it clean. We don't want any good Samaritans stumbling over it. Think you can handle that?"

Of course he could handle that! He was handling it fine.

He was supposed to be alone out here tonight, but Scooter had obviously fucked up, because five minutes after Zeke arrived, picking his way from a half-constructed house off Polpis Road through the dense bushes behind the clubhouse, making sure to leave little tidbits of evidence behind him, laid among the thorns and prickles with a careful, gloved hand, the cleaning crew arrived.

Most people would have panicked at this new development, but not Zeke. What could he say? Fear paralyzed some people. It inspired him. Zeke watched the men climb out of their trucks. Did these guys work every night? Scooter had to be told, they had to change the plan. Zeke had nothing against a bunch of immigrant workmen. He was no terrorist. Or was he?

Zeke glanced down at the steamer trunk-sized block of C-4 he had lugged through the moors on his back. He was sitting on it now—his own personal IED. Just like some cold-blooded Sunni insurrectionist, booby trapping a highway outside Najaf or Mosul. They didn't care who they killed. Zeke wasn't like that. He'd talk to Scooter, make sure he warned these guys, somehow, make sure they were safe.

But right now he had work to do. He cut away the square of sod he would use for camouflage, unstrapped his old army-issue entrenching tool and began to dig.

He was almost finished when one of the workers came out to his car for a cigarette. Zeke froze. The guy was no more than ten feet away. Zeke slid into his own hole, smeared dirt on his face, held his breath. The asshole was walking toward him. If he kept moving this direction he'd literally step on Zeke's head. Zeke tried to think of some explanation. He could say he was landscaping, digging the trench for a hedge. At this hour? How about a cop? Private security? It didn't matter. The guy would remember him.

The man was two feet away from him when the cell phone went off. For a crazy panic-glaring second, Zeke thought it was his own phone. He should have turned it off. What an idiot! What a criminally stupid, careless—but it was the cleaning guy's phone. Zeke fought to hold in a gasp of relief. The guy stopped walking. Zeke could see the New Balance "N" on the guy's scuffed sneakers. A quick exchange in Spanish, and then the guy turned around and headed back inside.

Zeke waited ten minutes before he resumed working. Finally he shoveled back the last of the dirt and laid the turf over his excavation, scattering more soil and walking over it to tamp it down. He checked it with the flashlight and added some twigs.

It was like so many things. If you weren't looking for it, you wouldn't see it.

He paced the square of loose grass again, thinking of something else his grandmother always used to say, "I felt like you walked over my grave."

Zeke stretched, took a few breaths of the sweet night air. They must have mowed the fairways that morning. He walked over to the kid's car and memorized the license plate. He'd need that to get the rest of the kid's information. When they had his cell number they could call him before the bomb went off, get him to evacuate the building, convince his friends to get out also. He'd be alive to testify, and the rest of the crew…they'd just be alive. Scooter didn't care about collateral damage, but Zeke did. That made Zeke different. That made him better.

He walked back to the corner of the building, picked up his entrenching tool, and took a last look around. The grounds looked frosted in the moonlight. Very pretty.

But not for long. Soon the captains of industry and the trust fund babies would be picking their way through the smoke and rubble and hopefully getting the message that they weren't quite so invulnerable after all.

He shot the place the finger with both fists, and disappeared into the night.

Chapter Nine
Fathers and Daughters

Franny closed the door behind us. Her eyes were wild, the way she had looked after our one stolen kiss in the Santa Monica Mountains. But this was her real romance, her real adventure. She had made a connection, figured something out. She was hot on someone's trail again, sniffing the dirt, quivering like a bloodhound.

"What's going on? Are you all right?"

"Have you met Debbie Garrison?"

"Sure. I gave her a tour of the station when she came in with Billy."

"She was hanging around with Billy Delavane?"

"That's right."

"And you didn't see it?"

"Franny, what are you talking about? Is something wrong with Debbie?"

"She's his daughter."

"She's—what?"

"She's Billy Delavane's daughter, Hank. The family resemblance is—it's almost comical. She has the same thin nose, the chin—or how about those ears? Small ears, tight to the head, no lobes. You don't see that too often."

"I can't believe you noticed Billy Delavane's ears."

"I can't believe you didn't! The no-lobes thing is so bizarre. That's not all, anyway—look at her eyes. She has the same little fold over the lid. There has to be a genetic marker for that."

"Franny, you can't be sure—"

"So it's a coincidence? You're the one who told me you didn't believe in coincidences."

"I said they were dead ends."

"She's on Nantucket, she sought him out. She came here today."

"Why didn't she identify herself as his daughter then? Jack might have let her in to see him."

She shook her head. "I don't know. Something's going on there. I'll talk to her and figure it out. That doesn't matter now. What matters is her age. And Delavane's story. It didn't add up. There was something he wasn't telling us, Hank. Seeing your old flame ten years later doesn't set you off like this."

"No, that's what I was trying to explain when—"

"But if Billy Delavane not only took her and slept with her, but he also got her pregnant and she actually had the child? The child that should have been Krakauer's and then that kid shows up and looks so much like Billy? It's eleven years later. She's eleven years old…you didn't put it together, but you can bet Krakauer did. "

"We saw her coming off the boat."

"Oh my God. How did he react?"

She touched my chest as if she could pull the memory out of my body. I felt her fingertips against my shirt with the same old physical jolt.

I did my best to ignore it. "He didn't react. At least not then. But I smelled booze on him, the next day at work."

"Funny that this is all about bombs," Franny said quietly. "Your friend is the real bomb. The time bomb with an eleven-year fuse. The watch clinches it."

"But he told us about it last night. Why would he do that?"

"Come on, Hank. I can think of a lot of reasons and so can you. He wanted to be sure Tornovitch asked the question. He knew I'd tell Jack what he said. This way he sets up Billy and distances himself at the same time. His watch was stolen, supposedly. So that puts him in the clear. It's the way a bomber would think—set the fuse, and be sure you're safe when it detonates."

I pulled back. "Wait a second. You can't prove any of this. It's all conjecture and guess work and—"

"Hank, listen to me. You're right. Okay? This is probably just some absurd red herring. I know that. I'm not going to tell anyone, not yet—least of all Jack. He'd go nuts. It was hate at first sight with him and Krakauer anyway. But I have to check it out. I have to talk to the girl, poke around into Krakauer's phone records, his movements over the last few weeks, his Internet activity—quietly, okay? It'll just be my private project for now. I earned that for myself. No one else saw the connection, not even you."

I shrugged. "It's not like I could stop you."

"That's right. I'm a juggernaut. That's what you used to say. It's one of the things you love about me. Remember?"

"You weren't going after my friends in those days."

She took my hands. "I'm not doing that now, Hank. If he's innocent I'll be able to clear him. I'll have proof if Jack comes after him. That's a good thing."

For some reason she reminded me of my daughter, soberly explaining that popping all the bubble wrap would make it easier to fit the plastic into the recycling can, when both of us knew she just wanted to do the firecracker dance.

"Tell me what you find out," I said finally.

She went up on tiptoes to kiss my cheek.

"Thank you."

She whispered it into my ear, hugged me quickly and then started for the door. I let her go. The door shut behind her. I stood listening to the streamlined silence of the new headquarters—my own breathing, the rush of the air-conditioning. The building had its own power, its own inertia. It was hard to get things moving at Valhalla. But once they were in motion they were almost impossible to stop. Franny's persistence had set our legal juggernaut rolling downhill. Now it was picking up speed, heading straight for my friend, and all I could do was watch.

◇◇◇

The judge set Billy Delavane's bail at half a million dollars. The hearing ended at two in the afternoon; by three, Billy's lawyer had posted bond and Billy was leaving the courtroom. Torno-vitch was furious, but there was nothing he could do about it.

"Why did no one tell me this bum was a goddamn million-aire?" he said to me on the street outside the town building.

I couldn't resist. "We assumed you'd done your homework, Jack."

"Very funny. But no one's going to be laughing if he sets off another bomb in this town. So I want him followed, and not by my people, either. They stick out like a bad haircut. Pick someone local, someone who can keep their head down and not get spotted. Krakauer's a local, use him. It would look funny if you didn't, and I don't want him to guess he's under suspicion. Let him pick a team. I want eyes on this little prick twenty four seven."

I nodded. "I'm on it."

"Is that so? Because at this moment he's walking to his truck, and in another two minutes he'll be driving away and you'll have lost him. Which isn't the most impressive way to begin the operation."

"Good point. See you later."

I sprinted to the station, ran into Haden at the dispatch desk and gave him his orders. Jack was more right than he could have imagined. No one on the force knew the island—or Billy Delavane—as well as Haden Krakauer. None of them had his experience or his military training. He was the best person for the job, though I wasn't sure who to replace him with on the night shift. I even considered buying some NoDoz and letting him work around the clock for a few days.

But it wasn't necessary. Events happened too fast for that.

This is how it went down, according to Billy's deposition and Haden's surveillance log. Billy drove out to the Lomax jobsite to tell Pat Folger he'd be back at work the next day. Then he drove to Cisco and checked the surf. He grabbed a board out of his truck bed and surfed for a few hours. Haden was watching him with binoculars from the widow's walk of a nearby beach house.

Billy drove home to Madaket. Haden parked behind Jack Rivers' house, took up his post in the outdoor shower, and settled in for the stakeout.

Half an hour later Billy burst out the front door, ran to his truck and drove away, tires spitting gravel. According to him, he had just received a frantic phone call from Debbie Garrison. There was some crisis with her mother. Debbie was hiding out in the scrub woods near the fourteenth hole of the new 'Sconset Golf Club. Her mother despised the club and its ostentatious members, but Debbie had friends on the staff and she often hung out there, playing Wii games in the locker room or cadging free food from the kitchen. Her mother knew nothing about this, so the club made an ideal hide-out.

Halfway up Milestone Road Billy became aware that Haden Krakauer was following him. Haden's car, a used Ford Expedition with a rack of PVC pipes bolted to the front grill for his fishing rods, didn't stand out on an island full of used cars, dump scavengers, and fly-casters. But Billy's eyes were drawn to the shredded roof rack pads. From a distance in the rear view mirror, they looked enough like the flasher bars on top of a police car to make him touch the brakes. The big car slowed down also, and that gave the game away. Billy turned off the state road onto the dirt track beside the cranberry bogs.

He lost Haden in the moors, but he never found Debbie at the golf course.

She denied making the phone call. There was nothing on her cell phone or her home phone records to indicate she was lying. I thought she might have used a pay phone, there was still a bank of them in the lot behind the old Masonic lodge downtown, as well as various other locations—the Stop& Shop, the airport. But we got the call records from every pay phone on the island. Nothing.

Haden found his way to Altar Rock and then picked his way among the ruts and puddles, backing up once for a hundred yards when a dirt road narrowed into a footpath through the brambles. Eventually he wound up skirting Stump Pond and emerging onto Polpis Road. He never caught up with Billy. He drove back into town and checked in at the station.

It seemed like a routine slipup, more fodder for Tornovitch's contempt. I didn't understand the real implications until later. But the fact remained—for whatever reason, neither Billy Delavane nor Haden Krakauer could account for their whereabouts that afternoon.

The town seemed to be settling down. The Army Corps was starting to work on the dock, and the Steamship Authority had reconfigured its schedules around one slip. Boats were running on time. That was all that mattered to most people. Even the disruptions were a sign of normality. Nantucketers dealt with such detours and delays routinely. Half the streets you turned into were blocked by dump trucks full of dirt, delivery trucks full of lumber, or fork-lifts and bulldozers moving the stuff around.

As dusk approached, it felt like a smooth-rolling summer night in America's premiere summer town. Restaurants were crowded. Nat Philbrick, Nantucket's most famous popular historian in the seven years since David Halberstam died, now was back lecturing at the Atheneum. The buskers had returned on Main Street.

Franny and I took the motor launch out to Wauwinet and ate at Topper's. Franny insisted on paying. I pulled out my wallet. She closed her hand over mine.

"Ask me about the case," she said.

I shrugged. "Any progress on Haden Krakauer?"

"Not yet. But I'm glad we had this talk. Now we can make Homeland Security pay for dinner."

"Including the cashew nut financiere and the fig foie gras crème brulee?"

She smiled. "Especially those things."

"Maybe we should get doggie bags for Tornovitch."

"Sorry, my rule is to piss him off only when absolutely necessary."

Riding the Wauwinet Lady back to the Hy-Line dock after dinner, leaning an elbow on the humming gunwale of the little boat, with the lights of Polpis flickering over the water and town gradually configuring itself out of the ground mist, I let her gripe about Jack—his passion for paperwork and his tendency to take her written reports and just sign them, turning them in as his own. I breathed the mild salt air and listened to her voice—the music, not the lyrics. I'd heard these songs before. Nothing much had changed since Los Angeles. It was higher profile now, with promotions and press coverage. She was making more money. And she rarely had to pay for dinner.

The talk circled back to Jack at my apartment later, after a world tour that included her marriage and mine, the virtue of the Colt 45 ACP over the nine millimeter handguns various government agencies preferred, her mother's lingering cancer and my father's death, by way of various regrets and missed opportunities, like unfinished novels, abandoned graduate degrees. We meticulously excluded our own relationship from that last topic. It was late at night. We'd been talking for hours. We were both tired, and neither of us had the stamina to launch a post-mortem on our time in L.A. I leaned across her for the bottle on the coffee table and poured us out the last of my sixteen-year-old Lagavulin.

She toasted the empty bottle and took a sip. "You died serving your country, sir."

"A true hero."

I took a swig, tasting the smoke and the peat bogs.

"Anyway," she said, "I felt bad, running down Jack before. People don't realize—he's had real tragedy in his life. No, I mean it. His wife left him when he was in the Army. She was a drunk. She was driving across country with their kid and got into some kind of horrific car crash. The kid died. She lived but she's quadriplegic now. Jack was having an affair in Kuwait. He had just divorced his wife. I guess he was planning to marry this girl. She died, too. He never told me what happened. But it must have been bad. The one time the subject came up, he lost it. We were in the Town and Country Lounge at the Mayflower a couple of years ago, getting a drink after work. Jack loves the place. J. Edgar Hoover used to hang out there. Anyway, right in the middle of talking about the girl, he excused himself and did a mad dash to the men's room. I was worried, I thought he was sick. I followed him, I listened at the door. He was crying. I scrambled back to the bar, and when he came out we both pretended nothing happened. But that was weird. Jack crying in the bathroom. Over some girl."

"Well, he was drunk."

"Not that drunk. Believe me. Jack never gets that drunk."

We sipped our scotch and let the specter of a heartbroken Jack Tornovitch fade away. Someone with a bad muffler roared down York Street and started the neighborhood dogs barking. Franny was looking at me with a quizzical little smile.

"What?"

"So when do I get to hear one of these poems of yours?"

"You don't."

"Come on, Hank. You may be the only poetry-writing law enforcement officer in the continental United States."

"That doesn't mean I'm any good at it."

She assembled a stern face. "Let me be the judge of that, Chief Kennis."

"I don't think so."

She slid her hand up my leg. "Poets are sexy."

"Are they?"

"I always fell for the arty types at school."

Her hand moved another inch.

"Okay," I said. "I never memorized too many of them. But this one sticks in my mind."

"Is it a love poem?"

"Sort of. I wrote it for my daughter when she was three. Actually, that's the title—'Three.' It might not be a great poem, but it's an excellent prophecy. It's already coming true."

She cocked her head, eyebrows lifted. "Well?"
I recited the poem.

There is a grace to parenthood,
And so there must be a fall.
I gaze at my daughter,
A self untested, uncertain, but pure
Wearing a purple dress
Looking not small but miniature
A cameo impression of a future self
Composed and separate
Going off to a dance
Or to college, or to work
Walking just as she does now
A little more steady
Posture just as straight
Striding without looking back
Across some future lawn
The same person, but bigger
And gone.
I miss her already
I cannot see her enough
Human perception is too small
It rattles like a pea
In the vast box of a single second
The loss cannot be reckoned
The predicament is too peculiar to mention:
I stand indicted by a future self
For the crime of divided attention.
So I stare
Grabbing at the swift flow of time,
Fistfuls of stream water
Standing five feet away from my daughter
Until my eyes begin to blur
Watching and watching
And watching
Her.

◇◇◇

Franny wiggled next to me and eased her head into the cup of muscle just below my shoulder.

"It's beautiful," she said.

"It's true, anyway."

She sighed comfortably. "Truth and beauty."

"So—you think poets who write about toddlers are sexy?"

"You know I do."

She was staring up at me with that little half-smile, and the silence settled in. It had its own authority. It seemed to prohibit conversation. Every hurtling second made talk seem more puny and meaningless. I cupped the back of Franny's head in my arms and kissed her. She kissed me back, pressing against me, pushing on my thighs to climb my body. Somehow I tipped over and she was lying on top of me on the couch. In the rush of feeling everything was new but also familiar. I was kissing her on that trail in the Santa Monica Mountains. It was the same kiss, interrupted by some indeterminate amount of time—a few seconds, to watch a hawk rising the thermals over the backbone trail? Or five years? I didn't know, and it didn't matter. Somehow we had found our way back to this same stream, both of us parched, heads ducked into the solid pulse of the current, gulping the icy water, drinking our fill.

I had just slipped my hand under her shirt, running it up the smooth warmth of her back, when we heard the noise.

We both froze for a second. Then Franny pulled away.

"What was that?"

My mind spun wildly, looking for a neutral explanation. Sonic boom? But no planes were flying at this hour. Thunder? But the sky was clear. Kids playing with illegal fireworks before the Fourth of July? But, faint as it was, the sound was too big, too deep, too wide for that.

"Shit," I said. "It's another bomb."

Then the phone rang.

I eased out from under Franny, rolled off the couch, and grabbed my cell from on top of the television. It was Tornovitch.

They had hit the new 'Sconset golf course, the Nantucket Golf Club. The bomb took out half the clubhouse and most of a cleaning crew, getting the place ready for a members' tournament the next day. Three innocent Ecuadorian immigrants, working the late shift for minimum wage. The other three made it out all right.

"Brief Agent Tate and get out here. This is our case now, Kennis. In my absence, you take your orders from her. Don't forget it."

He hung up.

I had a childish moment of thinking that whoever this bomber was, and whatever the ultimate purpose of these attacks, so far they were doing an excellent job of wrecking my love life. It was my last personal thought for quite a while, crumpled and gone even as it occurred to me, like a gum wrapper out a car window.

Everything was different now. There were casualties this time. This was murder. We were at war.

Chapter Ten
Disinformation

Two fire trucks passed us on the way to the golf course. We could see the glow of the blaze from the rise in the road, after the first Tom Nevers turn off. A sinuous length of smoke was rising from the fields beyond the cranberry bogs, dispersing against the high clear stars. It was almost two thirty in the morning. A full moon was casting a chalky light over the moors.

We drove east on Milestone Road without talking. I didn't want to say what I was thinking and I suspect Franny didn't either. You could make the case that Billy was out on bail because I failed to inform Jack Tornovitch of the Delavane family's financial status. If in fact he set off this bomb, then part of the blame would fall on me. It wasn't much of a case, but it was a real concern. You don't have to be found guilty to feel that way. Billy was the obvious suspect, running out of the house on the basis of that phantom "emergency phone call" from Debbie Garrison the previous afternoon.

Billy had been heading for the golf course, according to Haden Krakauer. He took evasive action, lost Haden in the moors—and twelve hours later the bomb went off. That was bad enough.

The other thoughts were worse.

Haden had been missing for part of the afternoon also. We only had his word that he was chasing Billy. He had plenty of time to set a bomb, and he knew the island well enough to approach the club from behind without being spotted. Could Haden have faked that phone call from Debbie? No, no, that was nuts. At least it sounded nuts. But was it really impossible? All he needed to do was bug her phone, get her on tape, then mix and match any usable quotes. Haden certainly had the technological know-how. He was a geek. I remembered him telling me about the 1960s phone "phreaks," using their black boxes to cheat the phone company. It had something to do with "supervision signals" and "Zener diodes." I nodded along, the way you do when someone in a foreign country thinks you speak their language, but I understood the most important part. Haden knew what he was talking about. That stuff fascinated him, which was a little odd for a cop.

This was ludicrous. It was late at night, I'd had a few drinks at dinner, I should have been home in bed, preferably with Franny. I stole a glance at her. She was looking out at the moon-washed landscapes streaming by. I had asked her about Haden at dinner—I was half joking, just giving her an excuse to put a meal on the government tab. She had joked back, but was she telling the truth? She kept things to herself until she had a solid case. Was she almost there? What had she actually found out?

I didn't ask her. I didn't want to know.

Two staties I'd never seen before were manning the yellow tape at the guardhouse at the bottom of the driveway. They let us through and we drove up the long series of curves toward the clubhouse.

The fire was mostly out by the time we got there. The left side of the big building seemed to be intact, but the right side was a smoking ruin. Gouts of water from four different hoses arced into the smoldering heap of charred timber. Bomb techs and forensic teams were swarming the blast site. Fraker and some local state cops were standing around drinking coffee.

We sat quietly in the car for a moment after I turned off the engine. Franny started to roll down her window but rolled it back up, hastily. Tornovitch appeared at my window. I dutifully rolled it down. The acrid air rushed in.

He looked past me and talked directly to Franny. "There are three survivors," he said. "Two of them can talk, but only one of them speaks English. Apparently he got a call a few minutes before the bomb went off, telling him to vacate the premises. He and his two pals believed it. The others thought it was a prank. Fraker is rounding up the groundskeeper and a couple of other locals who were in the vicinity. I want full statements from everyone. Speak that good Castilian Spanish of yours. They love the lisp. Make them comfortable. Get me some answers. Fraker has his people rousting the club personnel who were on duty yesterday. I want them deposed on a minute-by-minute timeline. I want to know if they saw anyone, any unfamiliar vehicle, any unusual activity, anything. The local cops can help with the transcriptions and the tape recording."

He turned to me. "Get your boys out here, Kennis. Your job is—keep the press away. Feed them some bullshit. The story is a gas main blew up. Stick to it. Put some summer specials out on the course. The press'll be cutting across the greens to get access. This is a world class PGA facility and I don't want those ghouls trashing it. My forensic team has already found fragments of the device. Residues indicate military issue C-4. I have a National Guard division on the way to Madaket right now to arrest Delavane, and an FBI team will be interrogating the brother within the hour. I want to know how he got his hands on this stuff."

Franny nodded and climbed out of the car, jogging away toward the makeshift field hospital at the back of the building.

"I can handle Billy," I said to Tornovitch. "You don't need a bunch of trigger-happy weekend warriors charging in there and—"

"You can handle Delavane? Are you drunk? I smell booze on you, Kennis. So maybe that explains your idiotic remark. Let me refresh your memory. You didn't want to arrest this lunatic in the first place, and then you withheld information which put him out on the street the same day we brought him in. Don't fuck with the United States government, Kennis. That's called treason where I come from."

This was pointless bullying. There was no way he could bring charges against me without admitting his own negligence. And it didn't matter anyway—he could never have gotten Billy held without bail at that hearing. The judge knew Billy too well and the evidence was too flimsy. Still, Jack never missed a chance to play the bully. It kept his blood pressure down. He let everyone around him suffer the strokes and the heart attacks. He'd be the picture of robust good health at their funerals.

The firemen turned off the hoses, and the place was quiet for a second after Jack strode away, apart from the murmur of hushed conversations, the dripping water, and the subsiding crackle of the burnt lumber. The scorched, sodden smell was stronger here in the aftermath of the explosion. The big shingled clubhouse had the look of one more McMansion under construction: half-finished, ostentatious, dominating the hillside over the golf course.

I called Kyle Donnelly and Charlie Boyce, gave them their marching orders. The entire press corps would be closed out— with one exception. When I called Haden Krakauer he was halfway up the driveway with David Trezize in the car beside him. David had been trying to get past the staties, telling them I had called him out to the crime scene. They weren't buying it. Haden arrived in the middle of the argument and backed him up, just to annoy the storm-troopers.

"They made David leave his car at the guardhouse," Haden told me. "Too many vehicles up here. I can take him back if you want."

"No, no—it's okay. Let him come."

I liked the idea of David Trezize scooping everyone, including the *New York Times* and CNN, not to mention our own *Inquirer and Mirror*.

David Trezize was the editor and sole proprietor of an upstart local weekly called the *Nantucket Shoals*. He had named the little newspaper after the lightship station that served as a landing mark for transatlantic sea traffic off the island until 1983. That was typical of him. His knowledge of Nantucket history was almost perversely encyclopedic. Standing on a random spot in Polpis he could tell you it had been a commercial holly grove in the early twentieth century, a dairy farm before that, and the site of a Wampanoag village a century earlier. He had the arrowheads to prove it.

The *Shoals* was the most successful effort yet launched to provide an alternative to the *Inky Mirror.* The little newspaper had almost gone under the year before, because of a feud with a vindictive plutocrat named Preston Lomax. When the man was killed, David had found himself on the suspect list, but only briefly. And it had turned out well for him.

Rumor was, Lomax's daughter Kathleen had put a lot of money into the paper, and they'd been seen together at various high-end island restaurants. Good for him. She was a good kid, he deserved a little romance, and his newspaper deserved a second chance. The writing was sharp because David edited and largely rewrote every article. The photography was striking because he took most of the pictures himself. He also fixed the computers, laid out the paper every week, and sold most of the ad space.

David was small and chubby with thick glasses. He seemed pale and unimposing at first sight but he had a termite intensity. He would chew into anything that caught his interest. It made sense that he was the first one to the crime scene, and that he'd managed to talk himself into riding shotgun with the assistant chief.

They climbed out of the cruiser, and I was glad to see the look of shock and horror on Haden's face. "It's a fucking war zone," he said to me when I walked up to them. "I never thought I'd see another one. Casualties?"

I nodded, and told him to secure the perimeter with the troops as they arrived, coordinating with Boyce and Donnelly. For the moment, we were just crowd control. There was no real police work for us to do. The off-island experts had that side of it handled.

"That's a comforting thought," he said. Then he pulled me aside. "Can I have a quick word with you, Chief?"

"Sure."

We took a couple of steps away from David Trezize.

"We need to talk."

"Listen, Haden, I don't know if this is the right time. Maybe tomorrow morning, when—"

"It is tomorrow morning. Listen, something weird is going on here. I've been thinking about it a lot. I didn't want to say anything because it sounds so crazy. And now, with some SWAT team arresting Billy Delavane…I don't know. It's like…a *Twilight Zone* episode or something."

I put a hand on his shoulder. "I know you feel bad about this, Haden. We all do. But we're standing in the middle of a crime scene right now. We have a lot of work to do before dawn. That has to take priority. We'll talk about this later. All right?"

"All right. But soon."

"Soon, absolutely. Tomorrow or the next day. I'll clear some time."

He went off to do his job, and we didn't get around to talking until it was too late.

Trezize strolled up to me. No one noticed him in the urgent bustle. "Quite a mess, Chief."

I nodded.

"Another bomb?"

"Word is, a gas main exploded."

"Would that be a Semtex gas main or a C-4 gas main?"

"Very funny."

"On the contrary—I think we're both dead serious here, Chief. And you're a terrible liar. No offence."

I glanced around. No one nearby. "It's C-4. Military grade. They're taking Billy Delavane into custody right now. This time they're holding him without bail. And you didn't hear any of this from me."

"Absolutely not. You're the soul of discretion."

"I mean it, David. Homeland Security is on the warpath right now."

He gave me an ineptly playful punch on the shoulder. "Hey, I always protect my sources, Chief. Just as if I ran a real newspaper."

David wandered away, and I pulled my mag-light and some zip-lock plastic evidence baggies out of the car. I walked around the undamaged side of the clubhouse, skirted the medical tent and pushed into the dense bushes of rosa rugosa, pitch pine, and scrub oak and huckleberry. I found an overgrown path, not much more than a deer track, and started down it slowly, shining the light a hundred and eighty degrees ahead of me. Soon I was out of sight of the club grounds and almost out of earshot.

I didn't know what I was looking for, but this struck me as the most likely clandestine approach to the property. Maybe I'd find the spot where the perpetrator had parked his car. Tire tracks could help us, so could paint residues if the brambles had scratched the finish. A good foot print in the soft dirt with a unique tread pattern would help. So would anything he left behind. Once in L.A. we found a bank thief's cell phone at the crime scene. People were careless. They left messes behind. Cleaning up after them was one of the best ways to put them in jail. So I moved through the underbrush at a measured, deliberate pace, looking for what didn't belong.

What I finally found in the brambles made my stomach lurch.

It would have looked like an inconsequential scrap of litter to anyone else. I almost missed it myself—a little square of wax paper, caught on a thorn at knee level, a yard off the path. I got a swarm of tiny cuts reaching for it, taking one corner with my tweezers and delicately lifting it free. My knees cracked as I straightened up, holding the powerful light on the paper. It was the wrapper from a HALLS cough drop, Haden Krakauer's favorite brand and constant companion.

Had he been here, trudging along this path, sucking his cough drops, cradling the bomb in his hands, the plastic-wrapped explosive he was so familiar with from his Army days?

The thought brought a chill, a feverish little shudder.

Franny was right.

Haden was framing Billy Delavane for some long-ago sexual peccadillo. He held grudges, just as Billy said. Haden was the bomber. And now he was a murderer, too. He was nuts, but he was good at hiding it. He had fooled everyone for years. Most of all, he had fooled me. I hadn't seen it because I didn't want to see it, just like I didn't want to accept that people were jacking deer and turning the island into a toxic waste site.

I looked aside. I preferred the fantasy, I preferred to live in my own little dream world, just like my ex-wife always said.

Well, not anymore.

I fumbled for one of the evidence bags. My hand trembled as I slipped the wrapper inside. In the process I dropped the flashlight and stood in the dark for a minute or so, the beam cutting a tangled path through the shrubs. I pushed the on-off button with my foot and breathed in the darkness, deep breaths that pushed the first spasm of anger and confusion out of my lungs.

I had to start thinking straight. Haden wasn't the only person who used HALLS cough drops. And whatever else he was, he wasn't a litterbug. He ranted against the secret garbage dumps on Land Bank property and the beer cans floating in the harbor. Plus he was a policeman. If anyone knew the danger of a thoughtlessly discarded piece of evidence, it was him.

But he had been out here yesterday. We knew that from his own testimony. And the wrapper was fresh.

The wind shifted. I could smell the charred wood, hear the faint sounds of the investigative teams at the clubhouse, someone shouting orders, portable generators kicking on. I saw the sudden burst of light from the halogens reflecting over the rise in the moors, blotting out the stars. I was standing in the shadow of a low valley, hidden from everyone, alone with my find.

I knew my legal and moral obligations at that moment. I had to turn this new evidence over to Tornovitch. The wrapper needed to be dusted for prints, the rest of the area behind the club needed to be searched by a full JTTF team. But Jack still knew nothing about Franny's suspicions. If she cleared Haden as she fully expected to do, then this bit of random paper would mean nothing to anyone.

If Franny found something, that would be different. For now I had breathing space. I'd hang back and let Tornovitch carry the ball. He didn't want to hear from me, anyway.

I slipped the evidence bag into my pocket, picked up the flashlight, took in another raw gulp of the smoke-tainted air. Then I started crunching back toward the garish lights of civilization. The shock was wearing off. I was feeling better. I didn't have to fix this one myself. I had the whole Federal Government on my side, working the case. They had their number-one suspect back in custody by now. All I needed to do was cheer them on—police work as spectator sport.

With the proper attitude, I might even enjoy it.

Chapter Eleven

Fireworks

On the eve of the July Fourth holiday, the day after the worst crime ever perpetrated on Nantucket, with Billy Delavane in jail, the town on Orange Alert, the Steamship Authority terminal under repair by the Army Corps of Engineers, and the National Guard in full uniform roaming the town, my kids had only one question, and it concerned Billy's pug. "Who's taking care of Dervish?"

I had just picked them up from Murray Camp where they'd spent the day sailing, making clay bowls and doing yoga. We had barely pulled out of the slant parking at Children's Beach when the question came up. Fortunately I had the answer.

"Abby Folger is staying at the house."

"We could help," Caroline said.

I knew what was happening. The conversation would work its way around to my getting a dog myself, their second most pressing concern after my finding a bigger place to live. They preferred a beach house at Surfside and a pair of black Lab puppies.

To divert them I said, "I'll call Abby. I'm sure she'd love that."

"We could take care of him if she goes off-island," Tim added.

"Sure. That would be nice."

We drove in silence for a while, jolting across the cobblestones toward Washington Street. We were immediately stopped behind a line of traffic. A group of tourists wandered across Main Street, stopping to take pictures. They would never stand oblivious in the middle of a busy intersection at home, but Nantucket was like Brigadoon to them—a magical place that came alive once a year, where normal rules didn't apply.

"Is Billy really the bomber?" Tim asked, abruptly.

"I don't know. There's a lot of evidence against him."

"I don't think he is," Caroline said. "Billy's nice."

"But, if he isn't…" Tim started and trailed off.

I glanced over at him. It was his turn to ride shotgun. "What?"

"Then—it's just…forget it."

"Come on, what?"

"Then…it's someone else and they don't know who, and…"

"There'll be more bombs," Caroline finished for him.

I took a breath. "Everyone is working hard to make sure nothing bad happens. Not just me. There's the State Police and Homeland Security…and soldiers." A pair of them trudged up the street, weighted down with guns and ammunition belts, eating ice-cream cones with the fierce concentration of ten-year-olds. The image was absurd and perfect—welcome to the Orange Alert Nantucket summer.

"Can we get ice-cream cones," Caroline asked.

"Not now. Maybe we can go to the Juice Bar after dinner."

Back home, Caroline IMed her friends and Tim worked on some summer school math homework, while I made a twenty-minute dinner: salad from packaged mescal greens and an olive oil vinaigrette; herb-crusted, pan-seared boneless chicken breast (That's sprinkled with dry basil and fried, to you); and boxed couscous.

I could feel the tension of the day releasing as I worked. The little apartment on York Street was my sanctuary, especially when it was filled with the buzzing hectic imperative life of my kids. Yes, I enjoyed my nights off, but I loved having them with me, too. Their silly jokes and passionate squabbling, the drama of their moment by moment existence was a lifeline and a tonic. The murder and mayhem churning through the town, the fear I saw in people's eyes—that was real, but so was this. The outside world stopped at the front door.

Or so I thought. Tim was quiet during the meal. "You okay?"

"I'm fine, Dad."

"Because if it's about the bombs—"

"It's not."

"Did something happen at camp?"

"Can we change the subject?"

I pounced. "So there is a subject! I thought so."

"Shut up, okay?"

"Hey, don't be rude."

He looked up at me, put his knife and fork down, pushed his chair out from the table. "You're being rude. You're being pushy and mean. Can I be excused? I have to do my reading." This may have been the first time ever that Tim voluntarily took up his summer reading before the last week in August.

"Sorry."

"That's okay. Sorry I said shut up."

"Don't worry about it. I just wanted to help."

"Well you can't."

"Why not?"

"Dad—!"

Finally Caroline broke in. "There's a bully at camp. He was bothering Tim at school and now he's at camp, too—"

"Carrie!"

"I can't stand this! What difference does it make?"

"I'm going upstairs."

Tim stood up and stalked out of the room.

I turned to Caroline. "Who is this bully?"

"Jake Sauter. He's a big fat ugly jerk. I think he was left back a few times. Timmy thought he was safe for the summer—Jake's family don't have much money. And it's mostly pretty rich kids at Murray Camp. But I guess someone died or something? Because Jake's parents inherited a big house in Wauwinet. And now Jake's at Murray Camp."

I spoke slowly. "Has he actually—"

"No, no…he just sort of threatens him and pushes him around. Sometimes I wish he would do something. Then they'd throw him out of camp."

"I'll be right back."

Upstairs the door was open to the big room Tim shared with his sister. That was a good sign. Caroline's side was a mess, clothes, shoes, cell phone charger, books and magazines scattered all over the floor, the bed unmade. Tim's side—they had put down masking tape to make the division official—was aggressively neat. His bed was made with hospital corners. His clothes were hung up or folded, his books lined up on a small white book shelf, arranged alphabetically by author.

He was sitting on the edge of the bed, working his PlayStation portable. So much for summer reading.

I knocked. "Can I come in?"

He tilted his head, but kept killing aliens on the little backlit screen.

"Tim, you know there's only one thing to do with a kid like Jake Sauter."

"Have a mafia hit man come and kill him?"

I laughed. "Okay—two things. It's cheaper to stand up to him. Bullies are cowards. Everybody knows that."

Tim put down the video game, twisted to face me. "I don't know that. Maybe he's a coward with some other big kid, but that just makes things worse for me. It makes him want to beat me up more."

"Not if you fight back."

"Come on, Dad. That'll just make him angry. Then he really has to beat me up or he looks like a wimp."

"Maybe—but he'll think twice before he comes after you again."

"Forget it."

He picked up the PlayStation and resumed the game, thumbs flying, the master of a tiny electronic world.

I stepped to his side. "Tim—"

He spoke to the screen. "You always say a good parent remembers what it was like to be a kid. But you don't remember anything."

I sat down on the bed.

"So what are you going to do?"

"Exactly what you did when you were my age. Keep my eyes open and stay out of his way."

I watched him blow up a particularly spiky savage-looking alien.

"If only life was a videogame."

He shrugged. "You'd need better graphics."

◇◇◇

The next night was the Fourth of July. I had to put in an appearance at the AIDS fundraiser on Lincoln Circle. I had asked Franny to attend and was hoping to meet her there. I picked the kids up from camp and dropped them off at Miranda's house on the way.

Tim must have talked to his mother during the day, thanks to the miracle of cell phone technology. She opened the door with her game face on, thick brown hair pulled back into a tight bun and the skin of her face stretched, too, by her latest 'life style' facelift. She was forty years old, beautiful without plastic surgery. But I no longer had to argue that case.

The kids ran past her into the house, and she blocked the entrance as if I wanted to force my way in. I didn't.

"I can't believe you told Tim to fight with a bully."

"Fine, thanks. How are you?"

"I mean it, Henry. How could you say that? Fighting won't solve anything."

"Actually, fighting solves things all the time. World War II, for instance."

"Really? Viet Nam is the war that comes to my mind."

"Fighting solved Viet Nam. It doesn't feel that way to us, because we lost."

She pressed her finger tips to her lips as if to physically prevent herself from speaking a devastating truth that she would only regret later. "Tim could get hurt."

"That's true, whether he fights back or not."

"I don't believe this."

"What would you suggest?"

"How about talking? How about resolving issues verbally to avoid this kind of terrible situation?"

"There's only one issue, Miranda. This kid is bigger than Tim. Tim is afraid of him. The bully likes that. He's not a new-age, sensitive, politically correct bully. He's a plain, old-fashioned bully, and if Tim doesn't stand up to him he'll be dealing with the guy forever."

Her cool green eyes used to pierce me like a piece of meat on a skewer, with the coals ashing over for the main event. But not anymore. I started back for the car.

She called, "If Tim gets injured in this pissing match, I'm holding you responsible."

I waved. "Nice seeing you, too."

◇◇◇

That year's Nantucket AIDS network fund-raiser took place at Kathleen Lomax's new house on Sherburne turnpike, a lovely old pile perched on the cliff above the north shore, and perfectly situated for viewing the fireworks. A surf of blue hydrangeas surged against the brick foundation of the sprawling old house, offset by rows of day lilies. Roses climbed the walls, sweetening the air, and music spilled from the open windows. The driveway was crowded with cars and people, and the atmosphere was festive. Kathleen hadn't gutted and modernized the house when she bought it, so it remained a museum of the 1970s, from the baggy couches and bleached pine paneling and plate glass windows to the carved whales, ship-timber mantel piece and pickled floor boards. Kathleen had even kept the old rotary dial phones.

Inside she stood by the front door with David Trezize, greeting the guests. This party made it official. They had finally come out as a couple. They seemed like an odd one, but I was hardly in a position to judge.

"So great to see you," Kathleen said, hugging me. David added, "Miranda is lurking around here somewhere. FYI."

So she had gotten a babysitter, after all.

I pushed through the crowd in the foyer toward the comfortable, low-ceilinged living room with its panoramic view of Nantucket Sound. The space was thronged with the silk dresses and blue blazers of Nantucket's ruling class. Senator Kerry and his wife were in the center of a group, watched over by three Secret Service agents. I saw Gould watching them, talking to Tornovitch.

It was loud, the roar and rustle of conversation as dense as cigar smoke. Ecliff and The Swing Dogs were tuning up at one end of the room.

A few steps ahead of me, Miranda and her new boyfriend stood deep in conversation with her boss, the Queen of Nantucket real estate, Elaine Bailey. Dan Taylor and his wife hovered nearby. Dan nodded at me. I nodded back.

Elaine was saying, "It's fabulous—hide-hair and leather. It's an eight thousand dollar couch, but I got it on sale at Neiman's for sixty-two hundred. I couldn't believe that price! I just *snatched* it up!"

Miranda and Elaine, kindred spirits, sharing at least two essential beliefs: couches are sacred and nothing is expensive if you get it on sale.

I veered away to avoid Miranda's group and landed face to face with Pat Folger. The bullish little contractor had a bottle of beer in one hand and my arm in the other. "Chief, we have to talk."

I scanned the room, but no sign of Franny. I knew what Pat wanted to talk about. "Could you come into the station next week? Because right now I'm just trying to—"

"We can get these guys, Chief. Have you seen the Oxy Kills posters all over town? I put them up. I didn't know what else to do."

"Pat—"

"Come with me. Please. Just for a second."

I let him lead me into a small den and shut the door behind us, sealing out the party noise. "I'm giving you these guys on a platter, Chief. You can take down the whole bunch of em."

"Pat, listen…I've been meaning to talk to you about this.

We're working this case but you're not helping. Stalking these drug dealers, taking pictures, bothering them…it's making them suspicious. If they get nervous enough they'll go underground and we could lose track of them for another year."

"Then arrest them!"

I grabbed his shoulders. "Pat, stop yelling. We have no evidence against these guys. All right? We can't use the drug dog, they can't sniff oxy. It's not even illegal if you have a scrip for it. Anyone can bring a suitcase full of the stuff across on the boat and there's nothing we can do about it. We can't open everyone's luggage. Especially not this time of year. We have to catch them in the act, Pat, unless a user steps up and rats them out, which—c'mon, you're talking about drug addicts here, so…"

He fixed me with a tight little smile. For a second I thought he might break into tears, but his voice was steady.

"Doug will do it."

I knew Pat's son had been in rehab down in North Carolina but had run away. The last I heard he was humping furniture at his brother Rick's antique store. So he was using oxy again? That would explain Pat's obsessive interest in the dealers.

"'Doug will'—I'm not sure what you're saying, Pat."

"Doug's been clean for a week. Rick's watching him like a hawk, letting him sleep on the couch. Doug got the insomnia and the sweating and the puking but he rode it out. It's like Rick says, you either want to get off the stuff or you don't and he does."

"Great."

"I don't mean to share Doug's business. But he wants to help."

"He'll testify against these people?"

"He'll do whatever you want him to do."

I let out a breath, squeezed the tough old carpenter's shoulder one last time and released him. This was a huge break if it was true, if Doug would really go through with it. "Have him come in to the station on Monday, Pat. We'll work out a plan."

Pat nodded. "Get these bastards, Chief. Just—get them."

"We will." He stuck out his hand and I shook it. Then we both went back to the party, to the rich insular, entitled Nantucket

I served, where the drugs of choice were Chopin Vodka and Macallan eighteen-year-old single malt.

Ecliff started their set, playing an old Jimmy Buffet song. I walked over to the wall of windows as the fireworks began, blooming in the dark, illuminating their own spider-legged trails of smoke in the flash of light against the stars. Rockets and roman candles, bouquets and brocades, lovely but pointless, extravagant but ephemeral, conspicuous consumption etching its temporary fossil into the soft stone of the summer night.

"Sounds like artillery fire."

Tyler Gibson stood alone nearby. Had he already broken up with that striking blonde from Cru? I wasn't surprised. If she had dumped him, he was taking it hard. He looked pale and feverish.

"Having a good season, Mr. Gibson?"

"You remember my name? I'm impressed."

"Being a police chief around here is a lot like being the head-waiter at an expensive restaurant. Remembering names is part of the job description."

"Smile!" It was Gene Mahon, taking pictures for the Nantucket Foggy Sheet society photo gallery that ran every month in *N Magazine*. The camera ratcheted as Gene pushed the auto-advance button.

"Hey" Gibson shouted. "What the hell you think you're doing with that?" He pushed his palm at the camera: the classic defensive block of the harassed celebrity.

"Don't worry," Gene said cheerfully. "You look great. Move a little closer together—put your arm around him, Chief."

"Get out of here. I mean it." Gibson sidestepped me and advanced on the tall, slouching photographer. I couldn't imagine a more benign target for his anger. Gene stepped back.

"Hey, no problem. Chill."

I grabbed Gibson's arm. "That's enough," I said.

Gibson was locked on Gene. "You need permission to print a photograph. You don't have mine."

"Okay, okay—no problem."

Gene backed away. Gibson let out a breath through clenched teeth.

"How do you stand that? People jamming cameras in your face."

"Gene's okay. And people like to see themselves on the Mahon About Town website."

I could see he had no idea what I was talking about. But before he could ask me anything, another round of fireworks went off—pinwheels and fountains changing color halfway down. The last one sent off no sparks, just a deep echoing bang, a high-caliber gunshot like the bomb at the Steamship Authority.

Gibson flinched. "Jesus Christ. No one who actually served in a war zone—I mean, no one who actually lived through a fire fight—could stand listening to this shit."

"I think it's supposed to evoke the sensation of being at war. Bombs bursting in air. All that."

"Well, they do a great job. Very realistic. Which is wonderful, because we wouldn't want to forget what it's like to have our eardrums ruptured and our friends blown apart in front of us. Excuse me for not being more grateful, but I'm outta here."

He shoved and stumbled to the front door, bumping people, leaving a wake of annoyed faces and spilled drinks. I felt bad for him. I wasn't a veteran. I had no idea what war felt like, and I was glad I didn't. I'd been shot at a couple of times, working for the LAPD. That was more than enough for me. Haden Krakauer was the only vet I knew. He might have been able to help this guy, but he was supervising the fireworks security detail at Jetties Beach, and he hated parties anyway. No way would he show up here, despite the free booze. He did his drinking at home.

I had more or less given up on Franny when I finally saw her at the other side of the room. She must have just come in, looking around, trying to spot me. I couldn't catch her eye, so I excused myself across the floor to slip my arm around her waist. I buried my head in her hair for a second and kissed her neck, just below her ear. "Glad you could make it."

She twisted away. This wasn't the moment for kissing. She looked exhausted, the skin pulled pale and dry against the bones of her face. "Can we go somewhere? We have to get out of here."

"What is it?"

"Let's just go. I don't want to deal with Jack right now."

He was huddled with Gould. There was a crowd between us and he was looking the other way. But he could turn around at any second. Franny was tugging me toward the door. Various people greeted me, but it was clear I couldn't talk to them. A man being dragged out of a party by an angry woman usually meant trouble. But for whom?

"What's going on?"

"Not here, Hank. Meet me back at your house. We have a lot of work to do."

The look on her face gave me the feeling I used to get, looking at a full mail box after a week's procrastination. The bad news was there already.

I just didn't know it yet.

Ezekiel Beaumont: Ten Hours Ago

Vika Avandeyev rolled over onto the American and let her nipples brush his chest. She liked his long lean body against hers and she could feel him stiffen beneath her. He was so responsive, so young and healthy. She had been forced to lie with so many old men before she left Plovdiv to come here, men in their fifties, men in their sixties, men who wheezed and snored and seemed to draw the vitality out of her, ticks feasting on blood. Yes, she knew all about ticks now, after a year on this Nantucket Island.

Grigor had promised there would be young men here, rich American men who were sick of their demanding American women, men who could give her a better life. And he was willing to let her go. This was the wonderful thing about Grigor. He knew all things were temporary, he could not hold you and he didn't want to. There was always a new girl, a younger and prettier one to take your place. That was fine with Vika. She had picked her American, she had made her choice.

Just how catastrophically, tragically, fatally bad that choice had been she was going to learn before the end of this close and humid summer day. Whether she could survive the lesson was another question.

What had Grigor told her? "These fancy men with their Nantucket five-spots—that's what they call the fifty-dollar bills they give you for a tip, because fifty dollars means nothing to them and everything is crazy expensive here and nothing is worth what you pay." He had touched her face with a rueful smile. "Maybe except you. You are worth every penny, little Vika. But be careful with this American dream you read about. It becomes nightmare if you sleep too long."

But of course she wasn't thinking about any of this now. She was just sleepy and horny. She wanted coffee and breakfast, but mostly she wanted to feel the American big and urgent inside her. She found his mouth and kissed him. In a moment he was kissing her back, with a deep groan of pleasure. Vika liked to hear that. He was like a cat, purring. She squirmed on him, letting him feel her thighs against his thighs and her stomach against his stomach. The simple pleasure of skin on skin flushed through her nerves like overflowing stream water through new grass.

He ran his hands down her back, stroked her backside the way he knew she liked. Then he grunted and rolled over to pull a condom out of his bedside drawer.

He pulled out a small digital tape instead, and she felt his whole body go rigid. "Goddamn it! God fucking piss shitting damn it! What the hell is wrong with me?"

She rolled off him and sat up. "Tyler? Are you all right? Is everything okay?"

He swung his legs over the side of the bed, pounded his knobby knees with his fists. "No! I'm not all right! Nothing is okay. Goddamn it. I am so fucked. How could I—argghh. Shit! I have to think."

"Tyler—?"

"Shut up and let me think!"

She flinched away and studied the freckles on his back. At first she had thought he was having a stroke. But he was upset—and with himself, not her. She was frightened, so she made herself very still and small.

Finally he stood. "I have to go," he said. "I have—something to do. Something I have to do. Right now."

The anger was gone. He was nervous and scared, unsure of himself. He stood there as if he didn't know which way to move.

"I could come with you," Vika said.

"No."

"I could help."

"I said no."

She scooched herself over to the edge of the bed, reached out to stroke his leg. "I could be lookout," she said. Somehow she knew he might need one.

He turned and looked down at her. "Why would you say that? What do you think I am?"

"I don't think. I don't care. This is not who you are. This is something you do. I can do with you. I am with very sharp eyes. And a couple looks like regular people. A man alone, people are wonder about him. What is doing, why is alone? People make call on cell phone, people take picture. Then—poof! Trouble."

He was shifting from foot to foot. "I don't know."

"People look at us they think, such pretty lovers. All the world loves a lover, yes? They feel jealous maybe, but not suspect. Who would suspect lovers? Besides, you should not be alone now."

He seemed to decide. He grabbed his pants off a chair and started pulling them on. "All right," he said. "But you have to do what I say—and keep your mouth shut."

She widened her eyes and pressed her lips together dramatically. It made him smile.

"Jesus, you're cute. Come on, get dressed. We've got to get moving."

She slipped into her shorts, t-shirt, and flip-flops, and followed him out to his car. They had slept in—it was nearly ten in the morning and everyone in their quiet neighborhood near the junction of Cliff Road and Madaket Road on this balmy Fourth of July was already out and about, having breakfast in town or setting up at the beach.

They cruised out along Deacon's Way and turned left toward town, past the fat standpipe and the new houses and the open fields at Tupancy Links that had been a golf course a long time ago. Tyler said nothing for a while then out of nowhere, "I hate those flip-flops you wear."

"Why is that?"

"I don't know. The way they make you walk. Kind of—splay-footed and bow-legged and clumsy."

"Splay foot? What is that?"

"You walk like a duck in those things. I used to like it when I saw girls wearing them—you know, anything to make the jail bait less attractive. But, now with you…I want you to drive other guys crazy. And it ain't happening in those sandals."

"Maybe if I make shirt tighter?" She pulled the flimsy cotton against her chest.

"Okay, okay, I get the point. You could wear swim fins and a nun's habit and still make a ten-year-old hit puberty two years early. But high heels look better than flip-flops. That's a fact. Now quiet down. I have to figure things out over here."

He had started the conversation, but she knew better than to mention it.

They skirted the edge of town, following Sparks Avenue past the old mill and the hospital. Beyond Stop&Shop to the rotary, and then east along the Milestone Road toward 'Sconset. Tyler kept looking around—for the police? For someone he knew? But he seemed to see no one and nothing and no one that concerned him. He was starting to relax.

Vika rolled down her window and enjoyed the breeze.

They drove past the winding driveway that led to the big new golf course and then up into 'Sconset. The road seemed to widen, lined on either side by lawns and maple trees in the pale sunshine. The day called out for romance, for picnics and walks on the beach. But Tyler was all business.

"Nothing's going to go wrong," he said, turning onto Morey Lane. "But if there's a problem, let me do the talking. Worst case scenario? We both let my friend do the talking." He lifted his shirt a little to show the gun tucked into his waistband.

Vika felt her stomach lurch. The glint of metal gave her a jolt out of proportion to the glimpse of brushed steel. She had been with men who carried guns before, and it was always bad. Guns made the bad things happen. They had some malignant spirit in them, haunted by the ghosts they waited to make.

But no. America was the land of guns. The NRA and the Second Amendment to the Constitution. Many people carried guns here. It didn't mean what it meant at home.

He pulled the car to the side of the street, beside an unkempt hedge. He cut the engine. "Stay put. Honk if you see a cop. Don't interfere, don't say anything. Just honk."

"Okay," she said.

"I'll be right back. Sit tight."

That meant be patient. Vika had an excellent grasp of American idiomatic usage. But she still made mistakes. She would have said "sit tightly," and Tyler would have laughed at her.

He disappeared through the arbor in the hedge. The street was empty—no cars, no pedestrians, no police, just the drowsing summer morning. She was restless. She wanted to know what he was doing inside the house. Maybe she could get a glimpse through one of the windows. She'd still be on guard, just not sitting tightly. It would be better to find him than honk and call attention to them.

She slipped out of the car and closed the door quietly. She was still alone on the street. She trotted through the arbor and up to the house. It was a gloomy old house and the windows were dirty. She tried the door. Open. She pushed it a little and listened. Footsteps from the far end of the hall.

She eased inside, closed the door gently behind her, and started up the dark corridor. It smelled of mildew and burned coffee, dust and pine resin bleeding through the wood. The captured heat seemed to push the air out of the hallway. She would suffocate if she had to live in this house. What was Tyler doing in here? What did he want with this place?

She saw him going through a door at the far side of the kitchen to the basement stairs. He'd be able to hear her footsteps above him now. She tiptoed along, sticking to the side of the passageway. Boards didn't creak so much along the edge of the floor.

When she got to the door she heard his voice.

"... I moved it behind a bunch of boxes and some big metal shelf full of paint cans. No way, not unless he suddenly decides to clean up the place—or redecorate. No way he's gonna talk his way out of this one. Nobody's gonna care. They'll be too busy counting the bodies. Right. That's what I'm saying. Yeah, yeah, I know. Paper covers rock. For once! Sure, I get it. Now let me go, I gotta finish up in here."

He was heading for the stairs. Vika raked the kitchen with a desperate glance. The only place to hide was the broom closet. She darted to the little door under a high cabinet and yanked it open: a mop and a vacuum. She squeezed herself in and pulled the door shut, digging her nails into the little gap between the flat surface and the raised edge of the panel. She stood hunched over, one shoulder pressed to a vacuum hose, feet pushed in among the clutter of canister bags, cords, and a plastic dustpan. She held her breath and listened as Tyler crossed the kitchen. Was he going outside again? Was there a back door? Could she get to the car before him?

She disentangled herself from the closet and stepped out. She heard his steps on the stairs to the second floor. She had time. She had to know what Tyler was talking about. What had he hidden in the basement? Something was wrong. There was no time to think about it. She had to move. She stepped to the door and down the bare plank stairs.

She saw the shelf right away, at the far end of the big cement floor, next to the hot water heater.

The big blond-wood box sat behind rows of paint cans, buried under liquor cartons. She moved one of them and saw the stencil: US GOVT. MUNITIONS

The cover moved when she tugged it up. The box wasn't sealed. She moved two of the heaviest boxes to the floor and lifted the lid.

She heard herself gasp—then almost scream a second later, when the water heater kicked on.

The box was packed with some kind of rocket grenades. They gleamed with oil, smelled of it. The stink of death. This man, Tyler, he had put these weapons here. He was hiding them from the owner. She didn't know why, but she knew he was going to use them and these were not the tools of sport or self-defense or even crime.

These were the tools of war.

Tyler was a madman. The thought exploded in her mind. There was no other explanation. Vika had experienced bombs going off. She knew how it felt. She had been walking back to her brother's flat in Sophia, two years ago, a cold clear February night, early morning by then, almost dawn, hurrying past the Galeria offices, shivering under her thin coat and more than a little drunk, when the explosion came. Across the avenue, she had been slapped off her feet as if by a giant hand. The silence afterward was the worst, the reverberating empty silence roaring in her head.

This silence was knowledge. Her charming American with his funny drawl was planning to kill people, many people, and somehow he was going to blame this man who let his coffee burn on the stove and kept old paint in the basement because he had hope for the future. This man who would not be able to 'talk his way out of' owning these terrible weapons.

Her thoughts surged forward. If these weapons were meant to be found that meant Tyler had more hidden somewhere else, somewhere safe. If these were the decoys, how powerful must the real ones be?

She could not breathe. She had to get back to the car some- how before he knew she was gone. But he might be there already. And if he was still in the house, how could she get out without him seeing her, hearing her? She clenched her fists, raging at herself: she had been given a perfect opportunity, when she saw the American going down the stairs. She could have run away at that moment, and she would be sitting in the car now, smelling the ocean, daydreaming, knowing nothing.

But that was not Vika. Vika had to find out. Vika always had to find out.

And now, Vika had to help. She was the only one who could. She had the chance to save this beautiful island, stop this terrible war the American wanted to wage on his own people. She could be the hero, perhaps become a full citizen and never leave this place, never go back to Plovdiv. She knew what she must do. She must convince Tyler to trust her somehow, she must prove she was on his side, until she could escape and run to the police. She had seen the glorious police building with its red brick façade and its twin flagpoles. She would go there.

She closed the cover and pulled the boxes back on top of the munitions crate. Then she sprinted for the stairs, working out exactly what she was going to say.

Good thing she was ready. He was standing at the top of the stairs.

"Jesus Christ, Vika," he shouted. "What the hell were you— oh fucking hell, you saw it, I can tell, you fucking snooped around and—"

Vika bounded up the last two steps, and flung herself at him, hugging him tight.

"You are make revolution!" she said into his neck between kisses. "I am strong with that."

He pushed her away a little, smiling now. "Oh, you like that?"

"I love that."

"You don't even know who I'm fighting."

"But I do. All fights are the same. All revolutions. You fight the ones who push you down, who laugh at you because they think they are better, who think they deserve to own the world because it came to them wrapped in pretty paper under the Christmas tree."

It was so easy. She had listened to her brother talk this way for years. The American stared at her for a few seconds. She held his glance without moving or even blinking, as if the pressure of her gaze could push the conviction into him, a stake into the dirt. Finally, he decided. He wanted to believe her and so he did. She could see it.

The tension left his face, pushed aside by a new urgency. "We've gotta get out of here. Come on."

He took her hand and started out of the kitchen. They had gotten half way to the front door when they heard the car. The engine growled to a high pitch and then cut off. In the chilling silence afterward, Tyler gripped her hand so hard she cried out.

"What the hell is he doing, coming home at this hour?"

Vika felt her mind clearing. She knew what to do, how to convince Tyler of her loyalty and get both of them out of this ridiculous situation.

"Go," she whispered. "Out the back door. I can take care with this. Wait for me at the 'Sconset Market." She pushed him. "Quickly! Before he comes in!"

Tyler walked back the way they came, taking light steps, and Vika dodged into the bathroom. She turned on the faucets in the sink all the way, and ladled water onto herself, drenching her hair, plastering the thin t-shirt to her breasts. The bathroom floor was wet, but she didn't have time to dry it, and there were no towels on the racks anyway. What kind of person had no towels in their bathroom?

She stepped out into the hall just as the front door opened. Vika listened for the back door, and heard nothing. Tyler could have slipped out while she soaked herself, but somehow she was certain he was still in the house, taking more crazy chances, listening to her, testing her. She thought of the gun in his waistband. "In case anything goes wrong," he said. Her spine shrilled with tension. She could feel the barrel of that gun pointed at her back. But perhaps it was just the water dripping down. It did not matter. She had to perform now.

She smiled as the man walked in.

"Hello?" she said.

He stared at her, with no arrogance, indeed with some regret. She knew it was quite a sight. Grigor often said her breasts were perfect and if he was truly an expert in anything—

"Who are you?" the man was saying. "Where did you come from? What are you doing in my house? How did—?"

"The door was unlocked," she said, stepping toward him, into the slab of summer daylight the open door had dropped on the floor boards of the front hall. "I was crossing someone's lawn, just walking to the market, and the sprinklers came on!

Just like that. They must be on timer, yes? But now I am soaked, and I thought…perhaps this person would have a towel, or a dry shirt, so I knock…but the door is open. I look…but you have no towels in your bathroom. This is funny, no?"

He couldn't take his eyes off her. This was good. Distraction was the secret to every magic trick.

"They—they're all…in the wash. Sorry…Listen…let me find you a towel from upstairs—and a dry shirt. Hold on—"

He scrambled up the stairs and Vika listened for Tyler. She heard no sounds, just the footfalls from the second floor. Was Tyler gone? Then she caught the snick of the back door lock engaging, the cough of the door against the jamb. She let out a breath. He was out. It was almost over. She liked the man who lived here. He was confused but kind. And he had lifted his eyes to hers when they spoke, which she knew required an honest effort.

He came down with a military green t-shirt and a big towel.

"Here you go," he said.

"Thank you so much…let me—"

She backed into the bathroom, stripped down, patted herself with the towel, and then used it to blot the floor. It came up dirty. What would he think of her? Or would he suspect something? And what if he did? She had nothing to hide. She was going to the police now, anyway. There were letters on the shirt, but there was always writing on American t-shirts—Americans were never happy unless they were advertising someone's product. Land of the logos, that's what Grigor said. He sneered at capitalism, but he did very well at it. The system suited him. He liked his Nantucket five-spots.

Vika stepped out of the bathroom, went up on her tiptoes to kiss the man's rough cheek, thanked him, felt his startled pleasure, promised to return the shirt very soon, refused a ride, and slipped past him out the door and into the hot steady late-morning sunshine.

She felt smart and shrewd and resourceful, but she had failed to notice a couple of small details. The letters on the t-shirt were NPD: Nantucket Police Department. And if she had needed some confirmation that the man was a cop, she could have checked the blue and red flasher lights concealed behind the front grill of his unmarked Ford Explorer. If she had paid attention in those critical moments, she could have turned back and told Haden Krakauer everything. Instead she hurried up Morey Lane. She would hitchhike to the big police station, talk to someone in charge, tell them her story, convince them to help.

Someone would stop for her, people always picked up pretty girls.

She broke into trot, feeling the heat of the day press against her. She was dizzy and out breath by the time she reached the Milestone Road. She started walking backward with her thumb out. It felt like a more open, more committed way to ask for a ride, facing the driver, subjecting yourself to the physical awkwardness of not looking where you were going.

The first two cars sped past. Did she look frightened, or crazy? She felt that way. She must be wild-eyed and disheveled, scarlet cheeked. She needed to compose herself. Tyler would be growing impatient, wondering what was keeping her, perhaps already climbing into his car to investigate.

Finally she saw another car. A quick flare of hope, then it was as if the man himself had grabbed her, reached into her body, clutched her heart.

It was Tyler's car, slowing down to pick her up.

She had to run. But where? Should she scream? There was no one on the road to hear her, and they would probably take his side anyway, the charming rich American trying to calm the hysterical immigrant girl.

No, no, all she could do was keep up the act somehow, get him to drive her into town, that much closer to the police station. But it was impossible, he had seen her hitchhiking, how could she explain that? She felt tears coming, the sting of despair pricking at her eyes.

The car pulled up next to her. "Get in," he said.

Hadn't she always heard that you should never climb into the bad man's car? But what choice did she have? He still had the gun in his waistband. She took a deep shuddering breath and wrestled herself back under control. She could do this. She was clever and strong.

She climbed in, assembling her story.

"What the hell is going on?" he shouted.

"I thought the man might have see you, you waited too long in the house watching us. I thought—he would be suspicious if he see you. Better—better we should get away, not together. Police would be look for a man and woman together. Apart we are safe. Did I do wrong?"

He seemed to relax a little, accelerating to pass three men in tight spandex on racing bikes. "Use the bike path!" he barked, but to himself. The cyclists were already gone, swept back behind the big SUV. "They're too good for the bike path. Too special. Assholes."

"What do we do now, Tyler?"

"I don't know. If he saw me we're both fucked. We'll know soon enough. This island is crawling with cops."

"I am very—with nerves. Nervous. Silly. I'm sure he saw nothing."

"Yeah, probably."

They drove along. He started speeding and then slowed down. No sirens in the distance, no police cars.

"That was quick thinking," he said. "You can think on your feet."

"Thank you."

"Game any situation, play the players, fool anybody. That right?"

"I'm not sure what you—"

"Tonight we improvise!"

He sounded crazy "Tyler—"

"So you're my partner in crime now?"

"I—"

"Bonnie and Clyde, that it?"

"I, excuse me? Who are these Bonnie and Clyde?"

"I was going to give you a cell phone back there, so you could call me if there was a problem. Jesus, that was a close one! You would have dialed 911 from that basement so fast! Then up and out the bulkhead doors, am I right? You'd have been gone like a rabbit in the bushes."

"Tyler, I don't know what you are talking now. This is not right for you to say. I only want—"

He could hear the tremor in her voice, she knew it.

He didn't answer. Instead, he yanked the steering wheel to the right. The big car skidded off the asphalt onto a narrow dirt road. Vika had to grab the plastic handle above the window to stop from being thrown into his lap. She could feel the car teeter. For a mad gleeful second she was sure it was going to tip over. But the American righted it, and they plunged into heart of the island, bouncing over the ruts, tearing past the dense shrubs that crowded the track.

She knew what he was planning and the knowledge burned off her panic. She was calm, now, staring ahead, waiting for her opportunity. She couldn't grab the gun, she would have to reach across his body and pull it free. She could lunge at him, make him lose control, cause a crash. But they would still be in the car together. And he was wearing a seatbelt. She wasn't.

She watched the American. His jaw worked, but he said nothing. Talking was finished.

Her moment came as they banged over a deep rut, swerving through a turn that kept turning, much sharper than it looked. Suddenly there was space between the car and the bank of undergrowth.

Now!

Vika punched the unlock button, yanked open her door and flung herself out into the brambles. The thorns tore at her arms and legs, cut her face. She didn't feel them. The big car skidded to a stop as she thrashed to her feet and started sprinting back toward Milestone Road and civilization. She cursed her sandals. Tyler was right. They slowed her down. They were foolish. She heard the car door slam, then his heavy footfalls. He was gaining on her. She heard his breath, then the impact pitched her forward into the dirt.

"Bitch," he croaked. "Fucking bitch."

He was on top of her. His hands closed around her throat, thumbs squeezing the air passages. She flailed and kicked. Her knee connected with his groin, and he reared up off her with an outraged whimper of pain. She kicked him again as she scrambled to her feet.

She had run a few steps when she felt the bullet sizzle past her ear. She heard the boom of the shot at the same second. She turned and he blundered into her. The gun went flying. She clawed at his eyes, but she was falling backward and those hands were around her throat again.

She thought, I will not die this way, I will stop him. She clawed at the big hairy hands uselessly. They were like wood, like two halves of a vise. She couldn't breathe. She thought don't let this happen to me, please don't let...

◇◇◇

Vika went limp under Zeke's hands and he staggered backward. His feet ran out from under him. He landed ass first, sitting down in the dirt. The silence echoed, full of the sharp smell of spent cordite.

She was dead. Oh crap, she was dead and he had killed her. He was shaking. He twisted around and vomited into the scrub.

He couldn't think, he had to think. He had to get her out of here, get her into the car, cover her with something, get the shovel out of the rental house garage, bury her somewhere—

And then he had to run. He had to get away from this place, walk away from this crazy plan, bury it with the girl. He was through, it was over. He just needed to tell Scooter. This had gone too far.

Scooter would release him. Scooter would understand.

Chapter Twelve
Search and Seizure

I let us into my apartment and turned on the lights. I hadn't cleaned Caroline's mess before we left the house. Couch pillows littered the floor along with discarded clothing, shoes, books, a school notebook, some pens, and the iPod she didn't use any more since it only held half a million songs. I started straightening up.

"My daughter creates chaos around herself. It's her mutant power."

"I was the same way at her age."

"Thanks, but I doubt it."

Franny sat down on the couch. I got a beer out of the fridge, tilted it toward her. She shook her head. "I need to keep my wits about me tonight," she said.

I sat down next to her. "Hey, it's a national holiday."

"Not for us."

I set the beer aside unopened. "Okay, what is it?"

She took a breath. "Maybe just a sip."

I twisted off the cap and passed her the bottle. She drank and passed it back to me.

"Come on," I said. "How bad can it be?"

"Pretty bad, Hank. The e-mails on Billy Delavane's computer didn't originate there. I traced them back to another ISP.

The service provider gave us all the details. There were firewalls but we got through them. Those messages were sent by Haden Krakauer."

"Wait a second—"

"I'm sorry, but—"

"How could he do that?"

"Easy. He probably used a spoofer with Billy's digital signature."

She talked for a while, about public/private key pair encryption systems, extracting the hash of an e-mail password with brute force cracking. "We run every combination of computer characters that could make up the password—upper and lower-case, numbers, and special characters—and compare the generated hashes to the one for the password until we find a match. It can take a while. It depends on your computer. With the setup they have at NSA, you can crack most passwords in about twenty minutes. With a regular computer it can take weeks—especially for longer passwords. That's why places always want you to use long ones with numbers and weird combinations of special characters. But they're hard to remember. Someone like Billy, who's not that comfortable with computers anyway, probably wouldn't bother. For him Haden probably used a 'dictionary attack'—that's running birthdates and pet names and that kind of stuff. It's a lot of work, but it's doable. Especially if you know the victim personally."

"So Haden wrote those e-mails."

"Well, he doctored them. Billy admitted to writing a lot of that stuff. Haden tweaked them a little. The best lie is mostly true."

"You're sure about this?"

She looked down. "I'm sorry."

"There's more, I can tell. Come on Franny. Get it over with."

"Okay. I used his cable Internet port for access and searched his hard drive. He keeps a diary. He tried to protect it, and he did a pretty good job but—well…let's just say he was overmatched. I printed out a piece of the diary for you." She pulled a folded sheet of paper from her purse and passed it over to me, with the feral pride of a cat leaving a dead mouse on my desk.

I love the bomb. More now then ever before. The sheer surprise of it, the light and the noise, the dislocation. It's the perfect metaphor. Things go bad in an instant. You are never safe. Everything is inevitable in retrospect, but you can't prepare. You expect the worst but you can't imagine it. All memory is ironic. You never knew then what you know now. You scarcely even know it now.

The bomb makes things fair. You think you're better then me? You're not. I've lost everything. What makes you think you deserve to survive the blast? No one survives the blast. It's a war and the losers will always be tried as criminals. They will always be shunned.

She said to me once, "I hate it when you're sick. I can't stand to be around a runny nose."

She was honest in those days. I loved that about her.

Billy never got a cold.

"He's a genetic immune," she told me once. As if that explained everything.

But no one is immune to what I have in store for him.

I folded the page, pressed my fingers along the crease to tighten it. "Jesus Christ."

"Yeah."

"And there's no chance…"

"The digital signature is a positive ID, Hank. Better than a fingerprint."

The word gave me a chill. Literally. The way you feel when you have a fever and someone lets a draft into the house.

Franny put a hand on my knee. "What? What is it?"

I stood. "I have to show you something."

Moving felt better. I walked to the peg board by the front door and took the plastic bag out of my jacket pocket. I returned to the living room and handed it to her. She took it tentatively, with a raised eyebrow—she could raise just one, like a parody of skeptical curiosity.

"I found it behind the clubhouse at the golf course. It was in the moors, along the best covert approach to the club. It's from a HALLS cough drop. Haden sucks them all the time."

"When did you find this?"

"That night."

She pinned me with a level stare. "And how long were you planning to hold onto it?"

"As a matter of fact, I was hoping to throw it away."

"I'm sorry, Hank." She stood and hugged me awkwardly, still holding the plastic bag. "This is bad. I didn't expect this. I didn't want this to happen."

I eased away from her. "It's okay. Let's do our job."

She smiled. "Protect and serve."

"Yeah."

She stepped away a little, and held up the bag. "Jack has a micro X-ray fluorescence setup at the station."

I knew about this technique. It used computer analysis of X-ray photographs to construct fingerprints out of the salts in sweat. It could detect potassium, for instance, which was a prime indicator for explosives. It picked up prints on surfaces that normal dusting didn't, like the wax paper of a cough drop wrapper. It was an expensive array of hardware. I'd never actually seen any of it up close. The NPD was lucky to get ninhydrin.

"Let's go," I said.

The streets were empty as we drove out to the rotary. Everyone was watching the fireworks. We could hear the finale stuttering and popping, muted by the distance. It sounded like the island was under attack—Gibson was right. The impression was particularly unnerving at this moment. I had reassured the kids that the actual bomber was safely in jail. Now I wondered.

Apart from a skeleton guard detail, the cop shop was deserted. Franny badged some drowsy night-shift statie and led me into the ad hoc computer room. We stood behind a lead barrier like dental hygienists while the X-ray scanned the little square of waxed paper. I waited while Franny booted the computer. I was looking over her shoulder when the image came up.

No prints. Nothing at all. Not even a trace or a partial.

"He must have been wearing gloves," Franny said.

"In the summer?"

She shrugged. "There's something else, Hank. No one looked at the blocked calls to Billy Delavane's house the afternoon of the bombing. Jack figured he was lying and it didn't matter. But I traced them today. One came from Haden Krakauer's number. And the timing fits."

"So what are you saying? He faked Debbie's voice somehow?"

"Why not? Come on, the thought must have crossed your mind, Hank. The call came from his number, Billy said it was the girl—and now we know he had no reason to lie. But Debbie knew nothing about it. She was with her mom that afternoon and we know she didn't call him. So what's left? It's like a dorm room at college—there are only so many ways to arrange the furniture."

I nodded. "I actually did think about this, but some ideas sound too ridiculous when you say them aloud."

"This isn't ridiculous. It's diabolical. He bugs her phone or hacks into it, and then pastes a recording together, like those ransom notes cut out of magazines. He plays it back to Billy and hangs up. Done deal."

I blew out a breath. "Do you really believe this?"

"The judge did. I got a sneak and peek warrant just before I came to the party."

"Judge Saunders?"

"Ted Saunders, yeah. Why?"

"How did you find him?"

"Jack has his personal cell number."

"So you went to Jack?"

"Not yet. Not until I'm sure. I know where to find the numbers."

Of course she did. "So you called Judge Ted out of a Yacht Club party to get what he basically believes is an unconstitutional warrant against a police officer he's known for thirty years. And he did it?"

"He looked at the evidence."

"So that's what this was about. You want me to do a B &E on my assistant chief."

"I'll go with you."

"Warrants are supposed to be presented to the subject, before you set foot on private property. That's the law."

"It was. Things are changing, Hank. I'm not saying for the better, but—they are. Cops learn burglary techniques at Police Academy now. It's standard practice."

"And we can seize tangibles if we can prove legal necessity."

"You know the law."

"I know it. I don't have to like it."

"Come on," she said. "Let's finish this. One way or the other."

I shrugged. It wasn't as if we had a choice. Either we went in there tonight or Tornovitch would sack the place tomorrow.

I looked at my watch, 9:15. "Haden gets off duty in forty-five minutes," I said. "We don't have much time."

We got to Haden's family house on Morey Lane with half an hour to spare. The place was dark behind its rough hedge, the door was unlocked. Franny gave me a contemptuous eye-roll at the clueless hicks who left their houses open. Inside, the peeling vertical bead-board walls displayed a clutter of family photographs—beach scenes and sailing races—dating back to the twenties. A threadbare Persian rug ran the length of the passageway. The place smelled faintly of that morning's bacon. A narrow staircase on the left led up to the second floor.

"I'll check upstairs," I said.

We both had flashlights; Franny had grabbed hers out of her car before we left, along with a leather wallet that held her superfluous lock-picking tools. She nodded and moved off toward the dark kitchen. I climbed the creaky stairs. Bedrooms lined the corridor beyond the second floor landing. Two of them connected to bathrooms, and there was a half bath at the far end of the hall. Haden used the master bedroom. Across the hall was the guest room. The last two served as office and storage locker. They were cluttered and chaotic. Searching them was a daunting prospect.

I started with the master bedroom.

I felt under the mattress, pulled out all the drawers. All I found was a little silver key, the kind Caroline used to secure the lock on her diary. I set it on top of the dresser between a lamp and a dish of coins. I checked behind the drawers, in case something was taped there. I almost tipped over the lamp, shoving the big cherry wood piece back against the wall. I moved on, testing the floorboards, examining the back of his mirror and his headboard, paging through the books on the low shelf under the window. I glanced at the armchair. I didn't want to slash the cushions, or cut open the mattress. Jack's boys would do all that tomorrow, if we didn't find anything tonight; and probably even if we did. They were nothing if not thorough.

I sorted through the clothes in the closet, shone my flashlight into a pair of vodka boxes he used for storing papers: tax returns, bills and cancelled checks—nothing sinister. I began to feel a tentative sense of relief.

Then I found the leather watch case on the closet shelf, tucked behind a wooden box full of photographs and a jumble of out-dated floppy disks, a blue plastic zip drive, a tangle of cables that Haden had never gotten around to throwing away.

The box was locked. A silver hasp, a tiny key hole. I held it for a long queasy moment, hoping I was wrong, manufacturing alternate possibilities. Anything could be tucked in there—cuff links, combat medals, rings. But Haden never dressed formally. He'd never mentioned any service decorations. And I knew him, he wouldn't wear a ring, even if he won the Super Bowl. Maybe the box was empty. But it had an ominous heft.

The key was on the dresser. Delay was pointless.

The key fit and the box opened easily on tiny silver hinges. Inside was a Patek Philippe watch with roman numerals. The watch that Barnaby had described, the same watch that Billy wore. The watch that Haden had reported stolen three weeks ago.

Haden, I thought, what are you doing? Who are you? Maybe I said it out loud. I don't know.

Franny called from downstairs. "Hank! Look at this!"

So there was more. I walked downstairs. Franny had turned the lights on. She didn't care. There was no reason for stealth now. She stood by the refrigerator in the kitchen. The gray linoleum held years of dirt. There were dishes in the sink, crumbs on the checked oilcloth cover on the table. Haden presented a meticulous façade, always clean shaven, his hair trimmed short, his uniform pressed, his shoes polished. But this jumbled house was a glimpse at the real Haden Krakauer. I felt chastised by it. I presumed to know my friend, but I was surprised and a little shocked by the state of his house. What other surprises did he have in store for me?

Franny was holding the first one: a little electronic recorder. "This was inside the baking soda box in the freezer. Check it out."

She pushed a button. "I need to see you today," said Debby Garrison's voice. "I'll be…at the golf course, behind the clubhouse…You have to help me. I'm in trouble. My mom is such a bitch. Please come right away. Just come."

Franny turned off the recorder. "If you don't mind a little federal law enforcement jargon, holy fucking shit," she said.

I handed her the watch case.

"This can only be one thing," she said.

I nodded.

She opened the box and let out a low hiss through her teeth. "He's finished."

"Yeah."

"Look, Hank…You feel betrayed. You feel like an idiot. It's humiliating. You're sad and angry and part of you just doesn't believe it. But the other side is…we solved this thing. He's not going to be able to blow up any more bombs. He's not going to wreck the island's economy or kill the governor at the Pops concert. It's bad, but it's over. And we finished it. That's what we live for. Some part of you has to feel good about that, Hank. There has to be some satisfaction there. It's bittersweet. But it's real."

I didn't want to discuss it. "Let's just finish searching downstairs."

Twenty minutes later we found Billy Delavane's wallet folded into a towel in the linen closet. Five minutes after that Haden

Krakauer came home. We read him his rights, handcuffed him, and took him into custody. Franny called Tornovitch and first thing in the morning, he sent a team to do a full search. They found a crate of rocket grenades in the basement behind a shelf of old paint cans.

It was like Christmas morning, all the evidence a greedy little apple-cheeked Homeland Security agent could have wished for, all wrapped up and tied with bows. All Jack needed was a dog romping in the wrapping paper and an empty cookie plate by the fireplace.

But it was too perfect. Haden might have been trying to get himself caught, but there are easier ways to commit suicide and smarter ways to get revenge. It wasn't his style anyway. Haden was smart and cautious. Festooning his house with clues this way, undermining a plot he must have been brooding over for the better part of a decade, just seemed incomprehensible to me. Even that sketch of Haden as the brooding master strategist fell short. If Haden was pissed off at you he'd tell you so. In Franny's opinion, he was secretive, brooding, diabolical. That explained everything.

Except, he wasn't any of those things.

Or maybe I really didn't know him as well as I thought I did. The chaos of his house remained a sharp reprimand. My opinion was irrelevant anyway. No character witness was going to get Haden out of this one. The evidence was too strong.

I didn't like it, but I was willing to be moved along by the momentum of the case, like a twig in a stream. I was just the local cop without a security clearance. I wasn't even allowed to talk to Haden.

Franny gave Jack the credit for the arrest, as usual. It was the best way to stay out of trouble for working behind his back. Jack played it up, and the newspapers were portraying him as the brilliant Homeland Security investigator who might just wind up saving America single handed. Next thing I knew he'd be running for office. He could probably win.

So I punched the clock, caught up on my paperwork, and stayed out of the way. I took on some of Haden's duties, so there was plenty to keep me busy. The regular police work was mostly futile. We raided the oxycodone pusher's house on Essex Road, after Doug Folger gave us the address and the layout. We found two Bulgarian guys with about-to-expire work visas and a sorority's worth of dangerous-looking Slavic girls cleaning the place. If this was the fabled Nantucket whorehouse, they were definitely multitasking.

We found no drugs of any kind apart from some convenience store packets of Advil. It was as if they knew we were coming, or didn't happen to be criminals. There were plenty of law-abiding immigrants on the island—the bulk of the immigrant population, in fact.

Cops see crime everywhere, I know that. Dealing with criminals all the time warps your perceptions. Still, the question remained, how had Doug Folger gotten it so wrong? I had guessed the answer to that before we ever showed up at the big cheaply-built house on Essex Road. Most likely the dealers had in fact been using the place—but had moved on, spooked by Pat Folger's snooping, just as I feared.

None of the Bulgarians knew anything and their English was terrible. Back to square one. It's the only numbered square, and I was beginning to see why. For the moment, I let it go. The island was quiet and I went back to doing a lot of not very much.

My inertia might have lasted through the summer, but the following Monday I saw something that tilted my perceptions about Haden Krakauer and brought everything into focus. The incident had no apparent relevance to his case. I had barely talked to Franny since Haden's arrest, and she was working around the clock. My little epiphany didn't even involve police work.

I was house hunting with the kids when I figured it out.

Chapter Thirteen
The Envelope House

For me the Fourth of July always felt like the beginning of the end of summer. The fleeting sense that the season was permanent, which took over in June, was always dissipated by the fireworks. The island had peaked. It was all downhill from here.

By the middle of the month, the second round of renters had arrived. Days were getting shorter again and Labor Day loomed six weeks away, casting its pall on the temporary perfection of high summer. The kids wouldn't feel the pressure until mid-August, when they realized they had to cram all their summer reading, and the mornings turned chilly again.

Shut out of the ongoing investigation of my assistant chief, with little to do on an uneventful Saturday afternoon, I decided to take the kids with me while I looked at real estate. They loved snooping houses. Pacing the perimeter of giant mansions closed for the season, squinting into the gloomy rooms and laughing at the tasteless 'interior design' on display there, was a favorite winter sport on Nantucket. As police chief I should have been strict about such trespassing; but I enjoyed it, too. The idea that these fortresses of privilege couldn't even be approached by lesser mortals was as pretentious as the German appliances and marble countertops we glimpsed through the windows.

Looking for a rental was less glamorous but more exciting, since summertime snooping was a rarity. Even better, the kids could actually get inside these houses and explore them; maybe even stake a claim to one.

We took my NPD cruiser for the drive out to the Tom Nevers area—a windswept barren chunk of scrub oak and coast, a mile or two west of 'Sconset, with no stores or amenities, zoned for cheap houses on small lots.

Tim got a kick out of the big police car, though it embarrassed Caroline. She had reached the age when everything about me embarrassed her, so it really didn't matter what car I was driving. We turned through a white gate and I followed the winding roads of a recent subdivision around to the house, pulled into the crushed shell driveway past a high clipped hedge, and got my first look at the place.

The house was big and angular, with a wrap-around deck, and I immediately got the feeling I wouldn't be able to afford the rent. But Miranda's boss, Elaine Bailey, had assured me it was a year-round lease and a "fantastic bargain." Yeah—like her six thousand dollar Neiman Marcus couch.

No sign of Elaine's Land Rover. She had insisted on showing me the house personally. My kids' theory was that Elaine had a crush on me. Terrifying thought. A hard, calculating woman in her early fifties, with the best hair and prettiest face that money could buy, pulled, tucked, tinted, dermabraded, injected and spa-pampered. Elaine had cold eyes and a humorless little incision of a mouth that rarely smiled. She was a petite woman who gave the impression of a battering ram, and Miranda laughingly called her "the Force."

She always got what she wanted, and it was blind good luck that she didn't want me. Elaine was always late. She liked people waiting for her. Today was no exception. I glanced at my watch.

"Dad, can I talk to you in private?" Tim said.

"Sure." I turned around to face the back seat. "Carrie?"

She sniffed "I know what he wants to talk about."

"You do not!"

"He has a crush on Debbie Garrison."

So Debbie's Mom had enrolled her in Murray Camp after all. Looking at Debbie, you could see that she was going to be a heart-breaker someday, but I didn't think it was going to start so soon—or that Tim would be her first victim.

"Shut up! You're such a jerk." He started over the seat, going after Caroline. I pulled him back.

"Oooo, that hurts! What a comeback! It's true, Dad. I heard him talking to Tommy Whitlock about it."

"Can I just talk to Dad alone for a minute, please?"

"I can't believe you even like her. She's such a little bitch."

"Carrie—"

I squeezed Tim's shoulder. "Come on. We can talk by the house."

Caroline sighed, giving up. Tim and I climbed out of the car and walked to the porch to sit on the steps, with the warm breeze on our faces.

After a while, Tim said, "Do you think Debbie's a bitch?"

"I only met her once, but—no. What I really think is…I hate to hear that word coming out of your mouth."

"Sorry."

"Actually, I got the impression she's a lot like Caroline. They're both bossy and people like that don't usually get along very well with each other. It makes sense. Only one person can decide which game the whole neighborhood is going to play. But you're perfect for Debbie. You come from a long line of men who actually enjoy taking orders from women."

He considered that. "I take orders from Carrie."

"And I took orders from your Mom."

"Then why did you get divorced?"

I looked up into the cloudless blue sky, piecing together the right words. A hawk was riding the thermals above us. "I guess there were some orders I couldn't obey. I couldn't be somebody else, for instance. That was basically what your Mom wanted."

"I like you being you."

"Me, too. Which is a good thing, because we're both stuck with me."

Caroline was out of the car by the time Elaine Bailey arrived. Both kids were playing with a neighborhood black Lab who had ambled over with a marshy tennis ball in his mouth.

"You are going to love this house," Elaine said as she climbed out of her car, followed by a billow of refrigerated air. She was wearing a white linen pants suit with a pale blue silk blouse. Her hair was cut short, a perfect blonde helmet.

The black Lab trotted over to investigate the newcomer and Elaine dodged back. "Where did that *dog* come from?"

"He's the welcoming committee," I said.

She sniffed. "There are leash laws on this island. Why don't you get your dog officer out here?"

I petted the Lab. He shoved the ball at me and gave me a little tug-of-war when I pulled the soggy mess out of his mouth. I threw it down the driveway, watching it spray a fan of spit as it bounced. The Lab bounded away after it.

"I like dogs." I wiped my palms on my pants.

"I figured it out, Daddy," Caroline said. Then, to Elaine: "Last week, I said I dropped something like a hot potato and my Dad told me to think of a better way to say it. He hates clichés."

Elaine cocked her head with a condescending exaggeration of interest. "And you thought of something now?"

Caroline turned back to me. "I dropped it like a dog-slobbered tennis ball!"

I laughed. "Good one."

"We really need to do this, Henry." Elaine started toward the house. "I'm just swamped today. And these renters won't stay at the beach forever."

We followed her inside. The rooms were big and sunny but the furniture was sparse: bean bag chairs and blond-wood tables; an uncomfortable-looking couch, toys scattered across the floor; wall -to-wall carpeting, no book shelves, no pictures, but some kind of hideous macramé rug dangled from a three-penny nail, a refugee from a 1960s hippy apartment. An enormous flat screen TV perched on a pedestal cabinet near the sliding glass doors. All the furniture tilted toward the gaping screen, like some

Renaissance painting with all the perspective lines converging on Jesus. The place smelled of burnt toast, sour milk, and the faint formaldehyde tang of new carpet.

"This is horrible," Caroline's pronounced. "It's like some creepy motel. Except with kids."

Tim was more practical: "Do we each get a bedroom?"

"There are actually four bedrooms in the house," Elaine said. "And a full basement—with a ping pong table and a juke box."

"What's a juke box?" Tim asked.

"It plays records, dummy," Caroline snapped. "It's from the seventies."

Tim brightened. "Like Dad," he said.

"Thanks a lot."

"We have an iPod hi-fi," Caroline told Elaine. "So we don't really need, like—vinyl."

I was looking out the window, at the view toward the ocean. There was a twelve inch gap and then another wall, with another set of windows.

"This is odd."

"I'll tell you what's odd. Some money manager telling me Occupy Wall Street should occupy Nantucket."

"When was this?"

"Oh, back in the spring. But I saw him in town today. I keep thinking about him. A very odd person—more like Hillbilly Hollow than West Los Angeles, where he said he was from, and kind of a creep. Scary."

"West Los Angeles?"

"Supplevita Boulevard, near the San Diego Freeway. I remember because the street sounded like some hippy vitamin product."

"It's Sepulveda, Elaine. And no one from L.A. calls it the San Diego Freeway. It's the 405."

She shrugged. "See what I mean? Odd. Something for the NPD to keep an eye on."

"Thanks for the tip."

She was all business again. She took two steps and stood beside me. I was still looking at the extra set of windows. "That's the wonderful thing about this place, Henry. It's an envelope house—a house built inside another house. The gap creates a thermal envelope. It's the most energy efficient structure in the world—state of the art. It's green. It's sustainable. All of that touchy feely stuff. But what really matters is—the place costs nothing to heat. You'll save thousands of dollars next winter." She waved a hand dismissively, reading my mind: "They'll get rid of all this furniture. You can decorate it any way you want."

A house built inside another house, like Russian nesting dolls, the outer one shielding the inner one. That was it. In that moment, listening to Elaine's sales pitch, I finally understood. I didn't have to think about it or put the pieces together. No leap of intuition was required. I didn't need to find the answer.

I was standing in it.

I saw exactly what was happening to Haden Krakauer. Someone had done this thing, someone had built an envelope house around him, caught him in a double-layered, perfectly insulated trap, sustainable and energy efficient. He was being framed, but not for an ordinary crime. He was being framed for something else, for something so eccentric it might never have occurred to anyone that it was even happening.

Haden was being framed for framing Billy Delavane.

It sounded crazy, but it made perfect sense. In fact, it was the only answer that made any sense at all, that actually fitted the jumble of contradictory facts. This was state-of-the-art construction, all right. Every piece of evidence that pointed to Billy had been built to blow back on Haden—the watch, the wallet, the fake message from Debbie Gibson, the e-mails, the voice machine…all of it, even that wild goose chase in the moors. Haden lived in 'Sconset, he knew the moors like his own backyard, because they actually were his backyard. If he wanted to set a bomb at the golf course he could have done it at any time. So why do it during the single two hour period when he had no alibi for his whereabouts?

It was diabolical. Franny was on the mark about that much. Except, Haden wasn't the Devil.

But who was? Who was doing this? And why?

"—because of the increased fire hazard they had to install a sprinkler system to bring it up to code," Elaine was saying. "But the house is perfectly safe and—Henry?"

"What?"

"Hello! We were hoping you could join us here on the planet Earth. The climate is lovely."

"Sorry, Elaine."

"Have you heard one thing I've been saying to you, Henry? Because I really don't have time to—"

I hugged her. "Thanks Elaine. This is great. You've been a huge help. I can't even tell you. But this—this is fantastic. This is just what I needed."

"So you'll take the place?"

"The place? The house? No, the house is bad. But thank you—thank you so much!"

I scooped up the kids and bolted, leaving her standing in the living room among the toy fire engines and the half-completed lego robots, no doubt more convinced than ever that the Nantucket Police Chief should be fired, ASAP. I wasn't worried.

I had bigger things to think about.

Chapter Fourteen

Conspiracy Theory

"That's preposterous," said Jack Tornovitch.

"Jack, listen to me for a second. I just—"

"You're loyal to your friend, Kennis. I admire that. But you're getting desperate. I had to deal with 9/11 conspiracy theorists who thought the U.S. Government brought down the World Trade Center, fired a missile at the Pentagon and moved all the passengers on American Airlines Flight 77 to some black site in Montana. They made more sense than you do."

We were sitting in Haden's old office, Jack barricaded behind Haden's desk, ignoring the forlorn beeps of incoming faxes, and his cell vibrating in little circles on the desk blotter with a weird animal urgency, bumping into the Steuben glass sculpture of an ice-fishing Eskimo that Jack had installed as part of his office makeover.

He turned the phone off and slipped it into his pocket with a terse, "Sorry."

For a few moments there I had thought I was getting through to him. But I was kidding myself.

"Are you familiar with the phlogiston theory, Kennis?"

"I studied it in college."

"Then you see my point."

"Not really."

"Let me refresh your memory. It was a seventeenth-century theory of combustion. Phlogiston was an element that got released when things burned, supposedly. The idea was shot down a hundred years later when someone noticed that ash weighed more than the log it came from. Something was being added, not taken away and that something was oxygen. Ring a bell?"

"I think so. Lavoisier had something to do with it, right?"

"Very good. He did the experimental work that debunked the theory. But the phlogiston supporters—particularly one Joseph Priestley—had their own explanation for his results. Phlogiston had 'negative weight.' Negative weight, Kennis. Do you see the point now? Negative weight! If the results don't fit the facts, make up new facts! Priestley's the poster boy for junk science. He's been a cautionary tale and a fucking joke for more than two hundred years."

I sighed. "And I'm Priestley. Because of my theory."

"You're Priestley because you won't let it go. Let it go, Kennis. You're wasting your time. More to the point, you're wasting my time, which actually has value. You're like my Eskimo here," he said, gesturing toward the sculpture. The sterling silver Inuit fisherman crouched on the frosted glass slab and drove his spear through a hole, stabbing at the fish in the clear glass below. "Striking blind, hoping for the best? That's not how we do things at the Department of Homeland Security. Now get out of here. I have phone calls to make."

◇◇◇

Crossing the parking lot to my car, I knew my next move. I still had one ally in the JTTF, or so I thought. When I called Franny, she was driving out to Sanford Farm for a walk. She always thought best in motion.

I beat her to the property, and was sitting in the dirt parking lot, listening to Diane Rhem on NPR discussing yet another 'extraordinary book' with yet another annoyingly successful author, when Franny pulled up in her rental Ford Focus.

I killed the engine, got out and stretched my legs. The lot was full today, and there would be dozens of people scattered along the seven-mile path to the ocean. A couple with two golden retrievers came through the gate. The dogs paused to greet an old man's standard poodle, and then trotted over to me. The old man tipped his beret, with a gesture not unlike picking up a puppy by the scruff of its neck. He and his wife ran an antique store in town. Someone had broken into the shop last month, but they refused to update their alarm system. I liked them for their stubborn opposition to the world of high-tech electronics and lower insurance rates. I also liked the sight of their big, tightly clipped poodle bounding into the field beyond the fence. I lifted a hand and the old man smiled. Everyone knew I wasn't there to enforce the leash laws.

Franny knelt down to rub the golden retrievers' heads. She was wearing a v-neck white t-shirt and cut-off jeans; I looked away from the glimpse of her bare breasts to face her thighs below the ragged edge of denim. It had been almost a week since I'd seen her last, and I felt a surge of inappropriate desire. It was like climbing the bluffs at Eel Point, the tilting vertigo as the sand gave way beneath your feet and you started slipping backward down the slope. And it carried the same belated knowledge: this was too steep. You shouldn't have even begun.

I righted myself, got my balance back, stood up. This was business. I needed to convince her to help.

"You got here fast," she said.

"I know all the shortcuts."

She straightened up with a wintry little smile. "A police officer shouldn't really brag about that, Hank."

"I'm not a cheater. I just know the island."

"Maybe you know it too well. You don't even recognize your own conflict-of-interest problems."

She had obviously talked to Tornovitch.

"This is no shortcut, Franny. Just the opposite. That's the whole problem."

"Let's walk."

She started away and pushed through the wooden turnstile, to the open fields beyond. I followed her. A quarter of a mile farther on, the path forked and took a rise into a stand of pitch pines that my kids always called the Hundred Acre Wood. People approached us along the path, couples, parents with their kids, old guys with old dogs, bird watchers. Everyone greeted me, with a word or a nod.

We walked through the pines on a carpet of brown needles and paused to take in the distant view of the ocean. Then we started down toward the loop path again, walking along the edge of Hummock Pond, among the milkweed and the Queen Anne's lace, past the osprey nests.

For the moment we were alone.

"What I'm asking you to do is start from scratch and rethink everything," I said. "That's not a short cut. It's a lot of work. It requires mental resiliency. You have to—"

"You don't have to do anything. You just blink and everything's inside out! That's all it is—throw away the photograph and look at the negative. Light is dark. Dark is light. But it doesn't mean anything, Hank. It's the same picture."

"It does mean something. It means you arrested an innocent man."

"Why? Because all the reasons we think he's guilty are the reasons he's innocent? He was alone for two hours on the day of the bombing, he has no alibi for the time frame when the bomb was set...and that's why he didn't do it? There was enough evidence in his house and on his computer for a two day trial and a double life sentence, and that's why we should know he's innocent?"

"Franny—"

"That's what you're saying. That's what you told Jack. Everything's opposite. The green light means stop on Nantucket."

"Actually, we don't have traffic lights on Nantucket."

"Exactly. That is so perfect. You refuse to install traffic lights because you want to feel special, but you have traffic jams and traffic accidents just like everyone else. You need traffic lights. You won't admit it."

"So we're all deluded."

"Maybe I'm just hanging out with the wrong people."

We walked along between low bushes. Some kids ran past. A group of women wearing University of Nantucket t-shirts ambled toward us examining a Conservation Foundation map of the property.

Finally the path was clear again.

"Haden is innocent," I said. "It's all too tidy. Someone is setting him up."

She was losing patience. She didn't want to be here. "Okay... so someone is setting him up to look like he's setting someone up? But who's setting up the person who's setting up Haden? That's the real question, Hank. And why stop there? Maybe somebody's framing that guy, too. Maybe it's Billy Delevane. He's been cleared, he's walking around free. So he must be guilty. That's your logic."

"So my theory is impossible."

"It's far-fetched. And it's contaminated, Hank. Because he's your friend."

"But that's the whole point! He's my friend. I know him, Franny. He's a bird watcher! They're the least violent people on Earth. We have a tradition here—the Christmas bird count. It started out as a hunt. Nantucketers went out on the day after Christmas and shot everything that moved, everything they could see. Birders changed that. They watch and cherish. They don't hunt. I watched Haden Krakauer spend almost an hour untangling a hummingbird from a spider's web. That's not a killer."

She wasn't buying it. "He takes his anger out somewhere else, that's all. He loves birds and hates people. Birds you can tag and study. They don't talk back."

"Actually, birders are the most sociable people I know. They travel in packs, they talk to each other constantly. They're enthusiasts. They like being outdoors and studying the world around them. It's healthy."

Franny took a breath. "Whatever. That's fine. But Krakauer admitted to planning this whole crazy scheme. During yesterday's interrogation. Turns out, he was thinking about it all through the Iraq war, all the time he was stationed in Kuwait—how to get Billy Delavane. How to frame him for a bomb scare."

"That's bullshit."

"It's true. I'd show you the transcripts but you don't have clearance."

"Wait a minute. There's no way—"

"Listen to me! Stop and listen to me, Hank. He worked it all out—the e-mails, the watch…stealing the credit card, everything. He obsessed over it."

"So what does he think of what's happening now?"

"I—"

"You must have asked him."

"No, I—it's…"

"What?"

"I just read the transcripts. Jack conducts the interrogations. No one else is allowed in there. It's just the two of them."

"That doesn't strike you as odd?"

"It's the way Jack works."

"And Jack didn't ask him? 'All your weird fantasies are coming true. Any thoughts on that?' No interest there?"

"No. At least not yet."

"Why not?"

"I don't know, Hank."

"Haden wanted to talk about it. That night, at the golf course, he brought it up—but there was too much going on, and it got lost in the shuffle."

"Did you follow up?"

"No. I should have. That was a mistake. But he didn't bring it up again either. I think he was embarrassed. You can see why, now. It was a long story, and he didn't want to tell it. Would you? It makes him look bad. He comes off as an angry loser. He sounds paranoid, like some kind of weird stalker type."

Her smile was cold. "My point exactly. Someone called, the night of the bombing—trying to make them evacuate the place. Sounds like a gentle bird-watcher type to me. He didn't want to hurt any innocent people. It fits. Every redeeming thing you tell me about this nut just makes him look better for the crime."

Checkmate. But I wasn't ready to give up yet. "Look, if I'm right, Haden has to know he's being framed. He might even have some idea who's doing it. Jack has to at least ask him. You have to convince Jack—"

"Have to?"

"No, I mean—if you could just—"

"Listen to me, Hank. Jack is the senior investigating officer on this case. He's an acknowledged expert on terrorist debriefing techniques. He wrote a monograph on it. They use it as a primary text at the Academy. Okay? He's the best in the world at this particular thing."

"But he couldn't get a confession out of Roy Elkins."

"That was a long time ago. And Haden Krakauer is no Roy Elkins. Look, if there's some line of questioning Jack's not pursuing, I'm sure he has his reasons. It's not my job to second guess him on this. I could lose my job doing that. All right? The point is, Haden was having every one of the bad thoughts you seem to think he's incapable of. Every single one. In fact, that was all he thought about, literally for years. He admitted it."

"Okay, fine. Maybe he did. But thinking about it is one thing. Doing it is something else. People fantasize about crazy stuff all the time. But we don't put them in jail for that."

"No we don't. Not until they start acting out. Until it stops being a fantasy."

We topped a small rise to where the old barn creaked in the steady south wind. I could smell the ocean. I sat down on the bench nearby. A tractor was cutting one of the fields. I listened to the faint insect buzz of it and let the humid air caress my face. We had been walking fast, Franny always walked fast. My legs were tired.

Jane Stiles trudged past, giving her eight year old a piggy back ride. Her face was flushed. The hike to the sea had obviously been too much for her. I knew how Jane felt. I had carried Tim halfway up Mount Batty on a trip to Maine a few years before.

She lifted a hand. "Hi, Chief."

"Hey."

Franny shot me a quick look when they disappeared down the hill "Who was that?"

"Just a local. Name's Jane Stiles. Landscaper, single mom. Excellent writer. I've heard her at readings."

"Attractive woman. Slim but strong. That's a lot of kid to carry."

"I guess."

We were getting sidetracked. We needed to focus. I had an idea. There was a possible loophole in Franny's argument.

"Who did he talk to?"

"What?"

"When Haden was in Kuwait, did he tell anyone about this idea? Because that's something else I know about him. He talks a lot, especially when he's drinking and he was drinking hard in those days. If he told someone, and that someone had some reason to hurt him, some grudge…"

"You're reaching, Hank."

I stood up. "Let's head back."

We were halfway to the parking area before either one of us spoke again. I was working out exactly how I wanted to phrase my final attempt.

"Franny, listen to me. The person behind this is evil. And Haden Krakauer isn't evil. He just isn't. I know him. That's not a conflict of interest. That's a tactical advantage you're throwing away. That's an investigative tool you're wasting."

She spoke to the ground: "You knew Roy Elkins, too."

"That has nothing to do with this."

"Are you kidding me? It has everything to do with this. It's the same situation, except this time you get to be the brilliant detective. This time you get to save your friend and win."

I looked around as if the proper tone of voice and the right words could be found in the thread of water at the head of Hummock Pond, or the silent houses on the other side, the empty fields, the fat white standpipe braced against the sky at the edge of the sound like a sentry. A few pale cirrus clouds sketched against the blue sky moved over us, pushed by a different wind in a different world. I wondered if this was what the ship-bottoms looked like to the creatures that lived on the sea floor.

"You never really know people. No matter what you think. You don't really know Haden Krakauer. You know what he chooses to show the world. But that's a mask."

I wasn't going to let her budge me. "I know him. And I know you."

"So this is about me now?"

"How could it not be? Because our positions really are reversed this time, Franny. That's what really bothers you. This time I've dug deeper than you, I've thought harder about the case, working it when you thought it was all wrapped up. You got lazy. You don't want to face the fact that I'm in the lead this time and if you admit I'm right you'll be following me."

"I just want the truth. I'm not twisting things. You're twisting things. I don't even think this is about your friend any more. It's all about proving how smart and cool you are. How you can be better than me, even though I've been promoted ten times since those days, and I'm actually responsible for this nation's security now, with fifty people working under me and I make ten times what you do. You're a guy who got fired from his only real job ever, marking time as a local cop in the middle of nowhere, wondering what happened to his career. You blew your career all by yourself Hank. Don't take it out on me."

I raised my arm, pointed a stiff finger at her.

"I am the Chief of Police of Nantucket."

"Right. The Mayor of Whoville."

I had to laugh at that. But I was touched, also. She remembered I'd been reading the Horton books to my kids when we first met.

I quoted the elephant's other motto back to her now.

"A person's a person, no matter how small."

She stuck her hands in her pockets and kicked a stone into the weeds. "It's a nice town, Hank. And you do a good job. You take care of your town. We'll handle the investigation. It's pretty much wrapped up now, anyway. A few more days of interrogation and we'll be moving Krakauer to a federal facility. Then we'll be out of your hair."

"I don't want you out of my hair, Franny. I want to help you solve this thing."

She stopped walking, pulled her hands out of her pockets and grabbed my forearms. She was strong. She squeezed, and then she squeezed tighter as she spoke. It felt like blood pressure wrap.

"Hank. Look at me. Listen. The case is solved. I solved it. It's over."

She released me.

"All you're doing right now is distracting me. And undermining me. It's not helping. It feels destructive and unethical and pathetic and…bad. I think we should stay away from each other for a while."

"You'll be gone in a while."

"That's probably for the best, Hank. I'm going back to the real world. I belong there. You belong here. You were looking for a home and you finally found one. That's good for you. I'm happy for you. It's your world. Live in it. Enjoy it, it's beautiful."

Mike and Cindy Henderson were approaching along the path, their new baby girl, Molly, hugging Cindy's chest in a snugly. They walked slowly, pacing themselves with their ancient collie, Gus. His muzzle was white and his hip dysplasia was worse than ever. But he wagged his tail and trotted over to me.

"You see?" Franny said. "You know everyone. And they all know you. That would be a living Hell for me, Hank. It would drive me insane. But not you. It's Heaven for you."

I had no answer for her. She was right.

"Hey, Chief," said Mike. "Did you get a chance to look over my bid? If you let those town buildings sit for another couple of years, it'll be too late for a paint job."

"Talk to Dan Taylor," I said. "It's up to the selectmen, now."

Franny lifted a hand, like she was swearing to tell the truth the whole truth and nothing but, then sidestepped the dog and started away. She was gone a second later, jogging toward the parking lot. She had used the crowded path, the flicker of social confusion, and slipped through the open moment like a door. It was already closing behind her.

I stood talking to the Hendersons, admiring the baby, Gus solemnly licking my hand, until I heard the engine note of Franny's car pulling out.

Maybe it was true: maybe I really was nothing more than the Mayor of Whoville, a small-time loser, living in a speck on a thistle. But I was right about Haden Krakauer.

And I was going to prove it.

Part Three:
Paper Covers Rock

Ezekiel Beaumont: Ten Minutes Ago

They met at Altar Rock, deep in the moors, less than a hundred yards away from the spot where Zeke had buried the girl.

This little hill was the perfect venue for a meeting, far from any microphone, solitude guaranteed, with a spectacular three hundred sixty-degree view of the island that meant you could literally see anyone approaching from a mile away. Zeke looked around. Altar Rock was the highest point on Nantucket, just over a hundred feet above sea level. He caught his breath, admiring the view. Rolling hills of dense scrub oak and rosa rugosa, wind-stunted pine trees and bayberry bushes, lush and green after the summer rains, cut by winding dirt roads edged at the horizon by the blue marker of the ocean. There was water everywhere. Half a dozen ponds glittered in the sunlight.

He stepped onto a flat slab of granite, gained an extra two feet. You could feel the smallness of Nantucket from up here and the island's isolation. A gentle breeze touched his face. The only sound was the faint ringing in the chambers of his own brain. He was going over and over what he wanted to say. He knew Scooter could be persuasive, overwhelming. The waiting was worse. By the time he finally saw Scooter's car he had almost lost his nerve

"I can't do this," he blurted as Scooter climbed the last few feet of the trail.

"What?"

"I can't do this. I can't go through with it."

"Stop."

"It's too much, it's too—and I'm losing it, I'm not safe, I'm not reliable now and I—"

"Stop!"

Zeke bit down on the next incoherent sentence, panting.

Scooter stared at him. "What happened?"

"Nothing! Nothing happened. I just—"

"Tell me. You made a mistake. You fucked up. What was it?"

There was no getting around it. Only the truth would convince Scooter. "The girl I was seeing—"

"That Bulgarian whore?"

"She—yes, I guess, but—"

"What about her?"

"She came with me when I—I forgot to plant the tape and when I went back she talked me into letting her come along."

"Shit."

"And she saw things, she saw the grenades in the basement, and she—I could tell she—"

"Zeke. Where is she now?"

"She's dead. I killed her." The words sounded insane. Scooter stared at him with shock and horror and something else, something rich and sweet. Respect? The beginning of a new respect. "I buried her right down there," Zeke went on. "I almost got caught. There were two rich jerks on fancy bikes…but they didn't see me."

"Are you certain?"

"Sure I am. I mean…she would have been dug up by now, and the cops—"

"All right."

"Then I had to go to this big party…I had met one of Vika's customers, at a restaurant, and he invited me to this big fund raiser and he called me, as I was burying the girl—on the Gibson cell, to remind me, to make sure I'd be there and I said yes—"

"Why? Why would you do that?"

"I was—I had to stay in character. And I was flustered. So I went. I just went. Jesus, I still had dirt under my fingernails, and I almost lost it, talking to the police chief. I never killed anyone before. I never…I didn't know what—"

Scooter reached out for Zeke's shoulder. "You almost lost it, but you didn't. That's the point."

"But the girl. If anyone—"

"The girl was illegal, Zeke. No one cared, no one's going to miss her but her pimp and he's not involving himself with the NPD. If those people live by any rule besides 'Hurt people who refuse to give you money' it has to be, 'Avoid the cops.' Am I right?"

"I guess so, but—"

"Forget her. The bitch played you, kid! You got taken by an expert. How does it feel to be on the other side?"

"But she said…she told me—"

"You're pathetic."

Scooter walked away, studied the roof lines of the houses at the edge of the moors, the sea beyond them. The breeze was freshening, out of the south

"This is getting out of control, Scooter," Zeke said to his back.

Scooter turned. "Stop it. Stop it and listen. Everything is fine! The plan is working fine. Yeah, the girl could have wrecked it, but she's history now. Forget about her. We're standing on the threshold of big things, great things, Ezekiel. Don't turn away."

"But all those people—"

"Those people? Those people have been sucking the blood out of this country for decades! They're leeches, Zeke, and you know that, and you know the only way to get rid of a leech is to burn it off."

"I know, but—"

"And don't forget your old commanding officer. The one who betrayed you, and let them ship you off to Miramar without a second thought. This is all coming down on him, Zeke. We've made sure of that. You've done well. You saved our asses when you terminated that girl. There'll be no way out for him now.

Think of it! He'll be vilified and hung in effigy and sent away forever so he can have a lifetime in some supermax jail cell to rue the day he ever crossed us. That's what he has to look forward to. If we stay strong. Can you stay strong, Ezekiel?"

He shook his head. "I don't know. I just don't know anymore."

"There's something else," Scooter said. "Something I haven't told you."

Zeke looked up.

"There's one more guest at the Pops concert, my friend. I just found out a few days ago. A member of the Joint Chiefs of Staff, invited by no less a dignitary than Vice President Joseph Biden himself. Oh, yes. Apparently they're old friends, ever since Joe became Chairman of the Foreign Relations committee, after 9/11. They go back a long way. A long, long way."

Zeke was alert now. Could it be? He felt the thrill in his blood. "Eddie," he said.

"Brigadier General Edward Claymore, your erstwhile partner in crime, that's right. The one who got off scot free. The one who made millions on your drug connections while you rotted in jail. He'll be front and center at the concert, my friend. Front and center. Could it be better than that?"

"No," Zeke whispered.

He breathed the word out and filled his lungs again, as much with hate as with the silky Atlantic air. The hate tasted better. You could feel it infusing the corpuscles like a drug, the best drug, the most addictive drug of all.

"Remember when we used to play rock-paper-scissors? Back in Iraq?"

"Sure. You were teaching me strategy."

"No. I was teaching you how to read people. How to predict their next move. I remember something you said one day—how rock blunting scissors made sense, and scissors cutting paper. But paper covering the rock you couldn't figure out."

"Yeah, right. I mean, the rock tears the paper, that's what would really happen. But in the game, paper wins because… the game says so. It's bullshit."

Scooter stepped up to stand on a flat rock and took a deep breath.

"It may seem that way, Ezekiel. But it's not bullshit at all. In ancient China you made your request to the emperor with a rock. If the answer was yes the rock came back sitting in a piece of paper. If he turned you down, the paper covered the rock. That's where it started. But it means something else to me. The game may be bullshit like you say, but in life, Ezekiel…in life, the paper really can beat the rock—the weak and flimsy and marginalized can take on the solid and powerful, and win. Just ask Gandhi or Martin Luther King. Think about those Lakota and Arapaho Indians charging the 7th Cavalry Regiment at Little Big Horn. Chief Gall and Crazy Horse took Custer down, my friend. I know they lost in the long run, but a Pyrrhic victory still goes in the win column. And goddamn, it does feel sweet when the fight is raging. But you already know that, don't you?"

"What?"

Scooter smiled, "I'll let you in on a secret about yourself, Ezekiel. I'll tell you the real reason killing that girl can't blunt your resolve. Do you think you're ready to hear it?"

He wasn't. But he knew what Scooter was going to say. Somehow he knew already.

"You enjoyed it. Zeke. You liked killing her. It was better than the sex."

Zeke stared at him, speechless, remembering the feel of her smooth throat under his hands, the spastic kicking of her leg as the light flickered behind her eyes.

"You see? I know you better than you know yourself. We should go our separate ways now, Ezekiel. We both have work to do."

He walked back to his car, climbed in, and drove away. Zeke watched tail of dust the big car kicked up. It was true, Scooter was right. He had the taste for killing now.

And there was a lot more coming.

Chapter Fifteen
The Best Defense

I knew what I had to do now: start over from scratch, question every assumption, pick apart every conclusion, re-examine every piece of evidence. We had all missed something. No frame is perfect. People make mistakes. Sometimes too much organization and planning is a mistake in itself. You get attached to the way things were supposed to happen, you tighten up and you can't improvise. This person framing Haden Krakauer must have slipped up at some point along the line.

I had to find out where.

I started with the paperwork—the police reports on both bombings, the evidence lists and photographs, the interrogation transcripts. I even reread the journal page Franny had printed off Haden's computer.

Going over it again, I saw the mistake immediately:

> *I love the bomb. More now then ever before. The sheer surprise of it, the light and the noise, the dislocation. It's the perfect metaphor. Things go bad in an instant. You are never safe. Everything is inevitable in retrospect, but you can't prepare. You expect the worst but you can't imagine it. All memory is ironic. You never knew then what you know now. You scarcely even know it now. Most of the important stuff you've already forgotten.*

It wasn't the style—for all I knew this was the way Haden actually wrote. I had never been privy to his journals before. But I knew he was a grammar hound and he would never write "More now then ever before." First of all, it was a sentence fragment. More importantly, he would never confuse "then" for "than." He had actually caught that same mistake in one of my poems. The line was underscored with a big red exclamation mark in the margin.

Whoever wrote that journal entry knew what they wanted to say, and they knew how they wanted Haden to look. The only thing they didn't know was Haden himself.

It wasn't evidence I could take to court, but it was a start. No one wanted to hear my theory, but they weren't stopping me either. That was my one tactical advantage No one cared enough about what I was doing to get in my way.

Or so I thought, until the attack.

Taking that morning apart later, the only leak I could find was my phone call to Billy Delavane.

"I didn't tell anyone and neither did you," he said afterward, when we were both safe and sound, drinking good single malt in his cluttered living room. "That means you had someone's ear at your door. Or else someone bugged the phone. The Feds found a transmitter on my line, Chief. How about yours?"

Tornovitch had made a show of checking all the phones at the station, personally. "Electronic surveillance is a passion of mine, Kennis." He had told me. I wasn't sure he knew what he was doing, but no one was going to question him.

Too bad, because someone had to have been listening that morning, while I told Billy my plan to revisit the golf course. I wanted to walk the moors behind the clubhouse, slowly and methodically, in daylight this time.

They knew I was going to be there.

So they made some phone calls of their own. And the Bulgarians were waiting for me.

◇◇◇

I couldn't have told you what I was looking for that day, in the moorlands beyond the golf club property. Looking for something specific is usually a mistake, anyway. Better to just wander around with an open mind.

I saw signs that the JTTF had tramped through—broken bushes and flat city-shoe footprints; a discarded take-out coffee-cup. They obviously hadn't searched with much care or precision. And why should they? They already had their perpetrator, along with that tidy pile of gift-wrapped evidence.

I quartered the dense underbrush north of the club, working my way back toward Polpis Road along the deer paths. It was nearly four o'clock when I reached the construction site. The crew had left for the day, but I could still smell the sawdust in the air. The house rose a full three stories, the open stud skeleton of its future self, built on a gentle rise in the land. The widow's walk would have a spectacular view of Nantucket Sound one day. I could see table saws, step ladders, and other equipment scattered across the plywood subfloor among the wood shavings and the tangled power cords, along with dropped tool belts and discarded bottles of Gatorade and bottled water.

I examined the parking area in front of the front deck. Half a dozen sets of tires had cut their pockmarked runes into the soft dirt, but the vehicles pulled up to the house didn't matter anyway. They had to be workers' trucks. I was looking for some-one else who might have parked at the edge of the cleared land and walked cross-country to the golf club.

I didn't have time to find anything though, because the Bul-garians found me first.

There were four of them, obviously foreign, with their bowl hair cuts and stubbly beards, tight jeans, leather jackets and brightly colored, flat-footed basketball sneakers. One of them wore a beret. Another sported a dirty New York Giants cap, obviously scavenged from the dump—not the best way to travel incognito in Patriots country.

I looked up from the tire tracks to see them standing around me in a rough circle. Two of them carried knives. One of them was pointing a Glock nine at me.

I recognized two of them from the Essex Road house. Drug dealers with no drugs to sell.

"Now you really are in trouble," I said.

The unarmed seemed unimpressed. He said, "Into the building," and pushed me toward the house.

The one with the gun stood back from the others—there was no chance of jumping him before he pulled the trigger. I'd been shot at before, and taken a bullet. I remembered the flat shock of impact, the nausea that spread along the nerves faster than the pain. Once was enough. A slick jitter slid through my arms into my fingers, down from my groin into my knees and my ankles.

There was no one nearby, no one coming to this job today, no neighbors close enough to help. The Glock was silenced, so they might not even hear the shot as far away as the golf club.

I looked into the Bulgarian's eyes. It was obvious to me and everyone else that he would shoot me just for fun, out of boredom, like Billy Delavane's father, potting rats at the dump.

I scrambled up to the half-finished deck and walked from stud to stud with the four men spread out behind me. When we were deep in the house, I said "What do you want?"

"You hear that, Grigor? He doesn't know what we want!"

"What we want? We want to get paid!"

They all thought this was hilarious.

"Man who pays us—what he wanting. That is question."

"Your English is good."

"I am study. Man who pays, he want you to stop."

The four of them backed me into a chest-high pile of strip oak flooring. There was a hammer on top of the pile, but no way I could grab it in time to use it. A plane droned by overhead. Did I hear something moving in the bushes?

"Stop what?"

"What you do. Make trouble. Ask questions. Poke where you don't be welcome."

"Sorry. That's my job."

"Then you need new job! Drive cab like everyone else!"

"Or sell hillbilly heroin to teenagers, like you do?"

"If I had this heroin I would use myself, not sell! Life is hard for us. We need to relax."

"So you never even grab a free ride with one of your prostitutes?"

"Prostitutes? Those are my sisters! Still—if you like, maybe we can make arrangement—once you heal."

Another round of laughter.

"Now listen Mr. Police—man who pays, he say to hurt you. Not kill you this time. But hurt you so you remember to keep out of other people business. Give him beating? But everyone would see. Break leg? Everyone would know. So I say, No. Do with secret. In Bulgaria I studied with Mohel. You know what is Mohel? He is man who performs the *brit milah*. You know what is *brit mila*? Circumcision. I leave Sofia because I kill this Mohel and rape daughter. What can I do? She would not marry!"

Another round of laughter.

"Now she marries no one. No one wants girl who is rape. But I know procedure. Yes? That is the word? Procedure."

He pulled a surgical scalpel out of the side pocket of his jacket. I flinched back involuntarily, and knocked against the pile of lumber.

"Today we perform the bris. Next time we take it all. Eh?"

One of the others edged up next to me, unbuckled my pants, and yanked them down.

"Good," said the leader, "Fear makes hard. Hard is easier for cut."

There had been a noise. I heard it again. My head was clanging, but somehow I heard it. Someone else was inside the building.

With two quick flicks of the scalpel the leader cut away my boxers. I could feel the air on me. That was the worst part.

The leader spoke again. "Hold him tight."

They grabbed my arms. I found my voice. "Don't do this."

"Then how we get paid, Mr. Police? Who will pay us for do nothing? Hold him tighter."

The two big men immobilized me. They stank of sweat and cigarettes.

The leader reached between my legs and grabbed me. I felt the cold edge of the blade against my skin. I shook my head, I tried to speak, but nothing came out. I begged him with my eyes.

He grinned. "Now we cut."

I sensed a movement and glanced over his shoulder. Billy Delavane gave me a maniacal thumbs up. The leader must have sensed something, too. He paused for a moment.

Billy Delavane. I had to be hallucinating.

A second later the air compressor kicked on with a deafening roar. Everyone lurched away from me, screaming like children, mouths gaping open. I couldn't hear anything over the ear-ripping clamor of the big machine. But I knew what it was. I grabbed the hammer and swung it at the leader's head. He ducked. I still connected with his shoulder. The blow knocked him sidewise, and I dove after him as the gun went off. Billy must have slammed into the shooter, because the next round went wild and they were both falling. I whacked the leader's neck and fell across him to chop the hammer into another one's knee. He dropped his knife and crumpled with a howl of pain. I kicked free of my pants and scrambled to my feet.

Billy was on top of the one called Grigor, pounding the hand that held the Glock against a hard edge of wood. The last one faced me, knife against hammer. We circled each other. Billy drilled one last punch, stood up, and the Bulgarian, outnumbered, dropped the knife and bolted. Billy grinned, stepping aside to let me chase him. I lunged forward, hit him full force in the knees, pitched him face-first onto the plywood. He went limp. When I looked up, Billy had the gun.

The compressor turned itself off. The sudden silence was explosive.

Billy let out a war cry that gargled into a laugh. "Goddamn, Chief! I haven't had this much fun since those Le Eme hoods jumped us in Rosarita." He looked around at the sprawl of inert bodies. "Seriously, though. Nice work. You'd have come in handy with those Mexican Mafia punks, Chief."

"Thanks." My voice was shaky. I stumbled past him, picked up my pants and pulled them on.

I leaned against the stack of oak boards, feeling flimsy and feverish. My body jerked, my teeth chattered. I wanted to grab the gun from Billy and empty it into the leader's head, a spasm of deferred shock and rage.

Billy got what I was thinking. "You don't have to kill him, Chief. But you could kick him around a little."

I stood up straighter, zipped my pants, cinched the belt. "Give me the gun. I have a bundle of flex-cuffs in the trunk of the cruiser. Grab them, will you? I'm parked at the golf club. I'll keep an eye on these guys."

I reached into my pocket and threw Billy the car keys. He caught them, stepped over the leader's body and handed me the gun, holding it by the barrel.

"Sure thing, Chief. Back in a flash."

Two of the Bulgarians were stirring, but the leader was still out. I saw the scalpel glinting in the sawdust, and I picked it up. Another shiver ran through me, as if the blade was an animal that could still attack. I held it by the edges of the handle and set it down carefully on the oak boards. It was evidence now, another part of the crime scene. I pulled out my cell and called Kyle Donnelly. I thought of calling Jack, but held off. I wanted the scene taped off and examined, but there was no need for the kind of advanced forensics the JTTF could supply. The criminals were already under arrest, caught in the act with an eyewitness.

Kyle drove out with Barnaby Toll. We left Barney to secure the scene and drove the Bulgarians back to town in two cars.

An hour later they were in jail, and I was drinking a single malt in Billy Delavane's living room. A swell had finally materialized, pushed by a low pressure system off New Jersey. We could hear the continuous boom of the breakers beyond the dunes.

"What were you doing out there?" I asked him

"Looking for you. Just bored and curious, I guess. Never occurred to me that someone might jump you, Chief. That kind of stuff doesn't happen in Nantucket. Or it didn't use to, anyway."

"It's a new world, Billy. We have three translators in the court house, now—Spanish, Portuguese and Russian. We get 911 calls in more languages than that. We go into every house guns drawn as if a murder was happening because we don't know from the caller whether it's a domestic dispute, or a burglary, or a bird trapped in the kitchen. It's crazy."

We drank our scotch and listened to the ocean.

Driving back into town, I had to pull over, just past the dump. There's a little dirt turnout that the NPD uses as a speed trap. I sat there while a sluice of nausea heaved through me. It was like being seasick on the ferry as the big boat pitched in the swells. I gripped the wheel, trembling, watching the cars slow down as they drove by. They could have been drag racing that afternoon, but they didn't know it. I read about some town that set up a replica cop car on the shoulder of the road. It controlled the traffic just fine for more than a month, until it got blown over in a storm. That was how I felt, sitting there—like a plywood cut-out of myself, knocked flat by the wind.

I took another five minutes and then drove the rest of the way to town.

Inside the station, Liam Brady was on dispatch, sitting behind the glass panel reading one of the *Left Behind* novels. Liam was a big chunky kid still fighting off the last of his adolescent acne. He had just been promoted from summer special to full-time. It was probably a mistake but I was shorthanded. He tried to cover up the book with some schedules. But he was busted and he knew it. Reading on duty was against the rules and those books were tragically bad anyway.

I said, "Not on the job, Liam."

"Sorry, Chief. Slow day."

"But even slow days require your undivided attention."

He slid the book into a drawer as I walked past him toward my new cubicle.

Charlie Boyce was waiting for me with an update. The Bulgarians had no working papers, and two of them had out-of-date passports. The one I recognized had his working visa, but it only gave him another week. All of them had criminal records and outstanding warrants in Bulgaria. And none of them had any idea who hired them. It was done over the phone.

"How did whoever it was get this Bulgarian's number?"

"I asked him that, Chief. He laughed. He said it was 'A referral.' Very American."

But not for long. I thanked Charlie and then took a few minutes to call the INS. I spoke briefly to a woman named Miriam. "Agents will be taking them to Barnstable detention tomorrow morning," she assured me.

She sounded tough enough to do the job herself. I hung up, and took the stairs up to the second floor and my office. I stood in the doorway for a few seconds, checking out the big room, seeing it with a fresh perspective, as a fifteen-by-thirty-foot surveillance grid. I knew what I was looking for, which made searching easy. I checked under the desk and behind my pictures—the Los Angeles Police Academy graduation shot of Chief Bratton shaking my hand, a pair of diplomas and a some prints—a Winslow Homer watercolor of a whitewashed wall with tropical flowers, Hockney's *Mulholland Drive*, a print from a museum show.

Miranda said to me once, "You'll know you have real money when your pictures cost more than the frames." I didn't see that happening any time in the near future.

The bug was under the desk telephone.

I found it as soon as I turned the thing upside down. It was a magnetized chip of metal about the size of a breath mint. I was furious, but it somehow struck me as funny also. I heard the old Certs ad in my head, some surreal new version of it: "It's two, two, TWO mints in one! It's a candy mint! It's a criminal conspiracy to conduct illegal surveillance mint!"

I pulled it off the phone. It was wireless. There was probably some sort of transmission booster attached to the building. I'd find it later. Now I had to figure out who put it there. I booted my computer, logged on the NPD site, and scrolled through the visitor logs, every notation since early May.

An hour later, I found him.

Chapter Sixteen
Procedural

The lists were tedious: names, dates and topic references, meetings on everything from town wetlands override warrants to circus permits to fire alarm infractions and police charity donations. Dan Taylor's was marked "Various complaints."

I smiled at that. Everyone knew Dan too well to itemize his grudges. The list went on and on, page after page. I remembered most of the meetings. Nothing struck me as significant. None of the various aggrieved private citizens, realtors and town officials seemed promising candidates for position of mad bomber or criminal mastermind.

I had just reached the morning of June 27th, when I saw this notation:

"9:50, Tyler Gibson, re: parking permits."

I recalled the meeting. Dan Taylor had barged into my office without an appointment, causing a fair amount of confusion before Gibson finally left. I had turned my back on Gibson. If he had been quick-witted and cool under pressure, he could have stuck some little electronic component under my phone. Not many circumstances, among all the meetings in my cramped little office, presented such an opportunity. I thought back, assembling the choreography of it in my mind. Had he been standing at my desk when I turned around? I seemed to remember that.

Tyler Gibson. I pulled my computer toward me. I didn't have Franny's CARGO program, but the over-the-counter generic substitute would do just fine this morning.

I Googled the guy.

First I tried Google Images. No luck.

But the regular search turned up his investment newsletter, *Pigs Get Nothing*. There was a quotation at the top of the home page: "Bulls get rich and Bears get rich. Pigs get nothing."

The most recent entry was dated May 27th. Before that he had been posting two or three times a week. The May 27th entry promised a rundown of the telecom stocks and the legal ramifications of the proposed new regulations. But it was a month later, and the site hadn't been updated. No explanation, only a lot of annoyed readers in the comment trail.

At the Fourth of July AIDS benefit, Gibson had freaked out over the fireworks. It looked like classic delayed stress, which made sense. He had the harrowed, suspicious look I had seen on so many veterans' faces. He had practically hit the floor when the fireworks started. I'd seen Haden Krakauer jump the same way when a car backfired.

The NPD was hooked into the Department of Defense computer archives. We couldn't access classified material, but we could pull anyone's military record and get rank, serial number, promotions, infractions, type of discharge, all that stuff. I logged on and entered Gibson's name.

No record of service.

I spelled it every way I could—with an "i" and an "e" instead of an "o" in the last name; with an 'i' instead of a 'y' in the first name. I went back in time to the eighties; tried all branches of the service, including the National Guard and the Coasties.

Nothing.

I was stumped. I needed a photograph of this guy. I accessed the Los Angeles DMV. I got Gibson's driver's license picture. Same guy. I wasn't quite convinced, though. After all, this was a techie who could hack into Billy Delavane's e-mail and leave a trail back to Haden Krakauer—if my theory was right. So getting into the DMV database and changing a picture would be no problem. It sounded far-fetched, but that didn't affect procedure. I still needed another picture to corroborate Gibson's ID.

The license gave Gibson's address in the 10700 block of Wilshire, in Westwood, near the 405. I thought of the rental client Elaine Bailey had mentioned at the envelope house. I needed to know that guy's name. I called her and left a message on her voice mail.

Then I tried the building management office in L.A. Soon I was chatting with an affable southerner named Bo Tanner. He 'ran the outfit' at the building, with a crew of six. He sounded like another veteran, and indeed he had been in the 2nd Battalion of the 1st Air Cavalry Division in Viet Nam. He laughed at the idea of Gibson serving in the military.

"No way in the world, Chief. That old boy couldn't shoot a BB gun."

Their security cameras were still hooked up to a creaky VHS system—the building management was too cheap to upgrade. The tapes were erased every seventy-two hours, but the police had taken one of the cassettes as evidence in a burglary a few months before. There might be something on there, if I could get a hold of it.

I thanked him and hung up.

My first thought was Chuck Obremski. He still owed me a favor. He always would, no matter what happened, no matter how many favors he did for me.

Years ago, he had stolen some money from a major drug bust stash to pay his son's gambling debts. We argued about it, at one point getting into an actual shoving match. But I covered for him during the Internal Affairs investigation. My own son had just been born. Maybe that had something to do with it. Anyway, Chuck walked away clean—not even a departmental reprimand.

Now he was five years from retirement and his son was going to law school. He'd be glad to help. I figured he was still working out of the Sawtelle station in West L.A. I called and left a message. Ten minutes later he called me back.

"Henry the K. How are ya?"

"I'm good Chuck. How about you?"

"Breaking in a new partner, three weeks into the South Beach diet, quitting smoking while we take care of my mother-in-law in a two bedroom house I still haven't paid for. Couldn't be better. How 'bout you, K? Ever hear from that Franny whatshername? Tater?"

"Tate. We're actually working a case together now."

"Working a case! I've heard it called a lot of things, K. But never that."

"No, seriously—"

"I know, I know. You're in the news, K. Someone's blowing the crap out of your retirement village down there. Oh yeah—I keep track of you, buddy."

"Listen, Chuck, I need a favor."

"Damn! I took a crazy shot and guessed that. What dya know? I must carry that gold badge for a reason."

I didn't rise to it. Chuck had always used insults as terms of endearment.

I gave him the address and the date of the burglary. I needed him to work with the doorman and send me a decent grab off the surveillance video. I gave him the doorman's phone number. He grunted his assent as he scribbled the information.

"I'm on it."

"Thanks, buddy."

"Fuck you. Kids okay?"

"Great."

"Mine graduates from Boalt in June. Just what I need. Another lawyer in the family."

"At least you get free advice."

"Are you kidding? That punk charges me to read my insurance claims."

We hung up without saying good-bye, as always.

Getting the screen-grab would take a day or two. I could use the time to pursue other lines of inquiry. Iraq, for instance. Whatever triggered this baroque assault on Haden Krakauer

must have started there. His life had been uneventful before and
after the war. He grew up on Nantucket. I did some checking—
stable family life, no tangles with the law, no problems at school.

He went on to West Point—his Dad had been a general,
commuting to Otis Air Force base all through Haden's childhood—and Officer Candidate School after that. He had a bunch
of unpaid parking tickets that had cost him about six hundred
bucks when he tried to renew his registration last year, that was all.

It had to be Iraq.

Billy Delavane's brother had served with Haden in the war.
Actually Haden had pulled some serious strings to get Ed transferred to the Camp Doha motor pool. The MPs were closing
in on Ed in Jeddah, where he was screwing Muslim girls and
getting them drunk on grain alcohol from his still. At least he
wasn't making s'mores over a burning Koran.

Haden got him out of there, put him to work on the base and
kept a close eye on him. They never became friends. Ed didn't
appreciate the favor. He resented losing his business and his
harem. He never understood how close he had come to a court-
martial, a dishonorable discharge, and a term in the stockade.
Or maybe he didn't care. From what I had seen of him, Ed was
a textbook sociopath. He had almost killed me last winter, and
I had solved the case that sent him to jail. I wasn't his favorite
person. But if anyone could tell me what happened to Haden
in Iraq, it was Ed Delavane.

He was currently being held at FMC Devens, pending his
transfer to Cedar Junction, the old Walpole Maximum Security
facility, where he'd serve out his life sentence. I called the SIA at
the prison and set up an appointment for the next day.

I caught the early boat the next morning.

As always, driving through Hyannis I felt a quiet shudder of
relief. The town had the same flattened commercial sprawl as
Los Angeles—but without the palm trees or the prosperity. The
mall had turned Main Street into a dreary ghost town, though I
suspect the average ghost probably had better things to do than
hang out in junky furniture stores and dingy bars. Who needs

another 'going out of business' sale or bad 'Polynesian' diner? They have actual houses to haunt.

Devens was even worse—a dying husk of rust belt squalor and cheesy commerce: six places to buy pizza and no bookstore. The Army base at Devens had closed more than a decade ago, leaving the usual crumbling buildings and poisoned groundwater behind. Supposedly the town was having a commercial resurgence. The jury was out on that one. The gray drizzle didn't help.

The prison wasn't much worse than the rest of the town. I parked in the lot, went inside and signed the paperwork. A guard led me to the interview room. It was crowded and the waiting area was full of crying women, noisy kids, and harried lawyers.

The door at the far side of the room opened and Ed sauntered out, eyes narrowed under his Army flat-top buzz cut, handcuffed in his prison jumpsuit, escorted by two guards. The outfit didn't humble him the way it was supposed to. He wore it like a boy psychopath's Halloween costume. He grinned when he saw me, a wide gap-toothed, Jack O'Lantern warning, with one lunatic candle lighting it up from inside.

"Howdy, Chief."

I pulled up a chair and sat down. "Ed."

"How's the stomach?"

"Turned out I had an abdominal hernia. Lepore closed it up for me. So you did me a favor."

"That little prick Rafferty hadn't showed up. I would have done you a permanent favor."

"And the staties would have gunned you down where you stood."

"If they could hit what they were shooting at."

I shrugged. "One of them would have winged you eventually."

"Maybe."

We watched each other for a while. The guards were glad to step away. Even seated, his compact body had a kind of compressed tension, ready to explode if he took the pressure off.

"So, Mr. New Police Chief. I had my eye on you for quite a while."

"And nothing came of it. I had my eye on you for three weeks. And you're in here."

He nodded. "You nailed Parrish, too. That was good."

"He wanted to make a deal."

Ed laughed. "Wheeler-dealer."

"He's doing his deals in MCI Shirley right now."

"Minimum Security section?"

I nodded.

"Well, fuck him."

Another silence. Ed sat forward "Well, you're good, but you're no Ted McGrady."

"I hear that a lot."

"When he arrested me, he didn't have a gun. No deputies with him. No handcuffs. He just knocked on my door and said, 'It's time.' I went with him. I could have knocked him out with one punch. But I went with him."

"I wish I'd gotten that kind of respect."

He let out a raucous cawing laugh, like a seagull. He had the black, empty eyes of a bird, the comfortable slouch of a lifetime predator. "Good one. But you were just another cop to me." He flashed that grin again. I wondered what had happened to his teeth.

"I want to ask you a few questions."

"What do I get for answering?"

"The satisfaction of being a good citizen."

"I prefer cash."

"Can't do it, Ed. Not on my salary."

He shook his head. "Who else but a cop would brag about being a loser?"

"A priest?"

That laugh again. "Good one. I'm starting to like you, Kennis."

An assessing silence settled between us. The two guards shifted from foot to foot. One checked his watch. I had been given all the time I needed today, and they weren't happy about that.

"So, Billy's been to see you a lot lately."

"He's a good kid. He set me up with some work when I got back to the island. Car repair stuff. He talked to Chris Witte about me. I liked working on those foreign cars."

"You should have stuck with it."

"The pay sucked."

"What do they pay you in here?"

He shook his head. "It's a little late for that, Chief."

"Sorry."

"I got nothing to spend it on anyway. I quit smoking."

"Homeland Security thought you were helping Billy buy military grade explosives."

He crossed his arms. "And they never even apologized."

"So they're not just stupid, they're also rude."

He hacked out another laugh. "You're three for three today, Chief."

I let a few seconds go by. "How are you at taking orders, Ed?"

A level stare. "You've seen my records. You tell me."

"And yet you left the service with an honorable discharge. How do you explain that one?"

"Friends in high places?"

"One friend in particular."

"One was enough."

"Well, your friend's in trouble, Ed."

"Tell me about it. We watch the news in here, Chief."

I sat forward. "He's being set up. I'm trying to prove it. And I need your help."

"As a character witness?"

I ignored the joke. "This whole thing started in Kuwait. It's somebody he knew from the service. Someone who's holding a grudge from back then. You're the only one I know who was there. I can't track down everyone Haden served with. I'm running out of time. Think back. Did he have any enemies? Did anything happen that might have triggered this craziness? Did he hurt anyone? Cross anyone? Fuck anyone up? Something bad went down over there. I know it."

Ed was nodding, one arm still across his chest, rubbing the stubble on his wide jaw with the other hand, like a chess player contemplating the endgame.

"Well, there was the drug bust."

Chapter Seventeen
The Identity Thief

Ed had watched the narcotics investigation at Camp Doha from a comfortable distance. It was the best entertainment on base. "It beat playing ping pong at the Marble Palace, that's for sure."

Twenty miles west of Kuwait City, Doha was built on the site of an old warehouse complex, next door to an electrical plant. Smoke belched out of the four smokestacks—everyone called them the "scud goalposts"—all day, every day. The air stank, but Ed lived in a trailer with air-conditioning. And there was pretty good soft serve. "Just like Dairy Queen."

Apparently, Ed wasn't the only one dissatisfied with the recreational opportunities on base. Drug use was out of control and the MPs were cracking down. Haden was there in 2003, running the base on forward staff for ARCENT Kuwait, the Army Central Force command. It was like being the mayor of a small city. Drug investigations weren't his job, but Haden had never learned how to delegate, and he was a puritan. There were more than two thousand military personnel and contract workers from five countries at Doha. They needed to be action-ready at all times. The idea that some shockingly large percentage of them were impaired by drugs at any given moment drove him crazy.

"Didn't stop him from getting drunk at the OC every night, though," Ed laughed. "The officers club, Chief. And that's where he figured it all out. He didn't have to do shit—everything came right to him. Sat down on his lap like a stripper and rubbed its tits in his face. Excuse my French."

He must have seen me grimace. Words affect me like smells sometimes. Hearing Ed's little turn of phrase there felt like opening the fridge after a five day blackout.

"Can you explain that?" I asked him.

"Well, he was drinking buddies with this hillbilly staff sergeant and I guess some second looie showed up one night when they were in the middle of one of their gab sessions and the sergeant acted a little weird, like he didn't want the guy coming near him. This is how I got the story from Krakauer. The sergeant told him he owed the lieutenant money and he didn't want any shit going down in the OC. But Krakauer saw them together the next day—four days from payday. And they were all pals. Haden played a hunch and had some MPs follow them both. The looie was just a buyer, but they busted the sergeant with seven ounces of weed, two days later. And that was just the tip of the iceberg. That little cracker was building himself an empire out there. But Doha was a small town, just like Nantucket. You can't get away with anything for too long. Too many nosy people. So he went down, but he wouldn't rat anyone out and they never caught his distributor. Something happened, though. There was some scandal that got hushed up. I didn't ask. I was tuning up the carburetors. And believe me, with all the sand on the roads out there, it was a full time job. Ever see a Jeep after a few trips to Great Point, Chief? Kind of like that. Anyway, I didn't know this sergeant too well. His staff car threw a rod, I remember that pissed him off. But I was sticking to beer in those days, so we didn't do any real business. I must have known his name but who fucking remembers? He got a raw deal, though. I heard him shouting at Krakauer in the parking lot one day, that he was getting reamed real good, and Krakauer was telling him to bend over and grab his ankles. Krakauer just kept walking. He was stone cold, man. He didn't want to hear shit from that guy. So anyway, they gave the sergeant a court-martial, shipped him back to the states and he was gone—pow, just like that, like he was never even there. He was a smooth-talking good old boy, that one. Except he didn't sound so smooth, that day in the parking lot. Hey—fuck him if he thought the Army was fair."

Ed sat back, looked over his shoulder at the two guards, and pinched a little air between his thumb and forefinger to let them know we'd be done soon. The noise spiked. A woman was crying at the other end of the room. It was hot in there, and the fluorescent lighting made everyone look sick.

Ed turned back to me, rubbing his hands on his knees, as if to push off and stand. "I guess that's all, Chief. The court-martial records gotta to be filed somewhere—you can get that little cracker sergeant's name that way. Just poke around. You'll find it."

We were done. We both stood and I shook his hand.

"Thanks, Ed. This was a big help."

"Be sure and tell them so, Chief. If I'm a good boy, I get a gold star and an extra cookie at lunch."

◇◇◇

The file on the case was sealed. It required a sensitive compartmented information security clearance to even look at the cover page. An SCI is an even more restricted rating than Top Secret. I asked the records clerk why a routine drug-related court-martial required such extreme protection. He told me to fill out an SF-86—a National Security Questionnaire—and turn it in to the State Department with all required support documentation. The background check and investigation would probably take at least a year. They were kind of backed up at the moment. But he'd be happy to talk to me when I had my paperwork in order.

I presented the request as a law enforcement priority, implied that I had powerful connections and even threatened him with an obstruction of justice charge if he didn't cooperate.

He didn't cooperate.

He knew I was bluffing and he'd heard it all before. "Refusing access to court documents for angry big shots who try to push me around?" he said to me just before we hung up, "That's the main perk of this job. That and the dental plan."

There was some forward progress to greet me at the office. Chuck Obremski had e-mailed a few frames from the security camera, identified by the doorman as Tyler Gibson—bulky like an ex-athlete, wide-faced with a bad comb-over, five foot six at most.

No resemblance to my Tyler Gibson, the one who was renting a house off Cliff Road and freaking out at the fireworks. My Tyler Gibson was just over six feet tall with a long bony face and lots of straw blond hair. The urge to drive out there now and arrest him loomed and subsided. I wanted him for much more than identity theft. If I picked him up now, he could raise bail in an hour and be gone. I didn't want him disappearing on me. We were less than a week away from the Pops concert, with the wrong man in jail. We couldn't afford any more mistakes.

Anyway, I wanted the JTTF involved and to convince Tornovitch I was going to need something more solid to show him. I checked my watch. Almost six o'clock in L.A.

I called the building security office in Los Angeles and caught Bo Tanner just as he was clocking out.

"Hey, Chief. Did you get that picture?"

"Yeah, thanks, Bo. Listen, I have a couple of questions, if you have a second."

"I got all night, son. I'm going home to the History Channel and a Stouffer's lasagna. Both of em can wait."

I glanced around my office, that shot of Chief Bratton giving me my Police Academy diploma. I was about as far away from Los Angeles as I could get and still be in America. I felt every mile of the distance tonight.

"Chief?"

"Yeah, Bo…sorry. I guess what I wanted to ask was—when was the last time you saw Gibson?"

"Funny you should mention that. We were talking about that a few days ago. He kind fell through the cracks lately. Mike was on duty when Gibson went out for his walk in the canyons, but he was off by the time Gibson got back. Kenny was on duty by then but it was real busy and he didn't recall seeing Gibson come home. Mike would have noticed if he never showed up, but Mike was gone."

"And when was this? Do you remember the day of the month?"

"Well, I can check—but I'm pretty sure it was late May."

"So no one has seen him for a month?"

"Well—he travels a lot. Sometimes we don't see him for three months at a time."

"But doesn't he leave instructions for his mail and his newspaper when he goes away? You have a housekeeping staff. Doesn't their schedule change when he's not around?"

"Hey, we have a lot of tenants in this building, Chief."

I released a breath and backed off. There was nothing to be gained by pissing off Bo Tanner. I decided to try a different tack.

"You said he walked in the canyons. Is there any special one he ever mentioned to you?"

"Oh sure, we talk about that stuff all the time. He used to go to Temescal and Sullivan sometimes. Now mostly he just goes to Will Rogers—or Rustic Canyon. Apparently you can get in there from the Will Rogers estate. There's a path next to the polo field. He knows those hills inside out. Me, I'd rather sit home with a beer and watch the National Geographic channel. I don't like them rattlesnakes. Oh yeah, he's seen 'em up there. Coyotes, too. Even a mountain lion one time."

"Thanks, Bo. You've been a big help."

"I'm sure Gibson'll turn up, Chief. He always does."

"Well, keep me posted. I'd like to talk to him."

"Sure thing."

I called Chuck Obremski on his cell.

"Oh brother," he said, first thing. "Here it comes."

"You have a possible 187 in Rustic Canyon. You have to check it out."

"Rustic Canyon's a big place, K."

"Take the standard walking route from Casale Drive. You can walk down in there from the fire road. It was his last known twenty, Chuck. As far as anyone can tell me, he went walking there and he never came back. A week later someone else is using his name, standing in my office complaining about parking tickets, and planting a bug on my phone. You're the one who always told me 'Check the time lines. Chronology is everything. A crime is a story and stories happen in order'."

"You remember that?"

"I wrote it down."

"I bet you did. Fuck! Asshole cut me off. I'm on the 405, trying to get home for dinner. I knew I should have gone over Coldwater. Fucking traffic."

"The time line makes sense, Chuck."

"Yeah, yeah."

"So you'll do it?"

"Yeah, but your name is nowhere on this. If it's real, I'm taking the credit. I need some notches in my belt. Our closed murder stats are in the toilet this year."

"Call me when you know something. And thanks."

"Mention it."

He broke the connection. A second later my phone rang again: Elaine Bailey.

"You're too late Chief. That house was snapped up two days ago."

It took me a second. Of course—the envelope house. Everybody lives in their own world, and Elaine's world was real estate. That might help me now. "Don't worry. We'll find something else. Listen, Elaine, do you remember the name of that client from Los Angeles? The one you mentioned to me, who creeped you out?"

"I checked my files that day, after we talked."

"So…"

"I think it was—Gibbons? No, Gibson. That's it—Tyler Gibson. Are you going to arrest him?"

"No, no, no—just curious."

I promised her we'd take another house hunting excursion and disconnected the call.

My shouted "Yes!" echoed in the empty room. I knew his name and Elaine knew his address. I jumped to my feet, feeling the old adrenaline rush. I had been ninety-nine percent sure.

Now I was a hundred percent sure and that tiny little one percent makes all the difference in the world.

All I needed was iron clad proof and an old-fashioned Chuck Obremski time line that made sense. I had a lot of homework to do. It was late, and I still hadn't eaten dinner. The excitement ebbed and exhaustion seeped in to take its place. I decided to drive into town. I parked on the apron in front of the old station house, a convenient perk until the town found something else to do with the building. Sheriff Bob Bulmer's official Ford Explorer with the fancy new rims—he had bought them as a gesture of amused defiance when people complained he was wasting his departmental budget—was already there, carelessly skewed sideways, taking up two spaces. Technically he wasn't allowed to park here, but Bob loved pushing the boundaries. He wasn't worth bothering with, and he knew it.

Climbing out of my car I realized that I missed the human contact and the sense of community we had when the cop shop stood in the heart of downtown, and you could step out into the lively summer streets any time you wanted and take their pulse.

The pulse was racing at ten o'clock—teen-agers putting off going home, couples returning from dinner, buskers on Main Street. A juggler had attracted a crowd, and further along a kid was playing the violin. Stores were open and people were shopping. They were relentless, they'd shop around the clock if you let them. How many t-shirts and bad paintings could you buy? The town had been built on whaling money. It survived on people's need to dispose of their disposable income.

A long jumbled line at the Juice Bar filled the sidewalk, spilled over into Broad Street and turned the corner up South Water. I never quite figured out the appeal of the Juice Bar. The only thing I liked there was the watermelon juice. But it was the only place in town to buy ice cream and monopoly capitalism ruled on Nantucket.

"Chief!"

I scanned the line and picked out Debbie Garrison and her mother. Joanne was a small woman, only a few inches taller than Debbie, with a perfect athletic body and severely-cut short brown hair. Her wide brown eyes and thin lips were pinched together, closing in on a sharp little nose. She looked like a scary doll— Harried Mom Barbie. This had been a tough time for Joanne. The secrets were out between Debbie and Billy Delavane, much to her chagrin. Debbie had dragged her mom to the station and they'd both been waiting when we let Billy out of detention.

"She threw her arms around me and shouted, 'Daddy, Daddy, Daddy!'" Billy had told me, later. "I figured the cat was out of the bag at that point."

Joanne grabbed Debbie's arm now, as the little girl started toward me.

"Debbie! Stay out of the street! It's—oh, hi Chief Kennis."

I smiled at her. "Having fun yet?"

"I saw a great bumper sticker yesterday. It said, 'If it's tourist season why can't we shoot them?'"

"Come on—it's lively. It's exciting."

"It's waiting in line for an hour to buy a five dollar ice-cream cone."

I shrugged. No way to argue with that. But I had an idea. "Can I borrow Debbie for a minute? We'll be back before the line gets to the front door."

"That gives you plenty of time."

I took Debbie's hand. "I want to ask you something."

"Police business?" she asked hopefully.

"Absolutely. Top secret police business."

We strolled up toward the Steamship Authority building. I thought about Chuck Obremski again, and his faith in chronology. "Why now," he always asked.

What had brought Debbie to Nantucket at this precise moment? Her grandmother had died, it was true, but Joanne could have handled the estate problems by phone or e-mail. And there was no need for Debbie to be here. Didn't she have a social life at home? What eleven-year-old girl wants to lose a summer with her friends, wandering around some sandy tourist town as a complete stranger? It made no sense.

But according to the evidence against Haden Krakauer, Debbie's arrival had set his whole revenge scheme in motion. Seeing her had turned his passive resentments active. No, it was more than that, much more. His hatred turned imperative when he saw this girl, when he realized who she was and what she meant about the waste and failure of his own life.

So, I could begin to generate the time line I needed. Tyler Gibson disappears, late May. A couple of weeks later Debbie arrives on-island and the Nantucket Police Department receives its first bomb threat. If Gibson was dead and the man who killed him was the staff sergeant in Kuwait that Ed Delavane had told me about, then the ten year delay had to be a jail sentence.

The prison term started the time line. Haden had sent this guy away. Now he was out, and making his moves.

Ahead of us, a crew was setting the new dolphin in place with a crane. The bright lights made it look like a stage show. Debbie was staring into the glare of the reconstruction, the aftermath of chaos. "I hope you catch that bomber person soon," she said.

"That's why I want to talk with you tonight," I said.

We walked along. I was still working out how I wanted to broach the subject.

To set Haden up, the staff sergeant needed to use Debbie for 'motivation'. That meant getting her to Nantucket, somehow. The first contact was crucial. But how would he go about it? A face to face meeting was out of the question. A phone call could be overheard, or written off as a crank or a prank. A letter was so twentieth century, not to mention encumbered with all kinds of potential forensics problems: finger prints, saliva DNA, postmarks. As we walked, another possibility blindsided me, like finding the last line of a poem, unexpected but unimpeachable. I ambushed Debbie with it.

"You can settle a little bet I made with myself," I said.

She glanced up at me. "Okay. Was it for a lot of money?"

"I have to buy myself dinner if I lose."

She smiled. "Uh oh."

"It has to do with you and Billy. When I showed you around the new station house, you said someone was calling Billy a terrorist. But you wouldn't say who. I think that's because you didn't know. I think you read it in a posting on your Facebook page."

She dropped her eyes, sidestepped a pizza crust.

"Whoever it was told you Billy was your father. He told you people suspected Billy of wanting to bomb all the rich people off the island. He said Billy needed you, maybe? To stabilize him, give him perspective, show him there were more important things in life than his grudges? I'm not sure about that part. Except, it got you here this summer, for the first time in your life, just ahead of the bomb scares."

She stopped walking, dropped my hand. "How did you know that?"

I shrugged. "Just a guess."

"No, I mean it. Just tell me the truth. How could you possibly know that stuff?"

I raised both hands a little to calm her down.

"I didn't know, Debbie. I've been trying to figure it out. I knew this guy could get past your Facebook firewall, friend himself somehow. I knew he'd been reading your e-mails, and your mother's e-mails. He knew Billy was your mom's secret and you were bugging her about it."

"Wait. How could he know that?"

"He had probably gotten access to your mom's computer as well—all her private e-mails. You were pressuring her to tell you who your dad was. She must have mentioned it to someone—"

"My Aunt Polly. They talk about everything."

"There you go. So this man wanted to get you here, and he had the perfect item of information for bait. The only question was—how to tell you. Do you remember any new friends you couldn't explain?"

"I have like two thousand friends now, and I block most of them. It was someone from school, I think. Maybe Tom Conena or Shawn Kennelly? They're here in the summer a lot. Not this year though."

"So he just picked a friend with some Nantucket connections and used the link."

She squinted in thought. "I wrote to Tommy—his family moved to South Carolina last year. He denied saying anything and got all weird about it. I figured he just felt bad about it. He always needs to have the 411 on everything and he's a total Chatty Cathy."

I nodded. "The guy lucked out there. Tommy was the weak link. Picking someone who had moved out of state was a shrewd move, though."

"Who? Who are you talking about? Who knew all this, that Billy was my dad, and my mom not telling me and—and reading my e-mail, all our e-mail, and watching us and spying on us and—who is this guy? Is he here now? Is he watching me or something? Is he following me, did you see someone following me? What's going on, because—"

"Debbie—"

"Because if someone is watching me you have to—"

"No one is watching you. You're safe here."

"I don't get it."

"I'm not sure I do, either. But if I'm right, this guy got what he was after. He's happy now. He has no reason to bother you."

"So this person, he tricked me and used me, and he got away with something. He hurt somebody, or did something bad, or… and I helped him."

"You didn't mean to. And he hasn't gotten away with it yet."

"Are you going to catch him?"

"Yes."

She stared up at me, unblinking. "Promise?"

"Absolutely."

"Okay. You better."

Caroline was right—she was bossy. I led her back to her mom, said my goodnights and went home.

The next morning was a Purgatory of delay. I was waiting for Chuck Obremski's phone call, checking in with my people on the ground at Jetties Beach. But we'd already organized the security for the Pops concert—the town's part of it at least, which was mostly traffic control and crowd management, going through the SOP binder with Fire Chief Ted Deakins and the Secret Service people, reps from the hospital, the WAVE buses, the taxi companies, Lonnie Fraker, and the harbormaster. The concert had been a smoothly running machine for decades before I arrived on the island. No one needed my help.

The beach would be closed as of Friday morning, when the stage sections were off-loaded from the ferry. The carpenters would assemble the big platform, while other crews put up the tents, set up the tables, organized the crowd control barriers, the porta-potties. I could feel the countdown in my head—three days until the concert. The only encouraging thought was that no one could frame Haden Krakauer for bombing the Pops concert if he was sitting in jail. And if they couldn't frame Haden for it, there was no point in doing it.

So maybe nothing was going to happen after all. Maybe it really was over.

I managed to take a few positive steps. I called Gene Mahon and asked for a copy of the photograph he took of Gibson and me at the AIDS benefit. He e-mailed it and I printed it up between phone calls. I wanted Haden to give me a positive ID on the picture, though how I was going to get it to him, I had no idea. There was a rumor circulating in the station, Kyle Donnelly had heard if from Lonnie Fraker, that I would be driving the police car that took Haden to the airport—the lead vehicle in a JTTF motorcade. It would be a typical Tornovitch gesture if it was true: a slap in the face disguised as a courtesy. Normally Sheriff Bob Bulmer got that job, but supposedly he and Tornovitch had hated each other on sight—good judgment from both of them.

If Jack's plan worked out, I'd be able to show Haden the picture on the trip. If he recognized it, I'd have my identity thief's name and a vital piece of evidence to support my theory.

I must have dreamed about another way to track him down—the idea was in my head when I woke up the next morning. It didn't take long to find out that in most noncapital crime cases during Operation Iraqi Freedom, the convicted offenders were shipped off to the Naval Consolidated Brig at Miramar, California. I knew enough about my identity thief—slight southern accent, physical description, computer skills, approximate date of release—to get a possible match from someone on the brig staff. I put a call in to the commander's office, and got bumped to voice mail. Of course: it was six in the morning there. I left a detailed message and got back to pacifying some CEO who objected to the north end of Beach Street being closed for the concert.

I heard back from Miramar as I was leaving to pick up the kids from Murray Camp.

They knew my identity thief. The dates and descriptions matched up. They couldn't tell me much—after one bad incident, he had been a model prisoner, working in the brig office and doing IT work on the computers. In fact, they were a little lost without him. He had dropped out of sight after his release—no contact with approved halfway houses or designated social workers. He hadn't used any of the job placement services.

"I may have found him for you," I said.

His name was Ezekiel Beaumont.

"Zeke to his friends," the commander's chief of staff told me.

"If he has any," I answered.

The chief of staff laughed at that. "Hey, everybody has a friend or two, sir."

I hung up, thinking about that casual comment. It stuck in my mind all the way out to the Delta fields. The Murray Camp day had ended with a pickup softball game on the windy baseball diamond near the Sun Island storage facility. I drove slowly out the airport road, past the new commercial developments and the grim, dark little condos with sad names like 'Anchor Village,' built just ahead of the popped housing bubble.

I was late, but I was content with the sluggish traffic. I wanted to think, and it would be impossible once I had the kids in the car. I kept turning that Miramar chief of staff's phrase over in my head.

Everybody has a friend or two.

Friends, or allies anyway. Beaumont would need help for an elaborate scam like this. Someone else was involved, they had to be. Someone from the Iraq war days. Someone who'd been involved with the drug bust that sent Beaumont to Miramar.

I thought of Dan Taylor, bragging about commanding men in Iraq. When had he actually come to the island? A self-righteous gasbag who had almost single-handedly pushed the funding for a drug sniffing dog through at a Town Meeting, he was the perfect candidate, the obvious choice for the role of military drug runner. Guys like Dan Taylor always had some kind of dark secret, and they always managed to skate. He blustered his way through.

So, how would this work? Dan Taylor was the front man, arriving years early to lay the groundwork for this plan? Doing what exactly? He had no real power or influence. No, it didn't make sense. Beaumont needed someone inside the investigation. But there were at least sixty people in the JTTF on-island—more like seventy-five if you included the Army Corps of Engineers crew and the Coast Guard transfers. There was no way to vet all of them in the time I had left.

I turned down the short drive to the softball fields. A little girl broke out of a crowd near the concession stand and started running toward the car.

It was Caroline.

"Daddy, Daddy!" she was shouting. "You have to help Tim! Jake Souter is beating him up and no one's helping!"

I pulled into a space and scrambled out of the car.

"Where is he?"

She pointed at the crowd and we took off.

"You're late," she said, between ragged breaths. Her tone was accusatory, but she was right. I should have been here ten minutes ago. Blaming traffic was pointless: you automatically added a few minutes to any drive in July on Nantucket—you leave time so stuff like this won't happen. I'd been tempted to use my flashers, but that was a needlessly trivial abuse of power. Pushing through the crowd with Caroline right behind me, I wished I'd done it.

Jake Sauter was a fat kid, twice Tim's size, with close-set eyes and a slab forehead under rank long hair. He had Tim's right arm forced halfway up his back. Tim was trying not to cry, but the tears were squeezing out of his eyes. I stepped to the struggling boys, and grabbed Jake's arm just above the elbow.

"Okay. That's enough. Let him go, Jake. Pick on someone your own size."

He released Tim and turned on me. "What about you! You pick on someone your own size!"

I pulled Tim over to me. "Let's get out of here."

"My dad's gonna kill you," Jake shouted after us. "You wait and see!"

Driving home, Tim was quiet.

I said, "Are you all right?"

He made a contemptuous little bleat, still turned away.

"Tim?"

He faced me. "I was handling it, Dad? Okay? I was doing fine—but now…"

"Tim—"

"Why did you have to do that?"

"I didn't think about it. He was hurting you."

"So now everybody's seen me being rescued by my dad. I thought this couldn't get any worse."

"I'm sorry."

I wasn't though. I felt anything and everything but sorry. I felt angry and humiliated. Still at scalpel point in a deserted jobsite, still driving a hammer into a man's knee, hearing his high pitched scream over the roar of the compressor. Proud of myself for not flattening Jake Sauter a few minutes ago, ecstatic and light-headed with the momentary immanence of that violence. Relieved that Tim was okay, and heartbroken at the look of bruised pride and chagrin on his face.

There was no way I could say any of that. So I said nothing and drove the car.

"Debbie Garrison was watching," Caroline added helpfully.

"Great," Tim said. "That makes it perfect."

My cell phone rang.

I pulled into the Fast Forward parking lot. By the time I had slotted myself between two big pickups, the phone had stopped ringing. I checked the received calls panel: I didn't recognize the number, but the 310 area code meant it had to be Chuck Obremski. He must have been using his own cell. The regular police phone number would be blocked.

"I have to take this call."

"Can we get sodas?" Tim asked. I had to smile at the redeeming practicality of the question. Humiliation and heartbreak notwithstanding, it would be foolish to ignore the chance to grab a Coke on a July afternoon.

"Sure." I gave them some money and watched as they darted across Cherry Street to the Cumberland Farms. Fast Forward sold fancy, hippy health-food artisan fruit-juice-sweetened sodas. The kids went straight for the junk.

I highlighted Chuck's number and pressed the call button, to a shiver of anticipation. Something had happened.

He picked up without any greeting. Cell phones had eliminated the need to identify yourself. "Thanks for the tip, K."

I took a long breath and felt it vibrate through my chest. "You found him?"

"What was left of him. But we got plenty of DNA and the guy gave blood two years ago. It's Gibson. Go arrest this mother-fucker, beat the shit out of him, add a resisting arrest charge, and extradite him to L.A. Fly out with him and I'll buy you a drink."

"Thanks, Chuck."

"You're thanking me? Thank you, buddy. This is why I'm still a cop, after all these years. Moments like this. You know what I mean?"

"Yeah. I know exactly."

Now I had it all. The pieces clicked together like Lego blocks. I called Miranda and told her she was taking the kids. She wasn't happy about it. She had a showing and Elaine was taking the whole office out to dinner.

I cut her off. "I have to arrest a murderer before he kills someone else."

"Henry—"

"I'm serious, Miranda. This guy set both bombs and he's going to blow up the Pops concert. Unless I stop him."

"Half the FBI is on-island right now. Why can't they—"

"They don't know what's going on and I don't have time to play catch-up. I need this guy in custody now."

"I hate this."

"I know. I'm sorry."

After a moment of silence, she said. "Take a gun. And don't go there alone."

Some people wonder why I still love Miranda, after everything we did to each other, after a bad marriage and an acrimonious divorce. Well, that's why—a comment like that.

I dropped off the kids and went back to the station to grab my piece. I called Elaine and got the address on Deacon's Way, texted Kyle Donnelly to meet me there. "I'm at the cop-shop right now," he texted back. "There's someone here to see you. Urgent."

Franny Tate was standing in my office, hair tangled, face flushed, leaning against my desk, grabbing the edge with both hands, fighting a smile, pushing it up into her eyes. Her voice was solemn when she spoke.

"Get ready for it," she said. "The words you've never heard from a woman. You were right. I'm sorry."

Chapter Eighteen

Inventory

"I finally talked to Haden Krakauer," Franny said.

We sped down Cliff Road, past the big houses perched above the harbor. You could see flashes of Nantucket Sound between the shingles and the hedges. We were alone. I had sent Kyle Donnelly to his uncle's real estate office—they handled most of the rentals on Deacon's Way—to grab a key and the alarm code. Franny had another of her Patriot Act no-permission warrants, but I wanted to avoid more breaking and entering. And I mean breaking: the way these new houses were secured, you'd need a battering ram to get in the front door.

"How did you do it?" I asked. "There must have been guards posted."

"Various techniques. I pulled rank, threatened them, bribed them with false promises. I flattered them. And flirted, of course. You always have to flirt a little."

"You learn that at Quantico?'

"I learned that in high school, Hank. Anyway, I was thinking about what you said, about Krakauer knowing the person who did this to him…I mean, assuming someone is actually doing this to him. Which I guess I'm assuming now."

"Did you get a name?"

"Barely. Tornovitch broke it up before he could say much.

One of the guards ratted me out. I guess my flirtation techniques aren't quite what they used to be."

We passed the big split-rail fenced parking area at Tupancy Links—lots of cars there today, lots of dogs at the old golf course. The fat white stand pipe at Washing Pond loomed above us. We were almost there. I stamped on the gas, pushing the speed-ometer toward sixty. The pond glittered in the sunlight as we swept down the hill, and we tore past a guy in a station wagon, shocked to see the big NPD cruiser whipping by, relieved that it was going the other way.

I glanced sideways at Franny as I slowed for the Deacon's Way turnoff. The big car fishtailed a little. This was bad driving. If I wasn't careful I'd skid in the sand at the intersection and hit a mailbox. But I felt a weird urgency, a premonition that we were already too late.

"The guy's name is Ezekiel Beaumont," I said.

She gawked at me, mouth open, jaw dropped like the old cliché, stunned, out-thought, out-maneuvered, out-detectived, if that was even a word. It should be. We need it for moments like this one.

We turned into the driveway, and I braked in front of the house. No sign of Donnelly yet.

She shook her head. "You must be psychic."

"Come on. I make phone calls and annoy people, the same way you do. I checked with Naval Consolidated Brig at Miramar, near San Diego. That's where they sent the Iraq war druggies. They recognized Beaumont from my description—not a hun-dred percent, but…"

"Now it is."

"Yeah."

We sat in silence for a few seconds. I looked around. The driveway was empty—not a good sign. The garage doors were open, revealing the usual surfboards and bicycles, step ladders and battery chargers, tool racks and bungee cords. No car.

We heard Donnelly's cruiser, and stood in the driveway to greet him. The crushed shell paving was new; it smelled of low tide in the afternoon sun.

Franny seized my arm, our last moment of privacy before Kyle pulled up. "I should have listened to you."

I put an arm around her shoulder and pulled her toward me. "You did, though."

"I guess. Finally. Maybe too late. Anyway, Jack was furious. He's talking about suspending me."

"What—for doing your job?"

"No, Hank. For doing his job."

"Well, someone has to."

Kyle pulled up, tires crunching on the shells. He got out of the car waving the key. Franny pulled away a little and we stood there in the sunlit silence looking at the big, shuttered house. It held its own secrets, but all these trophy mansions did. They gave you the sense of privileged lives unfolding quietly behind the tinted glass and the ten thousand-dollar window treatments.

Inside, Kyle turned off the alarm. The house was dark and cool, an upside down house, built so that the living room could have a water view, with the bedrooms downstairs, plush caves tucked along the tiled hallway. A family of six could live there comfortably. One lunatic knocking around all those rooms seemed bizarre. Did he just want to spend as much money as possible? Why not? He had Tyler Gibson's black American Express card, and Gibson wasn't going to miss it.

Upstairs, in the vanilla-colored, high-ceilinged great room, a wall of windows revealed a sweeping view of Nantucket Sound, stretching away to Hyannis. A ferry trudged across the wide blue expanse. The far end of the giant loft featured a fireplace with a grouping of furniture around it. The open kitchen gleamed, unused and pristine. The place felt uninhabited.

"Either he left a long time ago, or he had it set up for a quick exit." I lifted the lid of a big earthenware jar marked 'pasta' and glanced inside. It was empty. So were the 'sugar' and 'flour' containers.

I turned to Kyle. "Put out an APB for the guy. There's a photograph of him on my desk. Make up a poster and get the picture to the newspapers. Make sure everyone on the force has a copy. I want someone watching the airport and the Steamship Authority. The Hy-Line, too. And make sure all the charter boat captains have a copy of the picture. That would be an easy way off the island."

Franny was holding a hideous china rooster. She put it back on the counter. "Flight risk?"

"His plan worked too well. With Haden in custody there's no point in setting off another bomb. Unless he just likes bombs. I'd run if I were him. Let's work the surveillance and see if he turns up. And Kyle—make it clear to everyone. This guy is wanted for murder. He's a psychopath who kills for convenience. He's probably armed and extremely dangerous. If anyone sees him they call the police. No citizen's arrests, no heroics. Call the cops and get out of the way. All right? And that includes you. No one makes a move without backup."

"Okay."

"Get going. And thank your uncle for the key."

He trotted downstairs, slammed the front door.

"Now what?" Franny said.

"Now we work the case together. We talk it out, just like the old days. I'll make us dinner—something simple. Chicken, and a bottle of white wine."

"And we talk about the case?"

"I need help, Franny. I'm missing something, but I don't know what. I keep circling the same points over and over, like I'm stuck in an echo chamber here. I need to hear your take on it."

"You never did like thinking alone."

"Yeah, well. It's like playing tennis against a backboard. I always win but I never improve."

She shrugged. "Okay. A no-nonsense business dinner for two. When shall I come? Seven?"

"Come at six. You can help me cook."

Outside, Franny walked over to the open garage. I followed her and we stood looking down at the curved tire tracks coming off the oiled cement onto the driveway: an arc, ending in two little piles of dirt and shells. The driver had gunned the gas backing out, and jammed to a stop before straightening out. Ten feet farther on there was another, bigger set of piles.

"Looks like someone left in a hurry after all," Franny said.

"And they were towing something, some kind of trailer."

"Sounds right. But when did he leave?"

"That's the question. I'm betting recently. I'm betting, just before we got here today."

"Yeah."

We walked back to my cruiser.

"Drop me off at Fairgrounds Road. I have to deal with Jack. I know he's pissed I ran out on him. He was yelling at me when I left."

"That doesn't sound good."

"It's okay. I know how to deal with him. I apologize and grovel and promise to change my ways."

"Which you never do."

"No."

She kissed my cheek and climbed into the car.

◇◇◇

It was just after seven in the evening, and dinner was almost ready when Franny finally got to my house. She was wearing a short white summer dress and sandals. Her hair was down. The dress was almost transparent and her skin looked very brown against the lacy cotton. The sudden jolt of desire knocked the words out of my head. I stood stupidly at the door.

She lifted her eyebrows, performed a small curtsey. "Can I come in?"

"Of course."

I stepped back.

"It smells good in here" She lifted the bag in her hand. "I brought the wine. Really good wine. I need a drink tonight."

"Do you still have your job?"

"Barely."

I looked her up and down. "Speaking of barely…"

"What? Dress too sexy for a business conference? The other one I was thinking about was even shorter. Kind of like this."

She hiked the skirt up a little, flashed her thighs and let it drop. Warm, scented air drifted in the window carrying the sounds of someone's hedge clippers and distant dogs barking. The kitchen was paradise. Police work, the business she was ostensibly here to discuss, faded away like a memory of winter.

I said, "If you wanted to make love before dinner you should have come over an hour ago."

"That's okay. I'm happy to taunt and torment you for a while."

"Gee, thanks."

I took the chicken out of the oven, made the gravy and explained the fine points of whisking flour and water into a roux. She opened the wine, and we sat down at the little table in the kitchen. An NRT bus rumbled up the street.

It had been a rough week. We spent the meal catching up. We drank the wine quickly and I opened a second bottle. It was inferior, but I'd learned from my father long ago that you always drink the good bottle first. I told Franny about Tim's bully and my Bulgarians. She endorsed my approach to the little thug and had an interesting point about the big ones. Apparently federal law enforcement officials think of Bulgarians as absolutely the worst, most ruthless and dangerous of all Eastern European criminals; much scarier than the Russians.

"I can believe it," I said. "If Billy hadn't showed up…"

Talking about Billy Delavane led us to his daughter and the mysterious Facebook posting. Franny promised to investigate it as soon as she could get a FISA warrant.

"You really bother with those?"

"Yes, Hank, we do. Well, most of the time. Anyway, it's no bother. Just a form to fill out, really. With domestic cases like this you want everything by the book, when you turn it over to the Bureau."

I made a pot of de-caf and we took the coffee into the living room, poured two cups. "Are we off duty now?"

"Do you want to be?"

"It's been a rough week. I missed you."

"Me, too. Sorry—I know you hate that. I missed you, too, I meant to say."

She crossed her legs and the dress rose on her thighs. We drank our coffee. The crickets were chirping. Moths were banging against the screens. A gentle breeze moved through the room. Someone was playing music, but all we could hear was the baseline.

"I've been thinking about this teacher of mine at Quantico," Franny said. "Reynolds Crain. He was a forensic pathologist, he died a few years ago. Anyway, he was fascinated with bogus crime-scene data. He would have loved this case. There was this phrase he used, about perfectly cultivated, artificial evidence—stuff that looked real but tasted wrong. He called fake clues 'winter tomatoes.' Smudged half-prints on a ladderback chair: vine ripened. One set of clear prints on an otherwise clean gun butt: hydroponic. He always said, once you experience the real thing you always know the difference. I love that distinction. You can apply it to anything."

I put a hand on her knee. "How about us?"

"Us?"

"Sure—which are we?"

She cocked her head a little and gave me a long appraising look. After a few seconds she nodded.

"Definitely vine ripened."

"Ready to be picked?"

She pressed my hand to her knee. "Oh yeah. Maybe overdue."

"You know how I eat Bartlett farm tomatoes? I don't even cut them up. I just bite into them like apples and let the juice run down my chin."

"Sounds delicious."

"It's messy, though."

"Good."

Then she kissed me and the white dress came off and my shirt came off and so did everything else including the microscopic thong she had bought that afternoon just for me at the lingerie store on Orange Street, and we did everything we had ever imagined doing together, twice, and in between we ate ice cream in bed and talked about our most embarrassing sexual experiences and I told her my theory that people our age could use sex as a sleep substitute for at least one night, and she said probably two and we made love again and she dozed off and I hoped we were right, because I couldn't get to sleep at all.

There was one subject I hadn't brought up at dinner, one idea I couldn't get off my mind, one reason I had wanted to brainstorm the case with Franny, one professional reason for our date. I had let it go for the best of reasons—we both needed the untroubled time together. We had waited for years to follow up on that kiss in the Santa Monica Mountains. I had given up on it, myself. Probably she had too. Then the moment was offered, like money lying in the street, and we grabbed it. We deserved it, and we had made the most of it. I eased her hair off her forehead, behind her ear and studied her profile against the pillow, so peaceful in repose.

But that was last night. There was nothing we could have done about my idea at that point anyway. I picked up the watch I kept on my bedside table, pushed the button to illuminate the dial, 4:42 in the morning.

It was officially tomorrow.

I shook Franny's shoulder; she groaned and settled herself under the cotton blanket. I rubbed her again, more firmly, and she opened her eyes.

"Hank?"

"We have to talk."

"Is something wrong? What time is it?"

"Just before dawn."

"I—it's…are you all right?"

She sat up and let the covers fall to her lap. She looked gorgeous and tussled in the pale gray half-light of sunrise, but I refused to let myself be distracted,

She put her hand on my thigh and squeezed it gently. She was waking up now. "What is it?"

"I have a theory," I said.

She took her hand back, pulled it through her hair, twisted to face me. "Okay."

"I just want you to listen with an open mind."

"Okay."

"It's not too early?"

"I'm fine. What are you thinking?"

"There's someone else involved with this plot."

"Okay."

"Beaumont needed an accessory. It had to be someone involved with the investigation."

"I'm with you."

"I think it's Jack."

She crossed her arms over her chest, dug her chin into her palm. "Jack Tornovitch? Special Agent in Charge of Domestic Investigations, Department of Homeland Security? That Jack Tornovitch."

"That very one."

Her voice was quiet. "Okay."

"I did inventory, the way we did in L.A. All the key moments that pointed the investigation at Haden Krakauer. All those winter tomatoes. The way Jack jumped on Billy's accusations. It was a total 180, but he seemed totally on board with the idea that Haden was setting up a frame. And that wild goose chase before the bomb went off—Jack sent Haden on that one. If you wanted to create a situation where someone would have no alibi, you couldn't do much better than that. And why do you think he wouldn't let anyone else talk to Haden for all this time? Haden would have been telling anyone and everyone about Beaumont, and Jack couldn't afford that. Then today—you said it yourself, it looked like someone had just pulled out from that garage. Let's say that's true. Who else knew we were going there? Who else could have warned Beaumont? Nobody."

"Unless your office was bugged."

I hadn't told her about my discovery yet. "It was."

"But Jack checked out the whole station himself. He—"

"What?" But of course I already knew. She wasn't even putting it together, she was watching, staring at an airport departures board as the flights rescheduled after a weather delay. But every plane was headed to the same destination at this moment and they were all on time.

She looked pale. She stood and started getting dressed. I watched her pull on that tiny thong and button her dress. Was there a tremor in her hand? I had never seen that before. I stood up myself, grabbed my pants, and hopped into them. We stood facing each other across the rumpled bed.

Finally she finished her thought. "It's just…Jack insisted we take this case. It was out of the chain of command. Normally he wouldn't involve himself with this type of incident. I mean, at the time it was just one phone call, remember? But he was treating it like an all-out terrorist attack. And he hates field work, Hank. He delegates stuff like this. I've worked a lot of our cases alone and then shipped him the paperwork to sign. But he was all over this one. It didn't make any sense. I thought he wanted a couple of weeks' vacation on the government tab."

"So it's possible?"

"I don't know, Hank. I mean—why would he do this? What connection could he possibly have to Ezekiel Beaumont?"

"I've thought about that one, too. It started with something you said at my place after dinner, the night of the golf club bomb. Do you remember?"

"No, I have no idea. We said a lot of things—"

"We were talking about Jack. You said he really wasn't such a bad guy. You told me about that girlfriend of his that died. He wound up crying in the bathroom in some DC restaurant. And he wasn't even drunk, that was what you said."

She found her sandals, slipped them on while I grabbed a clean shirt from my bureau. She started making the bed and I stepped over to help her. She was in motion—that was a good sign. We were setting the pillows against the headboard when she spoke.

"Kuwait," she said. "He met that girl in Kuwait. During the war."

"And she died, and Zeke's beef with Haden has to do with a drug bust that cut off the supply of safe heroin for almost a month."

"So what are you saying? She was a drug addict?"

"And Jack was her pusher. Why not? Say he ran the networks that Zeke supplied. That would be the connection. And it explains why Zeke didn't roll over on him at the time. They both had bigger plans. They needed each other. For this."

"I don't know."

"What else can it be? How else can you fit the pieces together? Or arrange the furniture?"

"It's just…it's so creepy. I think of revenge as something hot headed and impulsive. Why would he wait around for so long?"

"Because if he waited, Zeke would do the dirty work for him. Zeke had the computer skills. Zeke had the balls to break into people's houses and plant evidence and steal things. He had the contacts to get the C-4 and the nerve to use it. Jack developed his position—the power to expedite things, to make sure the investigation went the right way, to run it from afar like a general. The way he does everything else. And in the end, if there's a problem he walks away clean and Zeke takes the fall. Just like in Kuwait. Because there's no real evidence against him."

"If it's even true."

"Exactly—if it's even true."

"There's one bright spot."

"Tell me."

"Well, in a sense they outsmarted themselves…if they're actually doing this, if Jack is really a part of it. Or maybe they underestimated us. We caught on too quickly. Most of the evidence we found was probably supposed to come out after the fact. Now with Haden in custody, their whole plan is ruined."

The thought had occurred to me—jail was the perfect alibi. But not the corollary. Franny must have grasped it at the same second.

"They'll try to break him out," she said.

"Impossible. I'm driving Haden to the airport, the first car in a ten-car motorcade. No way Jack could pull him out of that—and even if he could the blowback would destroy him. He could never talk himself out of that one, Franny. Mr. Law and Order."

"So they abort?"

"What else can they do?"

"So we win?"

"I guess so."

"So why doesn't it feel that way?"

"Because we're still missing something."

"Maybe. Or maybe we're just anal compulsive cynics who can't leave well enough alone."

"That's what Miranda would say."

"Which is why you divorced her."

"Actually, she divorced me." We stared at each other for a few more seconds. "It doesn't matter. She never understood police work. We both know something bad is going to happen today, and we're the only ones who can stop it."

"So let's go to work."

I nodded, "Protect and serve."

Ten seconds later we were out the door. Ten minutes later we were at the station, working the case, trying or find some scrap of evidence we could use to arrest Jack Tornovitch. We both knew it had to be airtight. We weren't going to get a second chance. Don't attack the King unless you know you can kill him.

We found nothing, and at ten o'clock in the morning our time was up. Haden Krakauer was headed for the airport.

Tornovitch strode up to me as I was putting Haden into the back seat of the cruiser.

I slammed the door and stood up to face my nemesis.

"You look like hell, Kennis," Tornovitch said. "You need more sleep. And cut down on the booze. My people don't drink. We celebrate with seltzer. That's a slogan I wrote. You like it?"

"It's great, Jack."

"Try living by it. You won't embarrass yourself."

I chose not to inform him that one of his people had been celebrating right along with me all night and with anything but soda water. I wouldn't have gotten the chance, anyway—he was already striding back to the first following car. He climbed into the black Expedition and we were set to go: three police cruisers and three DHS vehicles. The FBI agents were taking up the rear.

It was absurd, of course. Two cops could have taken Haden to the airport in a taxi. But Tornovitch liked ceremony, and in fairness, so did the town. The Wicked Witch was dead—or at least handcuffed and on his way to prison—so the Munchkins wanted to celebrate. They lined Old South Road to watch the motorcade go by, and I remained as baffled as Dorothy among the midget festivities.

I felt alert, but exhausted people often do when the adrenaline kicks in. And I was cocky because I was convinced Tornovitch had given up. Besides, I controlled the lock on the rear doors of the cruiser, and I had a small army of law enforcement professionals for backup.

Nothing could go wrong. But Tornovitch had perfect timing and the element of surprise. It happened at the Lover's Lane crosswalk. It didn't occur to me until after it was all over how appropriate that was.

Beaumont must have rigged Tornovitch a remote for the door locks. They opened with a loud click as I waited for a man and three small children to cross the road. Haden registered a moment of awareness and decision, then he brought both fists up hard into the throat of the FBI man next to him, lunged across the choking agent's lap, slammed the door open and dove into the street. He hit the asphalt in a tumbler's roll and was on his feet a moment later, sprinting for the woods.

He was gone before anyone could respond, darting ahead of a Marine Home Center truck heading the other way. I ripped my door open and plunged after him, banging my shin on the bumper as I ran around the front of the car, shouting his name. I was halfway across the road when someone tackled me from behind. I came down hard on the heels of my palms and rolled over to face the bulk of Special Agent Knightley, his throat already bruising from where Haden had hit him, pointing a gun in my face.

Tornovitch loomed above us.

"You're under arrest Kennis. Adding and abetting a fugitive, conspiracy to commit multiple felonies. And resisting arrest. Did he resist arrest, Agent Daly?"

"Yes sir. He sure did,"

"All right, then. Cuff him and get him back in the car. You know your rights, Kennis. Read them to yourself. You've got plenty of time."

The plan was on again. Haden Krakauer was an escaped criminal now. The genius of the remote was that everyone would assume I had unlocked the car doors. I was about to be thrown into my own jail, expertly framed, my word worthless and my options gone.

Now there was nothing to stop them from blowing up the Pops concert. The rage and frustration climbed my throat, choking me. No one was going to find the bomb—Jack would make sure of that. They were going to wipe out the business and political elites of the state along with most of the Boston Symphony Orchestra and a few thousand other innocent people. They were going to turn Jetties Beach into a smoking bloody crater—all to enact their psychotic vision of revenge. And they were going to get away with it, and Haden was going to take the blame. I was helpless, that was the real nightmare strangling me. I was powerless, futile, defeated. And all in the space of a few seconds. The urge to lash out was overwhelming, but my hands were lashed behind my back. Too tightly, Daly had made sure of that. The metal bite of the handcuffs was cutting off my circulation.

Through the rage and horror, the thought kept rebounding in my head—why had Haden done it? Why had he gone along with their plan? The safest situation—and the one outcome his enemies had to avoid at all costs—was him sitting in jail, with the perfect alibi that would render all their carefully laid plans worthless. So why go along with these men who hated him, sealing his own fate?

I had no answers and there was nothing I could do but sit in a holding cell, watching the clock tick down to zero.

Ezekiel Beaumont: Ten Seconds Ago

Haden Krakauer crashed through the scabby forest of pitch pine, cutting his face on the branches, stumbling over the exposed roots, catching himself, flinging himself forward away from the road and the police motorcade and the thugs who were taking him to jail.

He was wearing his police uniform, his hands unshackled as a professional courtesy. In fact Jack had just wanted to give him the best chance possible for a clean escape. But Haden had still wanted to improve his chances. He had seen a small oblong bulge in Knightley's pocket. A Swiss Army Knife.

It wasn't that he didn't trust the Department of Homeland Security. He didn't trust anyone these days, except his boss. Okay, Henry had been involved with the escape, but there was more than one way to unlock a car door. If the chief had been planning to work the remote, he would have said something back at the station. Maybe that was the wrong note that worried Haden. He had always been especially good at those "What's wrong with this picture?" puzzles, and something was definitely wrong here.

Slowly, carefully, using the swaying of the car as cover, he had slipped two fingers past the stitched flap and started easing the knife free, by a sixteenth of an inch when they swerved around a moped, and another fraction when they bumped over a seam in the road.

Then Haden heard the doors unlock. He knew the time had come, giving him a few seconds at most. He pulled the knife free and wrapped his fingers around it to brace his fist as he struck Knightley in the throat.

Now, running through the woods, he slipped the little red oblong of plastic with its nested blades up past the tight cuff of his uniform shirt. He ducked under a low branch, crested a hill, and saw the Range Rover. Homeland Security had a fleet of Ford Escapes and Expeditions—the fancy English SUV struck another wrong note. But he didn't have time to think about it. He could hear the curse and clatter of pursuit behind him. Jack couldn't call them back without giving away the plan. Haden was on his own until he got to the rendezvous.

He stumbled down the hill and almost fell into the man who stepped out from behind the car. Haden grabbed the roof rack to regain his balance. He stared at the grinning face in front of him, the crooked nose, the unruly blond hair, those radioactive blue eyes.

Ten years later and he hadn't changed a bit.

Staring at Beaumont, the sudden detonation of understanding collapsed Haden Krakauer's life like a building imploding. What did they call it? Controlled demolition. The perfect phrase.

He understood everything, but too late. Ten seconds too late, more or less—whatever, it might as well have been ten years, and in fact it was ten years, since Beaumont's court-martial. And now he was out, probably with time off for good behavior. That was certainly an error of judgment.

Haden listened to the approaching police, hoping they would catch him, but somehow knowing they wouldn't, and said the only word that mattered.

"Tornovitch."

Zeke grinned. "Yep. Looks like you trusted the wrong guy, Lieutenant Krakauer. The same way I did."

Then Haden saw a flash of metal, and the world went black.

◇◇◇

Haden woke up tipped over in the backseat of Beaumont's Range Rover, his wrists flex-cuffed together, his arms tucked into his chest, the Swiss Army knife nestled between the inside of his forearm and his bicep. At first all he felt was the headache, a drill boring into the base of his skull. Then the other voices joined the chorus—his back, stiff from the half reclining position, plus his face and neck burning from dozens of cuts and scratches. His knee was throbbing. He'd twisted it. But he had a weapon, at least, and that meant he had a chance.

"Stop faking," the driver said. "I didn't hit you that hard."

The voice brought everything back.

Beaumont and Tornovitch. How could he have not suspected Tornovitch? Actually, it made sense. Villains usually tried to conceal their true natures, they worked undercover. Jack had worked the reverse. He was too big a prick to be anything worse than that. But why? Why team up with Beaumont? How had they even met? Haden shifted position, releasing a new pain in his head—something sharp pushing at his temples. Red protoplasm swarmed in front of his eyes. He shut them. It didn't help.

Thinking distracted from the pain. Iraq, it had to have been Iraq. Tornovitch served in the war, Haden had checked his record. Jack had even been stationed at Doha briefly, but they had never met. Well, Haden must have done something to piss the guy off. God knows what. Maybe Jack was involved in the drug business with Beaumont. But it had to be more than that.

He thought back to the interrogation. Jack had been so convincing, following his lead, letting him talk. At first it seemed like Haden had gone crazy—blacking out and doing bad things and then not remembering them. But he knew where he was on the night he had supposedly placed the bomb at the golf course. He had been at home, talking to his mother on the telephone—it was her birthday.

So he wasn't insane, and if he wasn't doing these things someone else was. That led him to Beaumont. Jack had given Haden the benefit of the doubt, sending agents to the Steamship Authority and the airlines, the car rental places, the guest houses and hotels. They'd remember Beaumont if they saw him. But Jack had pointed out—looks like his were easy to conceal. Gain ten pounds, dye the hair, and put in some brown contact lenses—you blend right into the crowd. Beaumont was tall, but not freakishly so. It would have worked. Haden's hopes had dried up.

Tornovitch hung in there though, suggesting that it might be someone else from that time, someone who was eavesdropping at the officers club while Haden rambled on to Beaumont? But Haden had to demur. He didn't have an enemy in the world, apart from Beaumont. Jack had smiled at that, a strange squinting smile, lips crinkled like he had just bitten down on a kumquat. That smile should have been the giveaway. But Haden hadn't recognized it.

When he had finally given up all hope, Jack came to him with a proposition. A routine check by the DHS revealed that Ezekiel Beaumont had more or less vanished off the face of the earth, two months after his release from the Miramar brig. No contact with the halfway house personnel or the job search liaison office, no checks written, no credit card charges, no utility or rent payments, no phone calls or e-mails.

Apparently this disappearing act had convinced Tornovitch that Haden was telling the truth.

"That's right Krakauer," he had said, handing Haden a cup of coffee. "I actually believe your cockamamie story. People say 'Do the math.' Well, I actually do it and I stand by the results. I've been working the new intel, and I have a pretty good idea what this Beaumont is planning. But with you in custody—it's like you said. There's no point if he can't hang the bombing on you. Once you're gone, he's in the wind, and I'm not going to let that happen. It turns out we baited the perfect trap for this little sociopath, and he's not walking away from it because we're smarter than he thought we were, and we arrested you ahead of schedule. So you're going to escape. Make it look good, break for the woods. Someone from the JTTF will pick you up and get you to a safe house. You can be America's number one fugitive for a couple of days, watch it all on TV. Eat some take-out, drink a few twelve-packs. Maybe we'll get you a Homeland Security Distinguished Service Medal. We'll handle Beaumont.

All you have to do is run when you get the chance. You'll know the moment when you see it. Don't fuck it up."

Haden had believed him and Haden had run, because he wanted to believe it, because despite all his snide talk, he wanted to trust the Department of Homeland Security, because he wanted to clear his own name, because he wanted to be the hero.

Because he was a fool.

Haden squeezed his eyes closed and let the pain thrash him. He wanted to hurt. He deserved it.

A few minutes later, that grating drawl cut through the haze again. "Wake up, sleepyhead. We're almost there."

Haden used the slight centrifugal g-force of the turn to leverage himself to a sitting position. His back screamed as if he'd been stabbed in the spine. But it didn't matter, he had to get a look out the car windows—he needed every bit of visual information he could gather in the next few minutes.

He saw instantly that they were moving down Deacon's Way, off Cliff Road. They pulled up to a house at the end of the short street, a classic trophy home with a lattice of roses and a handsome widow's walk on the roof. There was a big, open garage with a Chris-Craft on a trailer parked in front of it.

He let the Swiss Army knife slip into the crook of his elbow, squeezed it against his bicep.

He had the beginnings of a plan.

◇◇◇

"So have you seen the woman again, Lieutenant?"

They were sitting in what the new people liked to call the Great Room. He glanced over at the big cracker, slouched down in the opposite chair. "What?"

"The woman! You know what I'm talking about! That sweet piece of ass your buddy knocked up, back in the day. You enlisted so you wouldn't have to see that big belly buying a flat of annuals at Bartlett Farm. Your exact words, Lieutenant."

Haden ignored the gloating little jape. "How does Tornovitch fit into this? I've been trying to figure it out."

Zeke shrugged. "Whatcha got so far?"

"Well…you served in Iraq together. You were probably in the drug business together. Claymore handled supply, you were sales. I'm guessing Jack was distribution."

"Go on, Sherlock."

"But that's where I stop. You took the fall, not him. If he had even a few of your contacts he could have been back in business within a week—and doing even better. It's always a sound move to cut out the middleman. So what's his grudge? I did him a favor."

"Yeah, but he don't see it that way since your little drug bust forced his girlfriend to buy from some local boys and she OD'd on a bad load. Guess he figures you killed her."

"This is nuts. I never even met the guy."

"But you signed off on his transfer papers when his tour finished out. One day he's going home, the next day he's playing whack-a-mole with a bunch Sunni insurgents in Fallujah."

"We signed off on hundreds of transfers! I had no idea who he was."

"Well, I guess that makes it OK then, Lieutenant. But Scooter thinks different. He sees you as the cause of all his problems. He sees you as the curse of his life. And I see his point. Anyway, I wasn't gonna try and talk him out of it. I needed the help. Never could have gotten this far without him."

Haden sat back in the chair and closed his eyes. "Jesus Christ."

Zeke stood up and stood over him. "The woman, Lieutenant. We got off the subject. I was asking about the woman. She still get your knickers in a twist?"

"I haven't even seen her."

"How about the daughter? She could have been yours. Sweet little thing. Quite the daddy's girl. That must smart."

"I'm over it, Beaumont. I've been over it for years."

"I don't think so, Lieutenant. I don't think you ever get over nothing."

"Stop calling me that! I'm not in the Army anymore."

"Yeah, well. Maybe not. But you'll always be that true blue, got-your-back commanding officer to me."

"So I betrayed you, is that it? I wrecked your fucking pathetic life? There are going to be ten thousand people on that beach tonight! Ten thousand people! That's more people than you've met in your whole life. There'll be families there! There'll be kids!"

He pushed his chair back and jumped to his feet, face to chest with Beaumont. It was ludicrous—mortifying. He wasn't even short! He stood five foot eleven, almost five foot eleven. Still this reptile towered over him. It wasn't fair.

But then inspiration hit.

Haden jumped up onto the coffee table. He almost slipped on a pile of *Architectural Digest* magazines, but he got his balance back and now they were standing face to face, and Beaumont was shocked into silence. Good thing, because Haden Krakauer was on a roll.

"What is this drama in your head—*The Count of Monte Cristo?* The tormented hero out for revenge? I have news for you, ass-face. You're the villain! And you always were. Self-pity doesn't change that. You went to jail? So what? You deserved it! Those were teenagers over there! Kids just out of high school, and you were selling them goddamn methamphetamine and cocaine! You know how you get over a meth addiction? Huh? Want to guess? You don't! Those kids are ruined forever, don't you get that? All they wanted to do was serve their country but they were weak and stupid and you took advantage of that and you destroyed their future—for money! For a few bucks you don't even remember spending. You're a criminal! They never should have let you out."

Beaumont stepped away, silent, but the creepy smile was gone—that was something. Finally he spoke. "I have things to do. Preparations for tonight. The front and back doors of this house are locked inside and out by electronic remote. The phone lines and the cable are cut. There's no basement and the crawlspace is sealed. I nailed the windows shut and disabled the alarm, so no one's gonna come running if you try to escape. Oh yeah, you'd like that wouldn't you? Back in a cozy jail cell with the perfect alibi. Forget it. You sit tight and think about what's going to happen—all those people dying and you taking the blame. Not just going to jail for the rest of your life, but knowing that everyone left alive on your precious little island is going to hate you forever. That's what you have to look forward to, Lieutenant."

Then he walked away, the length of the long high room to the stairs and down.

Haden stepped off the coffee table, feeling a first flicker of hope. So much depended on so much—if Beaumont was really as careless as he seemed, or as ignorant about the history and construction of Nantucket houses. If Haden could be swift and quiet enough. If he was physically up to the ordeal, and just as important—mentally up to it. He hated heights.

He took a breath. No time like the present.

He unbuttoned his cuff, shook the Swiss Army knife free, and cut himself loose from the flex-cuffs, bending his wrist inward to awkwardly saw at the hard plastic. It took a few minutes. His wrists were raw and red from chafing against the ridged plastic. He closed the knife and slipped it into his pocket, stretched his fingers, wiggled them. He was okay.

Cautiously, he crept past the fireplace to the third floor stairs. He waited, listening, leaning on a newel post.

The house was silent. He started up the stairs. On the third floor he climbed the wooden steps that led up to the widow's walk. The hatch had no lock. It was just a hinged square set into a square hole, meant for quick access in the event of a roof fire. Securing it would be difficult—and pointless, unless you were trying to protect your house from aerial assault by paratroopers.

Haden pushed with his shoulders and the slab moved up and tilted back to rest against the rail of the widow's walk. In a second he was on the roof deck, with a spectacular view of the Sound and the dunes. The gentle breeze touched his face, summoning a violent protective surge of love for this place, his place, his home.

Good, use it, he admonished himself. Get over this railing. Slide down the roof and climb down to the ground using the rose trellis. But the pitch was steep. Haden eased over the rail, let himself down, and his feet touched the wood shingles. Ideally he'd be wearing grippy rubber-soled sneakers on asphalt shingles. Leather uniform shoes on slippery cedar shakes? He'd skid like a car on black ice.

It was possible, though. The flat roof of one of the dormers began ten feet down. If he could stretch out flat, holding onto one of the platform's supports, the slide would only be a few feet. If the steep slope below him were sitting on the ground he could do it without a second thought. Right, because one mistake wouldn't kill him.

He took a breath and swung one leg over the rail, then the other one. Now his toes were pushed up against the spindles, resting on less than an inch of wood. He grasped the rail and leaned out a little, feeling the vertigo smother him. He had to step down onto the roof. It was no more than three feet below him, but he couldn't seem to reach it. His leg was dangling in midair. He bent the other knee, grabbed a spindle and eased himself lower. Where the hell was the roof? His shoulders started to cramp. He felt the first cold tentacles of panic curl around him. He refused to look down. That was what they always told you—don't look down. Great advice—until you actually needed to see something.

Finally, his foot touched the steep surface. Halfway there. He pushed hard with the sole of his shoe against the cedar shakes as he dropped the other leg. Then he was standing on the slippery pitch, gripping the widow's walk fence with both hands. Nothing to it! But the hard part was still ahead of him.

He gripped the spindles and started shuffling his feet down the slope. Immediately, they skidded out from under him. A scream rose in his throat, and he gagged to keep it in. This was like walking on wet marble—no traction at all.

It was impossible.

No, no, it could be done, he had to do it. Just breathe. He could feel his heartbeat pulsing in his throat like a wound. He went down on one knee, holding on to the end-boards of the decking and then the post that supported it. Another knee down as he inched hand over hand to the bottom of the post. He knees were taking his full weight, pressed to the ridged incline.

This was it. Now he had to stretch himself out flat and slide to the dormer roof. It couldn't be far, at the full extension of his body—maybe two or three feet, tops. Easy.

All he had to do was let go.

He took a breath, stretched out, released his grip on the splintery post, and let himself slide. Stomach churning seconds of slipping down the slick cedar…out of control…accelerating—then his feet touched the dormer roof. He took a moment to grab his breath and let his heart rate finally subside.

He slowly stretched up to his feet, turned, and gripped the edge of the dormer, haltingly shuffling backwards down toward the precipice of the main roof. That took him to a foot from the lethal thirty-foot drop. He edged around the corner, clinging onto the front of the dormer now, his back to the precipice. There was a tiny vertical gap between the storm window screen and the runner. He inched down, one hand still clutching the shingle at chest level. Was aluminum solid? Could he put all his weight on it and bring his other hand down, or would the thin, stripped screws pull loose and send him catapulting out into the vacant air?

Gulp and grip. He remained perched there, muscles locked onto the storm window frame by the fingertips of both hands.

Once more he lowered himself to his knees. This time, his toes extended over the edge of the roof. His foot pushed into the lattice and he exhaled.

He released one hand, stretched his arm down along his side. Of course, he couldn't reach the gutter. His hand brushed the rough grain of the third course of shingles from the brink. Not even close. Could he let go with the other hand? Hanging loose, attached to nothing, holding onto nothing, skittering over a hard rim into empty space. A few stomach-lifting seconds of free fall, then the shattering impact. Even if he survived, he'd be crippled for life. Nausea swam through him, schools of sluggish fish through dirty water.

Worse, he knew he didn't have the strength to pull himself back up. He'd just lie here on the warm ridges of resinous wood until he lost his grip and...

That was it. That was what he had to do. He had to work his feet out of the lattice and let go, snatch the gutter as he fell. He wouldn't have built up too much momentum, and as soon as he got a handhold he could jam his toes back hard into the lattice again...and climb down—if the lattice didn't tear off the wall. He had nailed his share of these trellises up when he was a kid, working for carpenters on summer vacations.

The nails were small. The setup was flimsy.

He was going to fall anyway if he waited much longer.

He gritted his teeth and let go.

It happened so fast it was as if it didn't happen at all. One second he sledded down, lurching off into the gulf of air. Next second the gutter bit into his palms and pain stabbed into his shoulders and he hung free, legs hitting the lattice, thorns biting him through his pants.

He dug his toes between the crisscrossed strapping and started down. Roses were blooming, perfuming the summer air. Stop and smell the roses? Some other time. He actually laughed out loud, more a nervous grunt of sheer physical relief than any actual amusement at his lame joke. Everyone hated his stupid jokes.

Fifteen feet above the ground, the lattice gave out. He heard a tearing sound and scuttled down for one more foot hold before he twisted around and jumped, landing face-first in a hydrangea bush. He struggled out of it, taking inventory of cuts and scratches, but otherwise okay.

He took a few deep breaths, loosening his muscles, looking up at the trellis above him, which leaned crazily away from the house. Scrambling out of the bushes, he stood up. Solid ground. Safe. He had made it. Now get back to Cliff Road, hitch into town, use the driver's cell phone to call the chief, and turn himself in again...

Ezekiel Beaumont stood three feet away from him with a taser gun in his hand.

Zeke applauded delicately, tapping his fingers on the heel of his hand. "Fantastic! That was a great show, Lieutenant. I wish I had it on video. It would definitely go viral. You'd get more hits than those Hitler cats. Well, I'd love to stay and chat. But we have a big night ahead of us and now it's time for me to live out one of my most cherished dreams—tasering a cop."

Before Haden could react, the conductive wires leapt out, the barbs dug into his shirt, and the voltage whipped through him.

He had time for one thought before he blacked out: He'd failed again.

Chapter Nineteen

Fugitives

They took me back to my own station house, walked me through to the holding cells from the garage, photographed me, fingerprinted me, and shoved me in one of my own cells. I glanced at the metal phone plate set into the wall. No way anyone would let me use it. No lawyer was coming to see me. I was totally cut off from the outside world. No one but Brad Pinckley at the booking desk even knew I'd been arrested. It was Miranda's night with the kids, though I was supposed to pick them up and take them to camp tomorrow morning.

Tornovitch came to see me, flanked by Daly and Knightley.

"Can you at least tell my family what happened?" I asked him. "They're going to start worrying tomorrow morning."

Jack grinned. "That's what all the terrorists say."

"I know what you're doing, Jack."

"Do you? Why don't you tell these law enforcement professionals then, Kennis? Share whatever outrageous story you've cooked up with them. They'll be taking notes for your slander trial."

Daly and Knightley looked at me like a sick monkey in some crumbling midwestern zoo. At least the chimp could throw his shit at them.

"I want to see my lawyer."

"Sure, Kennis. After the Pops concert."

"I'm going to stop you."

Jack laughed. "Are you talking to yourself now? Because that's a red flag for mental instability."

He followed the others out the door. They had taken my watch, wallet, and cell phone. No way of knowing the time. No television, no books, no magazines. Nothing to do but brood.

I had plenty to brood about. No one else in the NPD could possibly stumble on the tortured path of conjecture Franny and I had followed. No one in the JTTF would even be looking. Franny was still free, but coming to my defense would only get her thrown into a cell in the women's block. We had almost everything needed to take a case to court—a time line and a chain of causality, a motive and a plan, even a suspect. What we didn't have was proof, and Jack knew it.

I gave up on thinking. Whatever happened next, being well rested could tip the odds in my favor. I slept a deep hungry dreamless sleep on the hard cement that night, using my clothes for a pillow.

I woke up stiff, sore, and ravenous. No breakfast. No one came in at all. Lunchtime came and went. The orders were obviously to leave me alone. I paced the cell, went through sets of calisthenics and breathing exercises. Finally, I settled back on the slab to wait.

I'd been waiting there for most of the day when I heard Franny's voice outside the door, bits and pieces of a conversation. "Special detention," "heightened security," "enemy combatant protocols." Knightley answered, but his voice was pitched too low. I couldn't make out anything he said.

Finally the door opened.

"—and let's try to get this done quickly. Jack wants him out of here before the press conference."

"He didn't mention any press conference, Agent Tate, and I don't—"

"It's on a need to know basis, Knightley. I don't think he plans on having you talk to the press. Or would you like that? I can put in a word with him."

"No, no—it's just...I wasn't notified."

She stopped walking and cocked her head at him with a small quizzical smile that wondered, 'Is it possible? Can you actually be this stupid?' She said, "Consider yourself notified."

"Should he be cuffed?"

Franny produced a pair. "Unlock it and step back."

Knightley unlocked the cell and pulled it open. I moved into the narrow corridor and held out my arms. Franny snapped the cuffs on.

"Which vehicle will we be using for transport?" Knightley asked.

"I'll grab anything that's available. But I'm taking him alone."

"Are you sure that's a good idea?"

"I can handle it, Knightley."

"But it's not procedure. I'm going to have to check with Jack."

"Fine." She glanced at her watch. "Just be quick."

He pulled out his cell, turned his back, and took a few steps away to give himself the illusion of privacy. He was standing that way—with most of his weight on his right leg—when Franny attacked.

She drove a kick into the back of his right knee. He dropped the phone with a grunt and pitched backward. Franny caught him in a classic choke hold, forearm across his neck, yanking her own wrist with the other hand to cut off the circulation. It was swift and brutal. In less than five seconds, Knightley was unconscious on the floor. I gaped at her efficiency.

She pushed the handcuff key into my palm. "Let's go."

She opened the door and yanked me out, walked me across the booking room to a side door, nodding to Pinckley.

"Everything okay, Agent Tate?" he asked.

"We're running behind. When Knightley gets out of the bathroom tell him to meet me there."

Then we were outside in the dense heat of the late afternoon, walking past the big reserve oil tanks and into the green-fenced security parking lot. "Sorry this took so long. Jack had me running security at the airport all day. I just found out what happened."

"Franny, what are you doing?"

"What I can, Hank. The only thing I can."

"You attacked a federal officer and aided and abetted a prisoner escape. Franny! Look at me. You just flushed your career down the toilet."

"If we're wrong, that's the least of what I did. But we're right. And I—shit."

I followed her eyes. Jack's Expedition was skidding into the lot.

"Knightley must have hit speed dial."

Jack and Agent Daly piled out of the car. They both had their guns out.

"Franny, what the hell do you think you're doing?"

"I'm transporting the prisoner to a more secure location."

"Nice try. But this is the only secure location on Nantucket. He's going back into his cell and you're under arrest. Step away from him."

Jack hadn't used a gun in a long time, and he was at least a decade away from his last training course. He forgot the primary rule for controlling a suspect at gunpoint: keep your distance. Maybe he didn't think Franny was dangerous enough to be worth treating with caution. But he hadn't seen her in the detainment room with Knightley.

Franny stamped down hard on his instep, drove her shoulder into his solar plexus and twisted the gun out of his hand. The attack distracted Daly for a second, and I tackled him. We landed hard on the asphalt and his gun clattered away. We struggled briefly, but he had sixty pounds on me and my hands were cuffed. He rolled onto my chest, his fist pulled back for a punch, when Franny's voice froze him.

"Flat on the ground, both of you," she said. "Now."

Daly eased himself off me and lay down next to Jack. I scrambled to my feet. I was winded, but I had landed on top of the big FBI agent, which cushioned the fall. I scanned the building. No one was running out here, no shots had been fired. Someone would notice the ruckus in the parking lot.

"Go," Franny said. "I'll cover for you."

"Franny—"

"It's your island, Hank. Save it. You're the only one who can. "

I took off. I considered stealing Jack's SUV for the space of a few steps—the motor was still running. But my chances were better moving overland on foot. Within half an hour, state and local police, FBI and National Guard units would be patrolling every road and street on the island. I had to get under cover fast and formulate a plan. I clambered over the chain link fence beyond the concrete apron and made my way behind the businesses that fronted oñ Old South Road. I scrambled over fences and clattered through backyards, construction sites and parking lots. I stood listening for a moment or two, catching my breath. No shots, alarms or sirens, so far.

I lurched forward again. I was running hard when I almost fell into a trench Toscana was digging for a new sewer line. I managed to jump it but that slammed me into a dense hedge with a wood barrier on the other side. I grabbed the coarse bushes to regain my balance. There was no way through. I took a few seconds to unlock the handcuffs, threw them into the open trench, and headed for the street.

I was in plain sight then, clothes torn, bleeding from my hands and scalp, panting. I was about as hard to miss as a snapping turtle on a shell driveway, and I wasn't moving much faster at that point. A couple of cars had already slowed down to get a good look at me. Gossip traveled fast. The police chief was stumbling toward the airport, looking—as my mother-in-law loved to say—"Like he was dragged through a knothole sideways."

I was about to make a break for the other side of the road when a red Ford 150 pulled over. The driver honked twice and craned his head out the window. Pat Folger.

"Climb in, Chief," he called out. I sprinted to the truck. When I was inside and he was accelerating into traffic again, he took a good look at me and said, "Christ on a cracker! What the hell happened?"

I was still catching my breath. We slowed down behind a line of cars.

"It's a bomb, ain't it?"

We crawled forward.

"Yeah. You're going to hear that I had something to do with this, that I helped Haden Krakauer escape, but—"

He cut me off with a laugh that turned into a wheeze. "Sorry, Chief. That goddamn cedar's killing me. But you can't use the shitty pine they sell any more, so you're screwed either way." He grabbed a tissue off the center console and blew his nose. "So what are you asking? Will I buy their bullshit and turn you in? Forget about it. I may look stupid but we know better."

"How's Rick doing?" I asked him.

"Good, he's doing good. He knows antiques. And he got his business sense from me."

"How about Doug?"

"One day at a time, right? I just wish he'd get off this goddamn island. It's tough for the kids here, Chief. I'm telling ya. But at least you nailed those Bulgarian shitbags. Every little bit helps."

We drove through the intersection, and I directed him to turn in at the *Shoals* parking lot. It was my best solution to the immediate problem of getting off the street. David Trezize would hide me. He had computers and telephones, so I could contact my family and keep up with what was happening. He even had pals on the force. He tried to keep his sources secret, but it was a small town, and he was Barnaby Toll's godfather.

I climbed out of the truck.

"Thanks, Pat."

He wagged a finger at me. "Go catch these assholes. That's what we pay you for."

Then he backed into a two point turn and took off.

I was lucky. The office was deserted in the late afternoon. But David would be there. He was always there.

The ground floor of the small building held the advertising and circulation departments. There were no presses. The paper was printed off-island. Downstairs, David had converted the basement into a brightly-lit office space with five desks, a microwave, a mini fridge and a two burner electric hot plate. David was on the floor fiddling with the tangle of computer wiring behind one of the desktop monitors when I came down the stairs and knocked on the door.

"Come in, Chief," he called. "And tell me—why are you suddenly public enemy number one around here?"

I went into the cramped little bathroom and scrubbed the blood off my head, washed my hands and dried off. David was waiting with a mug of coffee when I got out.

"Fresh pot," he said. "Jamaica Blue Mountain. Chemex. The coffee nerd's holy grail."

I took a sip. The coffee was strong but not bitter.

"So tell me the story. It can be off the record. I just want to know what's going on."

Small and pudgy, he looked like an alert otter behind his thick glasses. I felt like a fish in a stream, waiting for him to pounce.

"I'll be happy to talk on the record when this thing is over."

"And when will that be?"

I looked at the big clock on the wall above the Xerox machine. It was just before four thirty in the afternoon. The concert started at seven. The fireworks were scheduled for eight thirty, to coincide with the William Tell Overture finale.

"Around four hours from now," I said.

He poured himself a mug of coffee, and swung his arm with it inclusively, as if he was showing me the office for the first time. "Look at this place, Chief. Here I have this amazingly efficient little news organization, single handed, in a place where *nothing newsworthy ever happens*! And what am I doing? The biggest story I'm following now is this Eastern European prostitution ring. Can you believe that? You know how the girls signify they're available? They sit at a bar drinking scotch on the rocks or a martini—through a straw. That's the code. That's how the johns find them. Little details like that make my life worthwhile. Chief? Hello? Anyone in there?"

I was staring past him seeing that tall blond guy at Cru the night of the first bombing, laughing with some gorgeous blonde, her scotch on the rocks through a straw. That guy was Zeke Beaumont. Another piece of the puzzle slipped into place. Now I knew how he'd found his little hit squad to attack me at the golf course jobsite. The Bulgarians were a full service operation.

I turned back to David. "When this is over I'll give you an exclusive, David. But I'm running out of time, and right now I don't have a clue."

I sat down in front of one of the computers, thinking about Tornovitch and Beaumont. I kept coming back to the military connection.

How would a military assault on the area work? An artillery barrage to cover an amphibian landing. But you'd need a mercenary army for that, not to mention landing craft and some serious air cover. Haden had told me he saw someone selling a rebuilt World War II DUCK on e-Bay. Could these guys have gotten their hands on an Air Force surplus bomber, too?

No, they didn't have that kind of money. They weren't pilots. They weren't mechanics, either. I was way off track. I went back. Something in that aerial train of thought resonated. Beaumont's behavior at the AIDS benefit had convinced me he was a veteran—that rant about the fireworks, the way they simulated an actual attack.

The fireworks. Was it possible?

I jumped up and pushed into David's private office. He was hunched over the computer. Behind him, on the poster from *The Great Escape*, Steve McQueen was still above that second fence, doomed to failure and not giving a shit.

"David." He looked up. "Have you heard anything about the security arrangements for the fireworks barge?"

"Uh, yeah—they're letting the locals take care of it. Drummond Brothers are doing the show, like always. The town's been using them for years. They've been in business since the fifties.

Old man Drummond served in Patton's Sixth Armored Division in the Second World War. He was an artillery expert and I guess it felt natural to—oh shit. Are you thinking what I'm thinking?"

I nodded. "That's why Jack let the NPD handle the security. He thinks we're incompetent."

"Jack? Jack Tornovitch?"

I nodded again.

"Okay, what the fuck is happening here?"

"It's a long story."

"I bet you could give it to me in three sentences. I can give you *Moby Dick* in three sentences. Whale bites off ship captain's leg. Captain goes insane and spends five hundred pages searching for the whale. He finds the whale and it kills him. The end. Three sentences. Look, I'm a newspaperman, Chief. Just give me the lead."

I took a breath. "Okay. It's a revenge story, David. Just like *Moby Dick*. Haden Krakauer killed Jack's lover—indirectly, maybe. But the girl is still dead. So he's framing Haden for the bombings. It was all leading up to blowing the Pops concert into the stratosphere, and Haden is on the loose now—perfect to take the blame for the attack. Everyone thinks I helped Haden get away, so I'm right up there on the Wanted poster with him."

He squinted at me. "Tornovitch can't be doing this alone. There has to be an accomplice."

"There's an accomplice. There's an Iraq war drug scandal. There's a military cover up. There's identity theft, and infidelity, and murder. But I'm out of time to talk."

"Tell me one thing. Did you actually help Krakauer escape?"

"Hell, no. I want him in jail. He'd be safe in jail. Jack pulled that little trick."

"He sounds tricky."

"He is."

"And he's winning."

"So far."

David took off his glasses rubbed his eyes. "What are we going to do?"

I smiled. "I'm going to stop him. And you're going to write about it."

"Fair enough."

"I'm going home to get my gun."

"Chief—"

"David, call Miranda. Tell her I'm all right. Tell her not to go to the concert. And tell her to spread the rumor that there's a bomb at the beach. You too. There's a couple of hours left. Tell everyone you can. There's no way to get the word out officially, but we still have gossip on our side. Spread the rumor. And stay away from Jetties Beach tonight. Just in case."

He shook my hand with an awkward solemnity. I went upstairs and slipped out the back door, across the parking lot, into the pine woods behind Valero's garden store, and gone.

Chapter Twenty

"… the bombs bursting in air"

I checked the clock on my way out. Six forty-five—I'd been at the *Shoals* office for more than two hours. How was that possible? I had less than two hours before the fireworks began. I needed a car. I needed a Coast Guard helicopter. And I had nothing.

I thought of David's Subaru, but I knew the emergency protocols. I had written them myself. With roadblocks at the Rotary and Fairgrounds Road you could close off all access to downtown from the east and south ends of the island, which included the airport and the inner harbor, as well as Squam, Quidnet, Polpis, 'Sconset, Shimmo, Monomoy, Madequecham…virtually the whole island. A single cruiser at the intersection of Cliff Road and Madaket Road would cut off access from the west.

If you were driving.

I was running, through the Naushop subdivision, behind the storage yards at Valero's and the Emporium parking lot, into the strip of dense undeveloped scrub oak and pitch pine beside the bike path, and finally out between the water company buildings to Milestone Road.

A roadblock had backed up traffic. I had to cross the street, which meant being seen. I crouched in the bushes beyond the bike path. I couldn't afford to choose my moment. Taking a deep breath I sprinted across the asphalt, dodging between the hood of one pickup and the tail gate of another and breaking for the trees, just ahead of a Yates gas truck heading out of town.

My breath was rasping in my throat as I skirted the wetlands at the edge of the harbor, parallel to Orange Street, behind Our Island Home and Marine Home Center, over railings and walls, through backyards, smelling the ripe marshy perfume of the harbor, scraping my hands on the rough wood of the fences, listening for sirens, the black clock ticking down in my head.

Eventually the shoreline curved away from my route and I veered back toward the street, maybe fifty yards from the duck pond where Union Street hooks its sharp left for the straight run into town.

Traffic was light and I saw no pedestrians. Most people were at the concert by now or eating dinner. I crossed the grassy vacant lot at the corner of Union and started up Orange Street. I walked fast, looking down or turning away when a car came toward me. Running would draw attention. When I passed York Street I expected to see a police car or two parked in front of my house. But there was just a gardener's truck with its trailer loaded with lawn mowers.

I didn't get it. Why would Jack leave my house unguarded? I jogged back down the street and ran to Dover Street—the next one over. There was a dark blue state police cruiser parked far up the road, almost all the way to Pleasant Street.

◇◇◇

I cut between garages, pulled myself over a crumbling retaining wall and crouched in the middle of my neighbor's wild blackberry patch. I scratched up my hands picking a few while I studied my backyard. The berries were delicious, tart and juicy, and I was hungry. I ate some more. I felt like a character in one of the fairy tales I used to read to my kids, miraculously surviving on nuts and berries in some enchanted forest. But my forest had scraps of toilet paper caught in the privet and beer cans in the bushes.

The yard was empty, the street was quiet. I held my breath, listening. Birds in the trees, a distant radio, leaves rustling in the south wind. Two mopeds grumbling by on Orange Street. Nothing else.

As I pushed through the hedge, a neighborhood dog caught my scent and yelped out the alarm. It turned into a chorus, but no one came charging out of the house. I crossed the yard quickly to the basement entrance, let myself in, and crept up the dark stairs to the door that opened into my kitchen.

I could hear the television faintly from inside. I opened the door a crack. Someone was listening to the NFL network. Where else could you watch the famous 1990 Redskins–49ers NFC playoff game on a summer evening? Whoever got the inside duty was taking it easy. Probably drinking my beer, too. All the better for me.

I eased into the kitchen. Maybe I could time my dash to the bedroom with Montana's big interception. One step inside and two men jumped me. They grabbed my arms while a third one put a gun to my head. He was young and eager, with the same storm trooper crew cut and heavy leather utility belt as the others.

"We got him, Captain Fraker! We got him!"

"Calm down, son," I said. "We don't want any accidents here today."

"Step away from the chief," Lonnie said, in his always surprising high-pitched nasal voice. It occurred to me that with a full head of hair and a baritone he could have been running the State Police by now.

The kid backed off.

"Do we take him in, sir? Should I handcuff him?" said the one holding my left arm. He smelled of Thai food and Old Spice cologne.

"Not quite yet. Let him go and stand down."

"Sir?"

"Just do it, Humphries."

"Are you going to read him his rights?"

"He knows his rights. Go inside and turn off the television." He turned back to me. "Those dogs gave you away, Chief. Tough to sneak around a neighborhood with dogs everywhere."

I massaged my arm where one of the troopers had grabbed me. "Four guys?"

"The order came straight from Tornovitch. Guys everywhere. There's a Red Alert out for you. Armed and dangerous, mandated use of extreme force. Seems like you're a regular terrorist now, Chief."

"You believe that?"

He laughed. "Hell no."

The kid came back from the living room and set the remote on the counter.

"Hell of a game," Fraker said. "Too bad they didn't have instant replay in those days. What a steal. Bad calls are the worst. Like today. The biggest asshole east of the Mississippi informed the whole JTTF that you and Krakauer are trying to blow up the island. *You and Krakauer.*"

"No one's going to argue with Jack Tornovitch. If the war on terror goes on long enough, he'll be running the whole show."

"Ain't it always the way. Assholes run everything."

The clock ticked. A noisy crowd of kids passed the house, heading into town.

"Here's what I think," he went on. "You came back for your Glock—come on, why else? You don't need your cuff links, Chief."

"So?"

"So I'm betting against the assholes, for once. Go grab your gun."

"Sir," the big trooper blurted. "You can't do this."

Lonnie's gun snapped in his hand, and his arm came up fast and precisely calibrated, like one sweep of a windshield wiper set on high. "I'm doing it," he said. "Step away from Chief Kennis. Now."

"But sir—that's insubordination, abetting a fugitive, obstruction of justice—you could lose your job, you could go to jail, and—"

"But only if it's true, Stallings. Only if it's true. Set your guns down on the floor. All of you."

He caught my eye and jerked his head to the left—get going. I sprinted into the bedroom, opened the gun safe in the closet, pulled out the Glock and a spare magazine. I pulled a knapsack from a high shelf and I snagged a change of clothes from the drawers—shirt and socks, pants and a sweater. I was going to be chilled to the bone by the time I finished my night's work.

Lonnie was waiting for me at the kitchen door, his soldiers huddled together by the sink. I pushed past them to grab a plastic trash bag and stuffed the clothes into it, then jammed the bundle into the knapsack.

I was ready to go.

Lonnie had his gray, wide brimmed police hat in his hand. He dug a set of car keys out of his pocket and dangled them in front of me.

"I parked a cruiser on Dover Street. Maybe you noticed. Take it and go. I don't want to know where you're going and you don't want to tell me." He pulled a pair of Maui Jims out of his breast pocket, extended the hat. "Put this on. Take the sunglasses, too. No one'll give you second glance."

I put on the hat and sunglasses. After a brief appraising cud-chew, like he was cleaning his teeth with his tongue, he nodded his approval. "Close enough for Nantucket, right? Don't stop. Don't talk to anyone."

"Thanks, Lonnie."

I paused in the kitchen one more time to grab a plastic freezer storage bag out of the drawer beside the fridge. Then I went out the way I came in, down the basement stairs, through the hedge, over the retaining wall to Dover Street.

It was full dark as I climbed into the cruiser and gunned the engine. The dashboard clock read 8:01. Time was tearing past. I resisted the urge to use the flashers. Traffic was light and I didn't want to call attention to myself. But I could feel panic tightening around my head like a metal band. If I was too late, if Beaumont launched those bombs…but it was crazy to think that way, stupid. I had to concentrate, and I had to keep moving—nothing else.

No distractions.

A National Guard Humvee rolled past me on Cliff Road, heading for town. The driver saluted. I saluted back.

Five minutes later I was pulling up in front of Beaumont's at the Deacon's Way hideout. The rose trellis was leaning crazily off the house. Had someone been trying to climb it? I glanced up at the widow's walk. It was possible. Beaumont had stashed Haden here, and he had tried to escape. He didn't make it though, or I would have heard from him. I took a breath. He had to be alive. Zeke still needed him. More than that, Zeke still needed to punish him.

I slipped the Glock into the plastic bag, and sprinted over to the open garage, unbuttoning my shirt. When I was down to my boxer briefs I grabbed the surfboard out of the garage. It was a nine-six, bright yellow longboard, the color dulled by layers of surf wax—perfect. I slipped the knapsack back over my shoulders, and jammed my feet into my heavy police brogans. I wouldn't have to run in them much more. I had blisters from the afternoon's exertions and the leather was raw against my bare feet. But that was better than trying to run barefoot through the bracken that lined the dunes.

I could see the lights of the fireworks barge from the beach, and hear the music, mysterious and romantic, drifting across the dune grass on the pale wind. The clear night spread across a dense crust of stars. I could just make out an embedded sliver of moon. With the low-tide smell of the salt water in my nose I took the plastic bag in my teeth, threw the board flat on the still water, and started paddling. The water was shallow and tepid.

I calculated the distance at half a mile. I dug in hard, tasting the plastic, breathing through my nose, watching the nose of the surfboard as it cut through the water, skimming just above the surface. There was no police presence in the harbor—not a Coast Guard cutter, nothing. It confirmed my suspicions. Tornovitch must have called them off. It was a good plan, but it was working against him now. He had emptied the Sound of anyone who might stall or impede me.

The music stopped and the crackle of applause floated out from shore. After a few moments of rustling silence, the orchestra launched into the William Tell Overture. I matched my strokes to the thumping beat of the music The fireworks were about to begin.

I was almost out of time.

A big motor launch bobbed at the side of the barge, tied off to a spar. That had to be Beaumont's ride. The barge was massive, riding high in the water. I slipped off the surfboard. The incoming tide would pull the board into the harbor. If some civic-minded yachtsman turned it in to the police, or some broke scalloper tried to sell it on the Nantucket Re-Use exchange, I'd know. And if some greedy surfer snagged it? I'd put Billy Delavane—and his daughter—on the lookout. It would give her another chance to play junior detective.

I pulled myself up on the deck.

Beaumont was at the far end, working a triple mortar on a tripod base. It looked like a giant's three-barreled shotgun, set into a hinged framework that Beaumont was cranking to horizontal using a wheel in the side. The whole thing had an ominously homemade look to it. The deranged hobbyist with his lethal toys.

Randy Ray and a summer special named Paul, along with the two Drummond brothers, were lying unconscious at my end of the barge. Closer to Beaumont's launcher, I could make out the unconscious form of Haden Krakauer in the flickering light.

It was exactly as I had predicted. Now it was down to me and Ezekiel Beaumont on this floating stage, surrounded by wood frames for the fireworks, filled with big clay cylinders and banks of cannons. With their basketball-sized heads they looked like racks of oversized ice-cream cones. I lay there getting ready to rush Beaumont as the first round of fireworks started going off on an electronic timer. They shot out of the three-foot mortars, each with the company logo engraved in the base. The booming fusillades left smoke trails hanging in the air. The small missiles flew to the top of their arc and exploded, bathing the barge in a flash of gaudy carnival light.

The music was swelling from the beach. I pulled my gun out of the bag and scrambled to my feet as another round launched.

Beaumont sensed my movement. He spun around and stared at me, dumbfounded. The rest of his features jerked back from his mouth, until his face was nothing but a blade of nose and two shrinking eyes, fast disappearing into his cheekbones. Beaumont couldn't fathom my appearance. How could I have figured him out, and caught him in the act?

He didn't even try for his gun, stuck into his waist band with the ski mask he wore during the initial attack. No one could testify later that he wasn't Haden Krakauer. Zeke was at least five inches taller, but it was dark and concussions scrambled eyewitness testimony. It could have worked, and it still might. I hadn't stopped him yet.

I stepped forward, gun leveled at him. "Move away from the mortar."

"You can't be here. You're in jail."

"Step away from the mortar, Beaumont."

"How could you possibly know my name?"

"I know all about you. Now move."

He tipped his head toward the launcher. "They're cluster bombs. Three of them. An antipersonnel unit and two incendiaries, all on a timer. Nothing you can do but watch the show."

I stepped closer.

"You going to shoot me, Mr. Police Chief? You can't do it. Not like some gangland execution. You're no killer."

I edged over to his side, past the rows of fireworks cannons, Beaumont watching me. The music from the beach was reaching a crescendo. We stood ten feet apart when the fireworks finale began. The cannons behind me jumped with a series of concussive blasts, like thunder and lightning ripping open the sky. I was stunned, deafened, immobilized.

Beaumont saw it and leapt at me.

I fired, but his movement rocked the barge. I missed. His shoulder drove into my chest, pitching us both into the water. I managed a breath before I went under, but I lost the gun. His shoes dug down on my shoulders, pushing me deeper as he clambered back onto the raft. I thrashed in the water and broke the surface. He wrestled his own gun out of his pants. The ear-shattering fusillade continued. He kicked at me and missed. I grabbed his ankle and he reeled backward.

I had one knee on the platform when he pulled the trigger.

Nothing happened—water had jammed his firing mechanism. His turn to be stunned. I took the split second advantage and lunged up at him. My head drilled into his stomach and knocked him over, slamming him hard on his back. I stomped his torso, stepped on his throat, and kicked his head lurching past him for the mortars. I heard him choking as I cranked the big barrels up toward vertical.

The wheel was stiff, turning too slowly. My arms burned, my throat seized, my body rocked with the effort. Too heavy, too much resistance, not moving fast enough. My skin crawled. Panic seized me. The blast could come any moment.

Beaumont flung himself at me, tipping the barge as he landed, his weight knocking the wind out of me. We struggled, wet, straining with effort, my arms aching, my shoulders cramping.

He pressed me to the deck, rasping, "Three seconds left. It's over."

A burst of sheer rage and hate rocketed me up to knock him off and crawl under the mortars. I heaved upward with all the strength I had left. I hit the barrels, punching them vertical just as they went off. The explosion battered me. The fire singed my hair, the hot metal seared my shoulders. The waistband of my boxers ignited. I rolled frantically on the planks to put out sparks as the bombs flew up. Haunted seconds of silence closed around me. Four seconds, five seconds, six. The other fireworks finished. The night sky hung soundless, trailing streamers of fading smoke, awaiting the big bang finale.

Then the explosions hit, booming and concussive. The sky burst into flame as the napalm rained down and sizzled into the harbor, well short of the beach. I curled and covered my head when the first blast wave punched. The force pounded me onto the deck. The next blast waves slammed down like sandbags dropping on me, hammering my knees against the deck, crushing the air out of my chest, smacking my face against the wood. My head was ringing and my face was bleeding. The air around me turned into a raging tantrum, flinging shrapnel and gobs of burning napalm.

I struggled to my knees, dazed, to look around. Boxes of munitions stood stacked near the wheelhouse, meant to be loaded as the finale progressed. If they caught on fire, the whole barge would blow. I heaved mysef to my feet, stumbled over Beaumont's prostrate body, hobbled through patches of flame to the wheelhouse, yanked open the door, sucking charred air into my lungs, and pawed at the wall for a fire extinguisher. I felt cold metal and grabbed the cylinder off its hook, starting to spray down the deck fires. My back burned, and I twisted something pushing up on the mortars. My ribs had shifted, I'd twisted my spine. I was scorched—my body shrieked in pain from my neck to my tail bone.

When I limped to the other end of the barge, Haden was biting and kicking Beaumont. I pointed the nozzle at Zeke, then dropped it. I was too shaky, and they were too close together. I might miss and hit Haden.

Haden didn't need me anyway. He held Beaumont around the neck, brought a knee up hard into the bigger man's gut, then stepped away and threw a roundhouse punch with his whole weight and all the torque from his bending body behind it. The blow exploded on the point of Beaumont's jaw, dropping him, but the scream of pain came from Haden, cradling his right hand.

"Fuck! I broke my hand!"

I dropped the fire extinguisher. "Are you all right?"

He grinned in the flickering red light "I'm great. We beat them, Chief. It doesn't get any better than this."

A cell phone rang from Beaumont's figure on the deck—that irritating, ringtone playing, and then playing again, louder and more urgent. I rummaged through his clothes to find it in a side pocket of his green camouflage cargo pants. The phone was a cheap throwaway, untraceable. The screen ID listed 'Scooter,' but the phone stopped ringing as I grabbed it. I pushed the SEND button, determined to fake Beaumont's reedy voice and slight southern accent. Two could play at that game.

Beaumont's accomplice answered with one word, the way he always did.

"Tornovitch."

It stopped me for a second, the gap between being sure of something and really knowing it, between theory and truth.

"Hey, Scooter," I drawled.

"I heard the bombs but no sirens. What's happening over there?"

I disconnected the call, as if brushing a bug off my arm.

"Jack?" Haden asked.

I nodded. "He doesn't know what's going on. My bet is he's still at the station, putting on his show. Fearless leader of the DHS."

His teeth gleamed through the smoke and soot. "Okay, it just got better."

"Let's get moving. It won't take long for him to figure out his plan went sideways."

My son Tim, who had watched the display from the roof of a friend's house on Lincoln Circle, summed it up perfectly the next morning. "Best fireworks ever."

We revived the Drummonds and our cops. Shivering, I shrugged out of the knapsack and pulled the dry clothes out of the plastic bag, grateful for the sweater. No shoes, though—I had been moving too fast, and left my brogans on the beach when I hit the water. It didn't matter. I'd live.

I shackled Beaumont with Barnaby's handcuffs, and guided, pushed rolled and dragged everyone into the launch, keeping Beaumont up front with me. Haden stayed behind to secure the crime scene. There was a phone in the wheelhouse, so he could make the necessary calls. The most important call, to the station house. Tornovitch had to be held there, by force if necessary, until I arrived.

Elvis wasn't leaving the building. Not on my watch.

The whole left side of Beaumont's face was starting to bruise. At first I thought it was from Haden's beating but the contusions were too severe. The blast waves must have slapped him against the deck. I probably didn't look much better. Enraged, Beaumont kept his mouth shut. We were all battered and half-deaf. My body felt like a tuning fork, vibrating with the others—one harmonic pitch of horror and shock. My hands trembled starting the engine.

I eased the boat away from the barge and headed for the Hy-Line pier. Patches of napalm were still burning on the black water, like campfires on a battlefield.

Three cruisers waited for us on Straight Wharf. Howie and Randy hustled Beaumont into one car and the Drummonds into another. I hobbled to the third and climbed into the passenger side of the front seat. Kyle Donnelly was driving.

"You look like shit," he said happily.

"Good to see you, too. Now get me to the station."

"Can't do it, boss. You're going to the hospital."

"I'm fine."

"You're trashed! You can barely walk. You were obviously— I'm not sure how to put this—*on fire* a few minutes ago."

He was right. I needed help. "Swing by my house on the way. I want to grab some shoes."

Tim Lepore was on duty that night. He had worked at Mass General treating gang war victims, and he had an amusingly astringent bedside manner. He bound up my ribs and rubbed some new burn cream on my face and shoulders. He even had a spare shirt in his office. While he was there he grabbed some Tylenol-codeine samples. "So you won't have to get a prescription." He refused to charge me for them, and when I asked about taking more than the normal dose to get to sleep, he was typically gruff. "Take as many as you need."

"They're not addictive?"

"They're for pain, Chief. When the pain goes away so will the pills. Relax. You're not going to be selling your body for Tylenol-codeine. Now get out of here. I have people with real problems to treat."

Kyle drove me back to the station. I wanted to brace Tornovitch and get some answers. Where did they procure the explosives? And the boat Beaumont used? Most of all—why did he do it? Was it really a girl in Kuwait? Was she so important to him that it still hurt, a full decade later? And how could he bear to wait so long for Beaumont's release, to plan so meticulously, and then set the plan aside for years? Did he care about the consequences of his reprisal? The people who would have died? Did he even understand it? Maybe not—for a true sociopath, no one else is real.

Still, I wanted to ask him and to see his face when he answered. I got my chance a few minutes later, not that it did me any good.

We turned into the parking lot of the station and stopped at a line of yellow crime scene tape. Crowds had gathered on the berm and both sides of Fairgrounds Road. All of my officers and half the summer specials were milling around the lot, barricaded away from the front doors by Lonnie Fraker, half a dozen staties and a couple of FBI suits.

Kyle parked the big SUV. I wrenched the door open, ducked under the tape and pushed my way past a jack-booted crew-cut off-island State Police storm trooper. Wearing a threadbare cotton sweater with chinos and a pair of topsiders, I didn't look particularly impressive—one more curious citizen. The trooper grabbed my arm as I brushed past, but I shook him off.

"Hey—!" he shouted after me.

"That's the police chief, asshole," I heard Donnelly say. "This is his house."

Nicely put, Kyle. Couldn't have put it better myself.

Jogging toward the big brick façade I saw Franny talking to one of the FBI guys. I shoved and shouldered up to them.

"What's going on?"

Franny spun around. "Jack's locked himself in his office. He says he'll shoot anyone who comes through the door."

"Shit."

"Well, we were right about him, at least."

"I have the cell phone he used with Beaumont. He's finished." I took her hand. "Come on." We jogged together to the big glass doors.

Lonnie Fraker was the last line of defense. "What are you going to do in there, Chief?"

"End this."

"I have a SWAT team scrambling right now."

"No! Tell them to stand down. I'm not turning this station in a war zone, Lonnie. Let me handle it."

He squinted at me. "You couldn't handle a hamster right now, Chief."

"Thanks. That's perfect. The more unthreatening I look, the better."

"But—"

"And he has me for backup," Franny said. "I know Jack Tornovitch. We've worked together for years. He trusts me."

Lonnie was still hesitating.

"Give us fifteen minutes, Lonnie. Okay? Fifteen minutes. Then you can storm the place."

He stepped aside, cocked his wrist to check his watch. "Okay. Starting now."

The big station was deserted in the spinning red and blue lights from the flashers in the lot. I thought back to a night in Los Angeles, that gangbanger in Compton, rap-battling me with what seemed like half the LAPD parked out front. The same angry lights, the same weird hush like the whisper of something big and heavy dropping from a roof.

I grabbed the key to Haden Krakauer's office out of the dispatch desk drawer and led Franny up the back stairs. Good to have her beside me. Poetry wasn't going to help me tonight, and I needed all the help I could get.

I banged on the door. "Jack, it's Henry. Franny is out here, too."

"Going to negotiate with me, Kennis?"

"I have the key. We're coming in."

"What's the deal? Immunity? Who do I trade for that? There's no one above me, Kennis."

"If you're willing to talk, not just about this…scheme of yours, but about the drug traffic in the Army, in Iraq. There was somebody above you there. You couldn't have moved those drugs into the country by yourself. Beaumont's probably ratting him out right now. You're going to want to get in on that."

Tornovitch laughed. "He's been trying to rat that turd out for a decade, Kennis."

"But now he has corroboration. Now you can back him up. You have nothing to lose."

"You can say that again, Boy Wonder."

He had called me that in L.A. I'd forgotten. "We can build a case together, Jack. Let's try."

Another laugh. "You are so full of shit. You'd say anything to get this gun out of my hand."

I fitted the key into the lock, turned it. My own gun was long gone, at the bottom of Nantucket Sound.

"We're coming in, Jack. Let's do this face to face."

I pushed open the door. He was standing beside the window in the swirling illumination from the flashers. Red and blue blobs of light traversed his white face. The all-American terrorist. The big Glock was pointed at the space between us.

"Jack—" Franny started.

"I knew you'd turn on me eventually," he said to her. "Just a matter of time. You probably have them writing your name on my office door already. But just check your dedicated DHS Command e-mail account. Seriously, come here—take a look. I have it up on the screen. It looks like you were sabotaging fireworks security. All the commands to clear the harbor came from you."

"You wouldn't—"

"Of course I would. If I have to go down I'm taking you with me."

"And if the plan had worked—"

"You'd be going down alone. You and Beaumont. I needed a conspirator inside the DHS so I could walk away clean. You were the perfect choice. Because you trusted me."

Out of control, she darted across the room to his desk. Jack knew how to push her buttons.

"Franny!" I shouted. Too late.

Jack grabbed her and jammed his gun against her forehead.

I said, "This is pointless. I have your phone. It stores the last ten calls, all them from you. I'm taking you down, Scooter. You're looking at twenty years to life."

Franny tried a different tack. "I know you're angry, Jack, furiously angry and brokenhearted and—"

"You know nothing!" He gripped her harder, drilled the gun into her temple. "Don't you fucking patronize me, you little slut. I'm not some mook you can talk down from a ledge. You're coming with me. You're my ticket out of here."

I edged a few steps closer, keeping myself between them and the door. "Don't do this, Jack. Put the gun down."

"You've got to be kidding."

"Put it down and I can help you."

"Listen to him," Franny said.

Jack roared, "Shut up bitch! One more word and I will shoot you in the face just to shut. You. The. Fuck. Up."

I took a breath and brought out my last weapon. It wasn't a gun or a knife. It was a name.

"Sarah wouldn't want this, Jack."

He froze as if I'd just told him he was walking through a mine field. "What? What did you say?"

I slipped closer, pushing the smooth soles of my feet into the thick pile wall-to-wall carpet. Baby steps. "You know it's true."

"What the hell are you talking about?"

I risked a glance at my watch. Six minutes left. I could feel the troops taking up their positions outside. Jack noticed the motion.

"How long did they give you, Kennis?"

"Not long. They're going to come in hard, Jack. You know the drill."

"Let them come. They're not going to risk shooting you." He stepped away from the window, though there was no perch nearby for a marksman to get a bead on him.

"I mean it. Think about Sarah."

"How do you know about Sarah? Who told you about Sarah? How could you possibly—"

"I figured it out, Jack. I did my homework. You were working the drug trade at Doha with Beaumont. It all went south because of Haden Krakauer. Someone died. Franny told me about that—you crying in the men's room over a girl in Iraq."

He shook her, bent her neck sideways with the muzzle of the gun. "You bitch." She bit back a cry of pain.

I pushed on. "What did Haden do? He shut off the flow of safe drugs. But your girl was hooked. She couldn't go cold turkey. She shot a bad load from some Arab street dealer and she died."

"You can't know that."

"I looked up the American ODs that turned up at the base hospital and the American medical facilities in Kuwait City. I had your service records and Beaumont's. I knew the rough dates. Late 2002, early 2003. Am I right? Four women, only two Americans, only one of them in the right age range. Sarah Lucy Constable."

"Fuck you. Don't you dare say her name, you fucking prick."

"She loved you, Jack. She wouldn't want you to end this way."

"Nice try, Sherlock, but she'd be cheering me on right now. She'd have blown you away the second you walked through that door. Now step aside. Franny and I are getting out of here. Move it."

He took another step toward me. We were as close together as we were ever going to get, actually within arms' reach of each other. I needed a distraction and there it sat on Haden's desk—Jack's prize piece of Steuben glass.

I lunged sideways. With a hard sweep of my arm I batted the ice-fishing Eskimo off the desk. The move pulled something in my back and the heavy glass banged my wrist—two blasts of pain. But it worked. Jack swung from Franny for one vital second, diving to catch the sculpture—too late. It bounced on the rug and the silver Eskimo snapped off. Franny staggered back. I flung myself at Tornovitch. We hit the carpet in a thrashing tangle of arms and legs. Jack still held the gun, twisting to jab it into my stomach, trying to get off a shot. We struggled, locked in place. I was too weak to dislodge his arm. I tensed, waiting for the impact of the bullet, but Franny pulled him off me.

The gun fired with an ear-splitting crack, burying the bullet in the wall. Jack knocked Franny away and kicked clear of me. She fell to her hands and knees beside me on the floor. He leapt up. Lonnie's men were banging at the door.

"Get back!" I shouted. "No one's hurt. Everything's under control! Stay out!"

"Jack—" Franny began.

"Shut up." He spun to face me. "You think I'm crazy, Kennis? Maybe I should kill your girlfriend here. Then you'd understand."

His gun swiveled over to Franny.

I talked to distract him now. "Don't make this worse for yourself, Jack. No one was seriously hurt tonight, no one died. They have you for conspiracy, but that's all. The DA will cut a deal. A couple of years in jail and then—"

He smiled. "Oh, I'm not going to jail, Kennis."

"There's no way out of this room, Jack. Whether you kill us or not."

"Guess again, Boy Wonder. There's *always* another way out. I'm free! Deal with it."

Franny cried, "No!" and launched like a runner off the starting block.

Jack jabbed the big gun under his chin and pulled the trigger. The 9mm bullet shattered the office window and sent a spray of brain blood and bone fragments chasing the shards into the humid night air, raining down on the crowd below, spattering on the big stone compass by the front doors.

Jack collapsed, the gun hit the floor and the SWAT team burst in, knocking the door clean off the hinges, all at the same time.

I threw up my hands. "Stop! Don't shoot! It's over!"

No one fired a shot. These kids were smart and disciplined. Lonnie Fraker pushed in behind them and gave the all clear.

Dazed and shell-shocked, Franny and I made our way downstairs and out through the garage into the security parking lot behind the building. The postmortems could wait until tomorrow. The town was safe. Jack was gone, and Zeke Beaumont was left alone to face the music, just like always.

Haden had arrived, shaken but determined, and I left him to handle the details. He could collect the evidence, make sure Beaumont was secure in a holding cell, organize the transport of Tornovitch's body, and start the cleanup.

I was done.

It took a while to reach the car. Franny drove. I closed my eyes and tipped my head against the window. I may even have fallen asleep for a few seconds.

When we got to my house, I invited her in for a drink. She poured us each a splash of vodka from the bottle in my freezer and squeezed a lemon over the ice while I walked around turning on lights. I didn't much like vodka—that bottle had been in there since Christmas—but the alcohol smoothed down the nap of my ruffled nerves.

There was no chance of our making love, even if we had wanted to. Sometimes a night of death and destruction can galvanize the limbic system, but I was too sore and we were both too rattled and numb to do anything but sip our drinks and sit quietly. When we finished, Franny got up and poured us another round.

She handed me my glass. "Don't worry about that e-mail trick. Jack must have left a trail. I can find it."

I nodded. "He must have thought he was smarter than you. After all this time."

"I thought I knew Jack. But I didn't. I didn't have a clue."

"You can't know a person like that, Franny. There's no way in. It's impossible."

Chirping crickets stitched the scented night air. She tasted her drink. After a while she said, "I'm leaving in the morning."

"Battlefield promotion?"

"Something like that."

"Washington DC."

"Horrible town. But I'm stationed there."

"You love it there. You belong there, just like I belong here."

"I could visit."

I took a drink, shook my head. "That would make it worse."

She spoke, rattling her ice. "I don't want to lose you."

The symmetry of it all could have made me smile, but I pursed my sore lips and squeezed my face into neutral. Facts were facts. This completed our role reversal. I had said those exact words to her in Los Angeles.

I took her hand, pulled her down onto the couch. "You found me, Franny. We found each other. I never thought that would happen. But it did. Jack told me once, 'Write it off as a victory and walk away.'"

"Hank—"

"I was married then. You're married now to the job. You'll never divorce it. You're about to get a huge promotion. And you deserve it. What would you do here? Buy new curtains and write parking tickets? That's crazy."

"I could transfer to the Boston office. I could commute."

"Come on. No one gets 'transferred' to the Boston office. They get exiled there." I pressed her knee. "'We'll always have Paris.'"

She clamped down on my hand. "I hate this."

I lifted my glass. "Here's looking at you, kid."

She put her drink down on the coffee table and leaned over to kiss me. It hurt and I let it. We held each other for a long time.

Then she stood up. "It's late. I have to go. There's paperwork and packing, and—there's a lot to do before morning."

I studied her. She was adding things up again, but the figures always came out the same.

"Good-bye, Franny."

"Good-bye, Hank."

She turned away and walked out of the house, making sure not to slam the screen behind her. I sat on the couch and listened to the car start, and the diminishing note of the engine as she drove away.

She never said, "I love you." I respected her for that.

Best to get away clean.

Chapter Twenty-one
Small Town Life

During the next week, Nantucket was overrun with network and cable news, reporters from the *New York Times* and the *Boston Globe*, stringers from newspapers as far away as Seattle and Los Angeles. Local stations from Boston and Providence brought their vans over, bristling with microwave antennas and bright-painted logos.

Yet David Trezize was the only journalist who got the whole story, which took up an entire double-sized issue of the *Nantucket Shoals*. His feature got picked up by UPI, Reuters, and various other news agencies around the world. He made quite a lot of money—what the *Shoals* normally brought in over the course of a year combining advertising and circulation, and he made his name in the world of big-time journalism. He got admiring letters and job offers. He deserved them. The articles he wrote were accurate and detailed. They were exciting to read. David had finally found a good story. He caught it like a screen pass and ran it eighty yards for a touchdown.

"The best part was getting a byline in Reuters," he told me a few days later. "I read that name in the newspapers the whole time I was growing up. Stories had that dateline—'from Reuters.' It was so glamorous. For years I thought Reuters was an actual place—this fantastic country where everything interesting happened. Now it turns out I live there." He shrugged with a little self-deprecating smile. "For a few days anyway."

We were standing in the steady roar of the south wind at the Delta fields, waiting to pick up our kids from Murray Camp. I nodded to Mike Henderson. Despite the fact that I had arrested him for murder briefly the winter before, we had stayed on friendly terms. His wife, Cindy, told me Debbie Garrison was spending half her time in Madaket with Billy Delavane now. Debbie was planning to move to the island in the fall, attend NHS, and live with him. She looked happy. Her mom, not so much, but she had given her permission.

"So the *Providence Journal* wants me to cover Homeland Security for them," David was saying. "They think I'm connected. I had to tell them—uh oh."

I turned to follow his look.

Pat Sauter was lumbering toward us. He must have weighed more than two hundred and fifty pounds, which gave him three inches and sixty pounds on me. His son was trailing behind him, crew cut like his dad, with the same slab face, the same wet lips carved from blubber—Pat's Mini-Me. My kids were running to catch up. Mike and several other parents moved toward us, sensing trouble.

Pat stopped right in front of me. "Jake says you pushed him around, Chief. That true?"

"He was beating up my son. So I separated them."

"You like pushing my son around, Chief?"

"That's an absurd question. Of course not. But I—"

"Remember what you told my kid? Pick on someone your own size."

"I don't see anyone around here like that. Just you."

"Funny guy. Big hero. Mr. Police Chief. Figure you're safe because no one wants an assault beef on a cop. That right? You gonna hide behind the badge? Suck your thumb behind the badge? Huh, Chief? That's how it's gonna be?"

My body still ached, but I was sick to death of these relentless bullies with their grudges and their agendas, their stupid pointless hatreds, their rage and aggression, prowling the world for targets, attacking the people I loved.

"Forget the badge," I said. "Take your best shot, lard-ass."

He shoved me hard, one-handed—a straight-arm jab with the flat of his hand. The effect was so extreme it was almost comical. For a second I thought he had dislocated my shoulder. The blow sent a flare of pain up my neck and down my arm, spun me around and sent me staggering backward. I tripped over my own feet and wound up sitting down with a jarring thud on the hot asphalt. I was an idiot. Certainly, no match for this guy. He was approaching me with the crabwalk preparation of a field goal kicker going for a thirty-eight-yard bomb. I knew the kick would do permanent damage, but I couldn't budge.

Tim screamed, "Stop it!" throwing himself at Sauter. The velocity more than the weight threw the big man off balance. Tim sank a fierce bite into the massive leg. Sauter yelped. He knocked Tim off with a flailing swat and my paralysis broke. I was on my feet and charging. I slammed into Sauter's chest as he was pulling back for a punch. We danced for a few seconds and then he got me into a stranglehold.

You see it in the movies all the time. What they don't show you is how to break the hold. It's one of the easiest moves in the whole playbook of hand-to-hand combat. I lifted my right arm straight up like a kid in class begging to be called on, and then twisted my body around.

His hands came loose and I drove a side-chop into the side of his neck. That startled him. He took a step back and we faced off again. My ribs were screaming—he might as well have stabbed me with an ice pick. My vision was going blurry. I had no more fight left while he was just getting started.

But as he jumped at me, Mike Henderson and three other parents grabbed him. One of them was the garbage man Sam Trikilis—Alana's father. I was stunned to see that David Trezize was one of them—he had Sauter's left arm. The fourth guy I had never seen before. The group of five thrashed and careened in a tight circle: Mike had Sauter's other arm, Sam had a grip on his waist and the fourth Samaritan was holding onto the giant's left leg. Somehow they managed to stop him.

"All right! All right! Get offa me!" he bellowed. He shook himself, like a dog after a swim.

"Fine," he said, catching his breath. "You win, Mr. Police Chief. But watch your back. Because these people won't always be around to protect you."

For some reason that moronic threat made me angrier than anything else.

"Yes they will!" I shouted at him. "Don't you get it? They'll always be here to protect me and I'll always be here to protect my son. This is our town and we take care of each other."

He glared at me for a second and then stormed off. I looked around for Tim and Caroline, huddled together near the parked cars. Debbie Garrison ran up and hugged Tim. He was too surprised to react.

"That was incredible," she was saying to him as I limped over. "You were so brave! I thought he was gonna kill you. O my God. I'm so glad you're okay."

She kissed his cheek and then bolted.

"She likes you," I said. "And she's right. You saved my ass today."

"I bit him."

"Good move."

We started for the car and Caroline gave her final verdict on the incident. "Boys are all insane. And this proves it."

The afternoon had lurched back to normal as the crowd scattered. I waved to Mike Henderson. He lifted a fist in solidarity. David gave me a thumbs up as his kids climbed into his car. Sam saluted me with a grin. The other guy waved. I had to find out who he was.

When we were alone, I sat behind the wheel of my police cruiser for a minute or so, battered and hurting, craving an aspirin or six, breathing with the wind that rocked the car on its springs, watching my friends drive off. Good friends, it turned out.

And I didn't even know some of their names.

I closed my eyes for a second, then keyed the ignition and drove my kids home for dinner.

To receive a free catalog of Poisoned Pen Press titles, please
contact us in one of the following ways:

Phone: 1-800-421-3976
Facsimile: 1-480-949-1707
Email: info@poisonedpenpress.com
Website: www.poisonedpenpress.com

Poisoned Pen Press
6962 E. First Ave. Ste 103
Scottsdale, AZ 85251